THE HORROR BEHIND THE DOOR

Eddie raced up the steps to the second-floor landing. Here he saw Elizabeth.

She was standing in the shadowy hallway, pale and terrified, her right hand cupped over her mouth, tears pouring down her face. She was staring unblinkingly into a room.

"Elizabeth?" Eddie called, his voice an injured whisper. "What's going on here?"

She shook her head in a quick panic. "No…no…no…," she sobbed, her gaze still fixed on whatever was in the room.

Eddie ran to her. He smelled something horrible. He grabbed her hand, still crusted with grime and blood. "What is it? What's going on?"

Finally she turned toward him, clearly in shock, her eyes wide and frozen. Her body was stiff as a board, the dirty robe pulled tightly around her waist. "We're…in…hell…," she muttered.

Eddie turned and looked into the room.

My God, we are *in hell.*

Other *Leisure* books by Michael Laimo:

THE DEMONOLOGIST
DEEP IN THE DARKNESS
ATMOSPHERE

PRAISE FOR MICHAEL LAIMO!

"Michael Laimo has the goods."

—*Hellnotes*

"Michael Laimo is a writer on the rise. He has a shrewd eye for macabre situations and knows how to draw the readers into the action."

—Tom Piccirilli, author of *A Lower Deep*

"Michael Laimo, in my mind, is the Alpha Male in the pack of new horror/dark suspense writers."

—P. D. Cacek, author of *Night Prayers*

"Laimo cranks up the fear quota several notches."

—Masters of Terror

"Michael Laimo's dark fiction creeps and cuts, calling as easily upon supernatural effects as psychological insights to disturb, startle, and just plain scare the living hell out of readers."

—Gerard Houarner, author of *The Beast That Was Max*

"Michael Laimo is able to draw out tension and suspense until it's almost unbearable."

—Edo van Belkom, author of *Teeth*

"Laimo is a delightfully twisted read. His work makes the dark scary and deliciously unforgettable."

—Linda Addison, author of *Animated Objects*

DEAD SOULS

MICHAEL LAIMO

LEISURE BOOKS NEW YORK CITY

*For Anna Rose and Emma Grace,
who'll never be old enough to
read their father's books.*

A LEISURE BOOK®

February 2007

Published by

Dorchester Publishing Co., Inc.
200 Madison Avenue
New York, NY 10016

ISBN 0-8439-5760-3

The name "Leisure Books" and the stylized "L" with design are
trademarks of Dorchester Publishing Co., Inc.

Printed in the United States of America.

Visit us on the web at www.dorchesterpub.com.

ACKNOWLEDGMENTS

The rituals performed in this book are based in part on actual magic rituals as detailed in the book *Summoning Spirits* by Konstantinos. Information about the author and his books on the occult can be found on the author's Web site: www.konstantinos.com.

Special thanks to: My family. My cousins, Joey Z. and Keith Caputo. Don D'Auria and Diane Stacy at Leisure. Shane Staley. Konstantinos. William Stechman, Jon Rogers, and Lacie Oakley of Burning Grounds Motion Entertainment. Heidi Meissner. Nicole Reinhardt at Horrorfind.com. The Horror Writers Association. All my friends on Myspace.com. All my friends at Shocklines.com. William M. Miller. Nanci Kalanta.

DEAD SOULS

PROLOGUE:
EVIL RETURNS TO WELLFIELD

August 24, 2005
11:45 A.M.

The man takes his break.

He is permitted outside once a day, at least for now, while it is summer, while the weather is cooperative. In the winter, it's a different story all together. Then he never gets to go outside. It's much too cold.

And today—what a nice day it is! The man can feel the sun's warmth against his face as he is ushered into the open courtyard. Alongside him is a nurse. She leads him gently by the arm, smiling warmly. Walking slowly in thoughtful consideration of the man who has a lame leg, a portion of his skull missing, and only one eye.

He looks around at the manicured courtyard. It is penned in by four three-story buildings that make up the Pine Oak Institute for the Mentally Insane. There are many trees here. Some of them have pretty flowers.

Their leaves rustle lightly in the gentle breeze. Beneath the trees are park benches where many of the patients sit and talk to themselves.

The nurse leads him to one of the benches. He sits down. She smiles again and says, "Lunch in forty-five minutes, David."

David smiles. He likes her. She is pretty.

The nurse leaves David. But he is not alone. There are guards here in the courtyard. Large men who wear white pants and white shirts with ID cards on them. They watch all the patients, some more than others. They barely pay any attention to David because he has been here for seventeen years and has never caused any trouble.

After some time, a voice calls to him: *David*. It is soft. Whispery.

He looks around, but sees no one.

David, the voice says again. He realizes that it is coming from inside his head. He's scared because he's never had this problem before. Some of the other patients have, but not him.

David looks down. There's a large blackbird on the walkway, a few feet away. It is looking up at him. David squints his one eye at the bird. The bird hops closer. Again the whispering voice fills his head: *It is time, David.*

"Time for what?" he asks out loud, brow furrowed.

The man who killed your parents, the voice in his head says. *The man who made you like this . . . his blood is returning to Wellfield . . . to the house.*

Although David feels frightened, he also feels a surge of excitement, of . . . sudden strength and power. He's been waiting for this moment since his first days in Pine Oak's crisis stabilization unit, seventeen years ago.

Go to the house, David.

David twists his head; the bones in his neck crack. He eyes the bird curiously. Then nods. "When?"

Now.

"Mr. Mackey?"

David rips his gaze away from the bird and looks up. The nurse is there, staring down at him. She looks concerned.

"Are you okay?" she asks.

David nods.

"I thought I heard you talking to someone," she says.

He points to the walkway. "I was looking at the pretty bird." He looks back down. The bird is still there. Only now it is dead. Maggots writhe in its eyes and on its head. Its feathers are thin and ragged.

The nurse shakes her head. She smiles insincerely. "Come, David. Let's go inside. It's lunchtime."

"There you are, Mr. Mackey," another nurse says. This one is a man. He is younger than David, who believes himself to be one hundred, but is really only thirty-one. David looks up at the nurse with his one eye. The nurse smiles at him. All the nurses smile. The guards don't, though. They never do. They are very serious.

The nurse places a tray on the lunch table. There are other patients nearby, but none of them talk to David. They don't talk to anyone but themselves. Unless, of course, they get angry. Then they yell at everyone.

On the tray is his lunch, a tunafish sandwich, a plastic cup of Jell-O, and some tea biscuits with pats of butter. Usually, David eats everything. But today he isn't hungry. He is thinking of the bird and the voice it brought, telling him to go to the house. To wait for the man's blood to arrive.

So while no one is looking—they don't pay much attention to David because he has never caused any trouble—he removes the plastic butter knife from his tray and tucks it into his pants.

David is allowed restroom breaks at any time. There is a bathroom in his room. He shares it with an old man who groans all night and swats invisible mosquitoes all day.

After lights out, he gets out of bed. He goes into the bathroom and shuts the door. He removes the plastic butter knife from his underwear (he'd hidden it in his mattress during shower time), and begins to gently rub it against the steel bolt connecting the drainpipe to the sink. The bolt begins to whittle away the rigid plastic. He makes certain to collect all the shavings.

He continues this activity for two days, never staying in the bathroom for more than a few minutes at a time. Eventually, he files the plastic knife down until the point is razor sharp. He then works on the edges, whittling both sides so they too are keen enough to slice.

He hides the knife back inside his underwear.

And waits.

He hasn't slept at all. He's waiting for the night nurse to make her rounds. At night, there's only one nurse and two guards on duty on each floor of the open-unit ward. They spend most of their time watching television or reading books.

He pretends to sleep. Finally, he hears the nurse come into his room. He hears her adjusting another patient's sheets. She then scribbles something down on his chart. Soon thereafter, he hears her leave the room.

He removes the knife from beneath his mattress. He touches the point and pricks his finger. Sharp as hell, he thinks.

He gets out of bed, tiptoes across the room. He peeks out into the dim hall. Sees no one. The nurse must be in one of the other rooms. He limps down the hall as fast as he can, all the way to the guard's station. The night guard, a muscular man with black hair and glasses, is seated at a desk. He is reading a magazine with pictures of pretty women inside. His back is to David.

He suddenly turns, eyes wide as he spots David.

David leaps forward and plunges the knife into the guard's right eye. The guard staggers to his feet. His arms rise. He tries to scream but can only wheeze. He falls to the floor with a heavy thump. David reaches down, yanks the knife out. Blood gushes onto the floor, black and oily. He removes the security card clipped to the man's belt.

Limping, he races to the Plexiglas security door. Swipes the keycard. The door clicks open, and he moves into the reception area.

From behind, the nurse screams. He looks back. She is at the far end of the hallway. She has a hand over her mouth. Her eyes are bulging.

David runs to the front doors. They are locked. He swipes the keycard. They make a buzzing noise before granting him access to the outside world.

He races outside, across the dark and empty parking lot, hurrying footsteps pursuing him.

The voice returns to his head: *Go to the house.*

Halogen lights on the outside of the building illuminate the parking lot. Now it's as bright as a baseball game at night. An alarm shrills. He can hear sirens in the distance. A white security vehicle appears from around the side of the building. It speeds across the parking lot, toward David.

Tires screech.

A man cries out; there is a loud, horrible cracking noise.

David turns. Under the bright security lights, he sees a guard rolling across the blacktop. When he comes to a stop, David can see that his legs are twisted into *L* shapes.

The security vehicle stops. There's a splotch of blood on the hood. Its front bumper is dented. The man, only a few feet away, is writhing on the blacktop in agony.

Go to the house, the voice repeats in his head. He looks up and sees a lone blackbird flying overhead, seemingly guiding the way. A feather drifts lazily down toward him. He catches it in midair.

David Mackey looks at the feather, smiles, then gazes up at the circling bird one last time before fleeing into the dark woods surrounding the Pine Oak Institute for the Mentally Insane.

PART I

THE DEAD, LIVING

*Now, upon the first day of the week,
very early in the morning, they came unto the
sepulchre . . . and they found the stone rolled
away, and they entered in and found not the
body of the Lord Jesus Christ . . .*
—Luke 24: 1–3

CHAPTER ONE

August 24, 1988
5:00 A.M.

It began with four bells tolling simultaneously through-out a large farmhouse commonly known in town as the Conroy House.

They rang once, their vibrations sounding much louder than usual. Thirteen seconds later, they rang again, stirring those in the house from their fitful slumber.

This early morning, a quarter moon beamed proudly in the sky, the winds blowing gently from the southwest, carrying with them the cries of blackbirds searching for the day's first worms. Rainclouds had dominated the skies the first two weeks of July, leaving everything in Wellfield gray and wet. Two days earlier, the power had gone out, and in parts of town the houses were still dark. The outage had only affected the Conroy House for twelve hours, an event soon thereafter considered a small grace from God.

At the tolling of the third bell, exactly twenty-six seconds after the first started, a man of forty-three years of age sat up in bed, swung his feet over the edge of the quilted mattress, and placed them in the perfect white circle painted on the oak flooring. The sweat-matted sheets drifted away from his naked form. He clasped his hands together, closed his eyes, and silently recited two prayers, the first to the Lord Jesus Christ, the second to the Lord Osiris. His lips moved gently against the hushed words escaping his throat.

At the conclusion of his prayer, the man stood in the circle. He set his sights on its intricacies, at the outer border of hexagrams, then at the inner border and the many sacred names of God etched into the bright paint. Upon each magnetic pole of the circle, penta-grams jutted. From the center of each, white candles rose like the stripped branches of ash trees. At the top of the circle, painted on the floor directly before him, was a triangle with the name of OSIRIS divided up, the *O* at the uppermost point, three letters at the lower right point, two at the left.

The bells continued to toll.

He gazed out the window at the wide stretch of land leading to the barn. A lone blackbird fluttered into view and landed on the sill, one oil-drop eye ig-nited by the faint moonlight, peering in at him. It cocked its head once, twice, then pecked a gentle message against the corner of the window. The bird hopped along the sill, then flapped its still-damp wings and flew away, leaving behind a sole black feather: a gift from Osiris.

At the thirteenth toll of the bells, the man, unsmiling, paced heel-to-toe about the circumference of the circle, knowing that in three of the other bedrooms, a woman, a girl, and a boy were carrying out the same exact procedure. He performed sixteen revolutions, then stepped away and paced to the window. He cracked it open and removed the feather from the sill.

After closing the window, he stepped to the bureau, where he struck a wooden match and lit a white candle. A yellow flame rose four inches high, its point flickering energetically, releasing a thin black line of wavering smoke. Alongside the candle, he lifted the pyramid-shaped top of a brass censer. Inside, loaded the evening before, was a cone of sandalwood. He placed the feather alongside the cone, then lit the incense and inhaled the escaping aroma as if sniffing a pot of steaming soup.

Still counting the toll of the bells, he waited until they struck thirty, then opened the bureau drawer and removed a leather parchment. He walked back to the circle, lit the four candles, then knelt inside the circle, hands resting lightly on his lap, palms facing upward and holding out the parchment like an offering. He relaxed his shoulders, facing the triangle. He began to breathe more slowly, inhaling deeply through his nose, holding the air in his lungs until the bell tolled thirteen seconds later, then exhaling for the same stretch of time. He repeated this process until he achieved a rhythmic state of reflexive breathing.

Concentrating solely on the spirit of Osiris, he unfurled the parchment and placed it flat inside the triangle. He studied the sigil etched in black ink on the worn leather, clearing his mind of all unwanted thoughts and worries. He repeated the spirit God's name for the toll of thirteen bells, chanting in unison with the voices of the woman, girl, and boy performing the same ritual in their respective rooms.

Following the tolling of the thirteenth bell, he recited a prayer, drawing out each word in a string of monotone notes: *"I beseech thee, O Spirit Osiris from the vast astral plane, by the supreme majesty of God, to allow the child Bryan Conroy an association to our purpose, so that he too may benefit from your empowering gift."*

As his words ended, the bells tolled again.

The Conroy House immediately grew hot. Beads of sweat formed on his brow. He closed his eyes and in his mind a warm glowing sphere appeared. He reached out for it, fingers extended. The golden light of the sphere seeped toward him in a thin tight line, as though it were composed of liquid. It entered his grasping fingers, quickly filling his body, snug and comforting, his legs, body, and head fully absorbing its fluid offering.

Once the light saturated his body, a slow vibration filled him, his body wholly accepting the powerful beat. He could hear it in his head, each encompassing cadence eventually forming distinct echoes. His ears popped with every echo, and he could see two dark misty spheres beside his head.

Windows to the astral plane.

The dark spheres expanded and faint gray holes appeared at their cores. He could hear sounds emerging, like the distant footsteps of a great and powerful giant. The man's lips moved of their own accord, his voice a long flat line as he repeated his prayer to the spirit God Osiris.

The golden light before him expanded, as did the dark spheres alongside him. A doorway appeared in the light, a glowing blue image on its metallic surface. The image took on a definite shape of curved lines atop an inverted triangle, bisected by a crooked arrow.

Slowly, the door opened. The pounding vibration exploded from the darkness beyond—from the realm of the astral plane into the physical plane.

The man gazed into the swirling black eddies, a storm of whistling winds that backed the slow, thunderous pulse. From within its murky depths, he could hear the spirit's message clearly, spat out one syllable at a time.

"Benjamin Conroy . . . proceed with the ritual."

CHAPTER TWO

September 7, 2005
12:56 P.M.

Despite the persistent rain and pain-filled thoughts that had kept him company on the bus ride into New England, Johnny Petrie was still able to unearth a bit of excitement—his stomach fluttered with invisible butterflies, his skin tingled with nervous anticipation. It was all so bittersweet: He'd spent most of his eighteen years, as far as he could recall, in Manhattan under the roof of a brownstone on the Upper East Side, 88th between Lexington and Park. Now, to see *this*: trees and mountainsides displaying their browns and greens in never-ending arrays; the hidden sun whose filtering daylight still managed to illuminate. Despite its simplicity, it was a grand feast for his city-bred eyes. Just south of Providence on I-95, he'd caught sight of a raccoon or possum that had met its fate beneath the tires of some unknown vehicle, but even this was something new and exciting to behold. The country, yes, that's what this was, and he cursed himself—and his parents—for never having gone farther north than Westchester County before.

Dear God, my parents, he thought, tears filling his eyes.

Regrettably, there'd never been any good opportunity to visit the country until now. Mary Petrie had kept a very short and tight leash on her boy throughout his growing-up years. With the city being a dangerous place and all, Johnny was forced to keep to the paths and schedules granted to him, attending (and eventually graduating from) St. Anthony's Catholic School (obedience school, if you asked him), instead of PS 35, which was more than ten blocks away. It might as well have been on the other side of the world. All summer he'd been made to continue his Catholic studies at St. Anthony's. On the weekends he was allowed recreational time in Central Park, but only if Mary or Ed came along, or if he'd had an adult chaperone joining him, preferably a God-fearing parent of a well-known school friend. Mary Petrie had done everything for Johnny's own good, at least in her own mind, treating him with all the love and protection a child could expect from a parent. That, and so much more.

So much more . . .

He thought of his mother, of how she would remind him every time he protested: *Remember, Johnny, everything I do, I do for you. Parents know much better than their children. God created us to steer you from evil, to teach you from right and wrong. To protect you from the evils of the world . . . it is my sole purpose to do so, praise God.* Despite his mother's idiosyncrasies, and religious zealousness, he loved her . . . he would always love her. He realized now, after spending his entire childhood and teen years controlled by her repressive discipline, that she did everything out of fear—a fear she was incapable of understanding.

But then he wondered: *Is she really incapable? There's so much more to the story she's not telling me. She spent her entire life trying to keep me from learning about it. No, she does understand her fears, and she's been keeping them locked away in the dark. Now, dear God, they're out in the open, and she's too terrified to face them.*

Ironically, Johnny had spent his entire life obeying his mother's every demand because he feared her. So, in a convoluted, roundabout way, he was able to empathize with her. But there was one chief difference between them: Johnny had finally found the strength to confront his fears, and was able to flee them, something Mary Petrie had never been able to do, in spite of her support from Jesus and the doctors and the church groups.

I've fled my fears . . . that, and so much more . . .

So much more . . .

The bus shifted lanes, jarring him from his thoughts. It passed a sign that read, DOVER, EXIT 43. Johnny kept his gaze out the window, nature's scenery blurring as he remembered the events that had changed his life— and his parents' lives—less than twenty-four hours earlier. . . .

September 6, 2005
3:38 P.M.

He returned home from the library (the only place he didn't feel guilty about sneaking off to without his mother's knowledge) and retrieved the mail from the clouded glass box in the lobby. He took the stairs three flights up instead of riding the elevator because the old man from 4F who smelled like cauliflower had just gotten in, and Johnny didn't really want to bear such undying torture. Once on the third floor, he entered the two-bedroom apartment and tossed the mail on the kitchen table, never once looking at it because nothing ever came for him except his monthly delivery of *Catholic Digest*—one of the few periodicals both Ed and Mary approved. He went into his room, dropped his knapsack on the bed, and changed into a pair of shorts and a T-shirt, thinking of how he might take pleasure in the next ninety minutes before his mother returned home at five o'clock. Maybe he'd read the copy of Wells's *War of the Worlds* he checked out of the library, or watch the talk show that came in on the UHF channel his parents didn't know about. It was a daily ritual, this time alone when he could take part in some of the simple pleasures of life (God-forsaken sins, if you asked Mary) before he was made to conform to the whims and ways of his mother. He'd have to perform his chores—every eighteen-year-old was expected to do *something*—either taking out the trash or helping with dinner; but Mary pushed further with Johnny, making certain that the bathroom was free and clear of the germs that undoubtedly festered while the house was empty; or the shelves in the fridge. God forbid some errant crumbs made their way out of the bread bag. After dinner, Johnny would be forced to perform his Bible studies, sitting at the kitchen table in plain sight so that his mind wouldn't stray. *There's more than enough to keep you busy until bedtime*, Mary would say, regardless of whether or not he had assignments. And then she'd add, more than once, *And don't forget to say your prayers before you go to bed!*

He went into the bathroom, washed up, then pulled open the medicine cabinet and experienced the same disheartening feeling he felt every day when he did this. The new bottle of the day was something called Lexapro, but Johnny had no idea what it was used to treat, not yet anyway. It was alongside a few dozen other bottles, the results of Mary Petrie setting aside her paralegal duties at three o'clock every day, so that by three-fifteen she could be seated in the waiting room of some non-discriminating doctor's office on the Upper East Side in hopeful search of that magic pill to cure all her woes. Johnny had performed a bit of research on his mother's tribulations, writing down the names of the scripts from the tiny brown bottles— Valium, Darvocet, Xanax, Celexa, among many others—then searching them out on the Web in the library. What he discovered was that Mom had a considerable number of personal issues, ones she never elected to talk about, at least with Johnny. Obsessive compulsive disorder, generalized anxiety disorder, panic attacks (he'd never seen her in a state of panic, so he wasn't quite sure what that was all about), attention deficit disorder, and some other serious-sounding mental ills. Johnny had wondered if there was a pill she could take that would alleviate her "iron-fisted control disorder" and "overzealous Jesus-worshipping disorder."

He pulled out a bottle of ibuprofen (one of the many over-the-counter bottles relegated to the lowest shelf in the medicine cabinet), popped the top and dry-swallowed two pills, a preventative measure to ward off the headache he'd be bound to develop when Mary returned home.

He closed the medicine cabinet and peered into the mirror. He frowned at the face staring back at him:

meek and mousy, skin peppered with acne, hair short and curly, hairline already receding, the promise of baldness perhaps six or seven years away. He rubbed his eyes, then paced out of the bathroom, the wood floor creaking noisily beneath him.

He unzipped his knapsack and removed his textbooks, thinking now of his father, an act not so commonly performed. He peered over at the photo of his parents sitting on the nightstand—a decorative choice on Mary's part. *It matches the portrait of Jesus on the wall*, she'd once said. It had been taken by Johnny a few months earlier, the day they all attended his mother's co-worker's funeral. An odd time, Johnny had thought, to snap a picture for prosterity. Ed Petrie was a big man, now losing the dark curly hair he'd passed along to Johnny. This single feature, however, was where their similarities ended. In contrast to Johnny's wiry frame, Ed boasted a gut that exploded over the waistline of his pants, making it damn near impossible, Johnny thought, to ferret out his privates in order to take a leak. Ed's shirttail was always out—as it was in the photo—and he was always in need of a shave. He held a job—a *union* job, he would brag—as a longshoreman on Pier 121 directly below the Brooklyn Bridge. He drank often and smoked even more.

Ed was big pushover when it came to Johnny's mother, giving in to all her idiosyncrasies and religious outbursts with calm replies such as "Yes, dear," and "Of course, hon." He'd rub his eyes at her every word, most likely hoping to find her gone when he opened them. Of course, she'd still be there in all her Bible-slinging glory, reciting the Lord's Prayer, or the Twenty-third Psalm, and he'd have no choice but to give in and let her run the household, as long as he was able to go to work twelve hours a day, Monday through Friday, and watch the latest sporting events at Glen's Tavern on the weekends. Ed had spent most of his time avoiding the wrath of Mary. And avoiding Johnny.

Johnny's relationship with his father was trifling, their conversations kept to a bare minimum. Sometimes weeks would pass without them uttering a single word to one another. The fact of the matter was that Johnny only saw his father on the weekends, usually between noon and three, after Ed woke up but before he headed out to Glen's Tavern on Second Avenue and 64th Street. It'd seemed obvious to Johnny that Ed Petrie had never really wanted a child in the first place—the man was a huge lazy ne'er-do-well who only showed attention to his son when he returned from The Food Emporium with arms full of groceries. (Strangely, Johnny would be allowed to the grocery store by himself, but Mary would always preface the two-block walk with a firm "Don't get lost" followed by an emphatic sign of the cross; it seemed that having food in the house was quite worth risking their son's life for.) Oddly enough, Johnny was always pleased with the smile on his father's face when he handed over the bags of food.

He tore his eyes from the picture, then dug out the H.G. Wells book from his knapsack. He tossed it on the bed and went back into the kitchen, where he took a quart of milk from the fridge and chugged it straight from the carton, an act, according to Mary, worthy of eternal damnation.

As he chugged, his eyes darted over to the kitchen table, where a light beige envelope peeked out from between the pages of a drug-store circular. He could see the return address clearly, printed in a dark, old-style font:

Andrew Judson, Attorney-at-Law
14 Main Street
Wellfield, ME 12789

There he stood, quart of milk in hand, staring at the envelope and wondering what a lawyer from Maine might want with his parents. He assumed that the letter had been accidentally mishandled, that it had gotten caught up in the circular and was really meant for someone else in the building. He put the milk back in the refrigerator, then stepped toward the table. Looking at the envelope, he felt strangely tentative, as if approaching a cockroach with a paper towel in his hand. He reached forward and touched the corner of the envelope.

He wondered incredulously: *Why am I so damn anxious? Maybe I've inherited some of my mother's problems? Lord Jesus Christ, come strike me dead!*

He slipped the envelope out from between the ad pages and realized instantly that his apprehensions were surprisingly justified.

The envelope was addressed to . . . him.

CHAPTER THREE

August 24, 1988
5:17 A.M.

Benjamin Conroy opened his eyes. The golden light hovering in the air before him slowly vanished, like a beam from a movie projector turning in on itself. The circles of gray mist alongside his ears performed the same magical feat. At the tolling of the next bell, he slowly stood, keeping his feet at the center of the circle, his eyes pinned to the flames rising from the candles in the pentagrams. He folded his hands together, feeling the beads of sweat running down his naked body as he silently recited a prayer of thankfulness to Osiris.

Flexing his muscles—first in his arms, then his legs—he stepped free of the circle, to his right, between the two pentagrams. The aroma of sandalwood incense filled the room, its rising smoke creeping out of the censer like lengthening tentacles. The candle on the bureau tossed its glow against the smoke-coated walls in quaint, nimble flickers. He stood before the bureau, listening to the vibrating hum of silence between the bells, feeling his nerve endings in heated anticipation and the eager beat of the blood in his ears. For a moment longer he peered longingly into the candle's flame, then opened the bureau drawer and removed a hooded black robe that had been folded in thirds. He immediately donned the robe, all the while keeping his tear-filled eyes on the flame, its golden depths drawing him deep into its comforting warmth. As he tied the braided sash around his waist, the perspiration on his body melted into the warm cotton fabric of the robe. Then he pulled the hood over his head. He brought a small black book out of the drawer. Its worn leather released a bitter odor of dry autumn leaves burning. He opened the book to a page scrawled with hieroglyphs and sigils, and silently recited the ancient prayer. Once the prayer was complete, he spread the robe at his chest. He dipped his finger into the censer, dousing it with ash, then gently ran it along the wrinkled scar tissue on his sternum.

"Bryan," he whispered. "May your soul live with us for all eternity."

He squeezed the book in his hand, the leather comforting despite the feeling of something heavy turning in his midsection. He turned and exited the room, then stood in the hallway as he awaited the next toll. The sun had begun to climb up over the horizon, sending elongated shadows down the hall, through the front window—the sheer curtains had been drawn, but were mostly inefficient in blocking the light. A bell rang. He looked both ways, up and down the hall, then went left. Hands groping the wall, he reached the first door, which was left ajar, and at the toll of the next bell, pushed it open.

Here in this room, the curtains were black and fully drawn. The light did not break through at all. The lingering mouth of darkness invited him, cool and welcoming.

He stepped into the room and closed the door behind him. Looking forward, he regarded his wife, Faith, who was kneeling naked in her own circle, hands upturned on her knees, beaded sweat glistening beneath the candlelight rising from the quartered pentagrams. He gazed about the room and smiled, seeing it perfectly prepared for ritual: the circle, drawn to precise circumference and etched with the many names of God, her personal triangle positioned on the floor alongside it in the southern hemisphere, its apex pointing south. Within the triangle, lines of hexagrams ran like soldiers along the edges, sandalwood smoldered in a censer at its heart, and a sole candle burned alongside. At her knees lay a leather parchment containing the seal of Osiris wrapped in black silk. Beside it sat two small chalices, one containing water, the other salt, both offerings to the spirit of the Lord.

Benjamin approached the circle. Faith's crystal blue eyes stared straight ahead, toward the curtained window. Within the walls, the bells tolled. A dull pecking sound surfaced at the window. Faith's unwavering stare fixed to it as her lips trembled in soundless prayer. Benjamin spread the curtain and cracked the window.

On the sill was a single black feather. *A gift from Osiris. Thank you, my Lord.* He retrieved the feather, then closed the window. He returned to Faith and knelt facing her. Gripping the feather between two fingers, he lifted the lid of the censer and placed it inside. Both husband and wife inhaled the pungent odor that developed.

He took her hands in his and allowed his eyelids to close, his heart now beginning to pound at the initial state of perfection the ritual had brought. He called out to Osiris: *"Come, thou all-powerful Lord Osiris, who exists amongst the Gods in the astral plane and governs the Realm of Resurrection and Everlasting Life. I conjure thee to bestow upon Faith Conroy your influence of spiritual re-birth, so that she may purely and honorably engage your powers for the purpose of ancestral afterlife, with utmost earnestness and commitment."*

Upon his utterance of the final word in the spell, a bell rang. Benjamin grabbed the candle at the outermost point of Faith's triangle and dropped it on top of the parchment containing the sigil of Osiris. The parchment immediately burst into flames. They held their hands over the flame, both reciting, *"To your service I dedicate water to cleanse your body and salt to feed your blood, oh infinitely powerful Osiris, in hope that you may find this an acceptable offering for your bounteousness."*

They broke their grasp, at which point Faith grabbed the chalice of salt and Benjamin the water. At the same instant, they overturned their offerings onto the flame, extinguishing it. Benjamin opened his eyes and gazed at his wife, naked and glistening with a passive grace in the flickering gloom. He suppressed the smile of satisfaction that attempted to form on his lips.

So far things were going perfectly. *God bless . . .*

A bell tolled, signifying the next stage of the ritual. Using his index finger, he rubbed it in the wet mess of ash between them, held it up and nodded. Faith closed her eyes and stuck out her naked chest.

On her sternum, directly above the breastline, was a mass of scar tissue exactly like her husband's. Benjamin pressed his finger against the bottom of the scar. He slowly traced the shape—a loop up, curving over, and then back down—leaving a trail of wet ash upon the ridges of gnarled flesh.

He pulled his hand away and admired his work.

"Osiris is with you, Faith," he whispered, standing up.

She nodded, then stood and put on her robe, which had been folded on the bed behind her.

The bell tolled.

Joining hands, they both left the room.

CHAPTER FOUR

September 6, 2005
4:03 P.M.

Downstairs on the second floor of the apartment building, someone began playing Jimi Hendrix at a high volume, sending vibrations up into Johnny's feet. The beat
of "Purple Haze" fought hard against the nerves that assaulted the rest of his body. He made a deep-breathed effort to ignore his thumping heart and his shaking hands.
He tucked an index finger into the corner of the envelope and tore the paper along the crease. Inside, a letter
folded in thirds peeked out. It was the same beige color
as the envelope. He licked his dry lips, and removed it.

He found himself hoping that the letter would be an
odd piece of junk, part of a mass mailer directed to future college students. Of course Mary had no intention of sending their boy to college; no, her grand plan
was to send him to work so he could play his part in

supporting the everyday foundations of the Petrie family, *thank the good Lord for my boy's presence*. Needless to say, Johnny hadn't worked a day in his life, with all the religious studies imparted upon him. He peered at the envelope again and saw that it had been manually stamped—no presorted postage marker here. This letter, whatever its contents, was deliberate and meant for him.

He unfolded the letter. Centered on the paper was Andrew Judson's heading, printed in the same old-style font. Below, just above the fold-line, was a date: August 25, 2005.

One day after Johnny's eighteenth birthday.

And all he kept saying to himself was that his mother would have two fits if she knew he'd opened a piece of mail without her consent; she would have *never* let him read this letter—despite it being addressed to him—without first opening it herself and inspecting its contents, and you can safely bet that if this had happened, Andrew Judson's letter would have never passed before his eyes, regardless of the subject matter. For once, Johnny Petrie was thankful for his mother's after-work ritual.

Still, he peered around nervously, into the bedroom, feeling paranoid and yet intensely curious at the same time. *This envelope is addressed to me. To me.* He grinned uncomfortably, wondering why in God's name he was behaving so irrationally, why he felt like such a criminal. *No one's watching me. I'm not doing anything wrong.*

Tell that to your mother, Johnny. If she saw you now, she'd wind up and fling the wrath of Jesus at you harder than a Roger Clemens fastball and make you spend the entire night reading passages from the Bible about how "Thou shalt not steal."

"Screw it," he murmured, quietly of course, just in case his mother had decided to come home early and had an ear cocked to the door.

He read the letter and at once, his head spun.

Andrew Judson, Attorney-at-Law
14 Main Street
Wellfield, ME 12789
(207) 555-0300

August 25, 2005

Mr. John Petrie
479 East 88th Street
New York, NY 10017

Re: Refunding Bond and Release
Perry County Surrogate Court
Dear Mr. Petrie,

In the matter of the estate of one Benjamin Conroy, it is my duty at this time to name you, Mr. John Petrie, residing at 479 East 88th Street, New York, NY, as the sole living heir of Mr. Conroy's estate, which has been willed in your name. As indicated in the last rites of the deceased, you, Mr. John Petrie, are to receive the entire estate bequeathed to me as executor, minus legal fees and taxes. The value of the inheritance is estimated at two million dollars.

I urge you to contact me immediately upon receipt of this letter so that we may

arrange for the properties to be legally and
rightfully transferred to you in full and final satisfaction.

Sealed with my seal and dated on the
25th of August, 2005.

Andrew Judson, Attorney at Law

Johnny felt incredibly scared. Of what, he couldn't tell.
He read the letter again, and then again, feeling his
heart and blood and nerves doing battle inside his
body. He closed his eyes and told himself to calm
down, that there was nothing at all to be scared of. Being chased by a mugger or beat up by the school bully,
these were things to be scared of. Not getting a letter
from a faceless lawyer telling you that you inherited a
fortune. Really, even Jesus would agree that this was a
good thing.
Benjamin Conroy . . .
But he *was* scared. Scared of his mother and of how
she would react to this, of how she would scream, *It's a
letter from the devil. He's playing a trick on you! Burn it,
Johnny! Burn it so you can be saved from an eternity in the
fires of hell!* And then she would tear the letter from his
hands and crumple it up, but she would also stealthily
slip it into the pocket of her housedress where she could
retrieve it later and try to figure out what all the mystery
was about. And upon eventually reading the hogwash
about Johnny receiving an inheritance . . . well, she
would charge out of her bedroom with her dress flying
out behind her like a flag in the wind, gripping the letter
in her clawlike hand and laughing at him for thinking
that it was anything more than a piece of useless junk

mail. *You know, a scam to bilk the meager savings out of hard working Christians. An unethical attempt to convince the "good people" that if they don't make some sort of donation toward the "retrieval of their good fortune," then the earth's rotation would double and launch everyone and everything on the planet far off into the darkest reaches of the solar system,* later adding that somehow those damn cockroaches would find a way to survive.

No, he couldn't let her read it. It'd be like forfeiting a baseball game without once stepping up to the plate.

Downstairs, Jimi Hendrix sang about a girl named Mary and how the wind cried her name. Johnny read the letter again, knowing that he couldn't allow himself to be scared, not one bit—not of the letter or of whatever lay ahead. There were only two possibilities: a quick return to the unremarkable routine that was his life, or a huge fortune and the resultant life that followed. Regardless of the outcome, however, he knew that he needed to be strong and confident and mature, like the eighteen-year-old he was. Again he told himself that the letter might turn out to be nothing more than a scam, a scrap for the trash. If so, then he would shrug it off.

But if it turned out to be authentic . . .

He remained skeptical. Really, how could this letter be genuine? It clearly stated that he, Johnny Petrie, was the direct heir. That would make him a family member, or at the very least a close friend or relative of this person he'd never heard of.

So who was Benjamin Conroy, and why did he presumably leave his fortune to Johnny? He didn't have to think about it very long: Never in his life had he ever heard of the man.

He gazed at the door, studying the calendar with the portrait of St. Luke that hung from a single brown thumbtack. Downstairs, Jimi stopped singing. An odd silence filled the apartment.

Holding the letter, Johnny paced to the phone on the wall next to the refrigerator. He gazed at it for ten seconds.

Then he reached for the handset.

CHAPTER FIVE

August 24, 1988
5:39 A.M.

Benjamin led Faith to the end of the hall, where they made a left turn, passing the entrance to the bathroom. They stopped and gazed along the corridor at the three closed doors that beckoned them like warm fires on a cold day, then silently acknowledged that the first door on the left, Elizabeth's room, would be their next stop. The bell tolled, then faded as they walked hand-in-hand to their daughter's room. A carved and painted *E* hung on the door, green ivy and yellow daisies winding about the shape, spring-warm and inviting. When the bell rang again, Benjamin gripped the knob, and they went inside.

Here, the bell's resonance hung in the air like a mystery. They both took deep breaths, drawing into their lungs the thick, spicy aroma of sandalwood.

They peered at the scene before them.

The room was dim, but not too dark. The curtains were open. Dawn light shafted in through the window and pooled on the polished oak floor. Candlelight flickered across the walls, faint but still alluring. The Monet print next to the sliding closet shimmered, its river seeming to flow, its trees seeming to sway, looking like a window into another world. Elizabeth's stuffed teddy bears, perhaps two-dozen in all, some of them older than Elizabeth's eighteen years sat looking up at them with their shiny plastic eyes.

Looking out the window, Benjamin saw the cherry tree in the side yard, its wooden bench-swing swaying back and forth from a brown, knobby limb. On the sill he spotted a black feather. The bird, Osiris's messenger, had already left its gift for Elizabeth.

Good.

Releasing Faith's hand, he stood in front of his daughter. Faith walked to the corner of the room, next to the armoire, where Elizabeth's censer and candle burned pungently. Elizabeth was seated on the floor, perfectly centered within her circle, naked and cross-legged, sheened in sweat. The soft glow of the candles jutting up from the hearts of the pentagrams shimmered upon her wet skin. Her eyes were closed, hands on her knees, palms facing upward. Her full lips trembled in soundless prayer. Her breasts were layered in gooseflesh, nipples dark and rigid.

Before her, at the top of the circle contained by the triangle, was her leather parchment, unfurled so the sigil could be delivered to the spirit. Beneath it lay a smooth cushion of black silk. Alongside were two chalices, one filled with ground rose petals, the other mud unearthed from the garden where the petals grew.

Benjamin approached the circle. Elizabeth opened her eyes. She beheld her father, staring down at her proudly, moist eyes twinkling beneath the cast of the candles. Behind him, she glimpsed her mother moving to the window to retrieve the black feather from the sill. Faith turned and held the feather high, gazing at it until the next bell tolled. Then, along with Benjamin, she sat cross-legged in the circle, facing Elizabeth. She placed the feather atop the leather scroll.

As if on cue, they all locked hands and closed their eyes. Benjamin could feel his heart pounding harder and harder as the ritual commenced. The bells tolled, and again he called out to Osiris, singing the verse in a flat tone: *"Come, thou all-powerful Lord Osiris, who exists amongst the Gods in the astral plane and governs the Realm of Resurrection and Everlasting Life. I conjure thee to bestow upon Elizabeth Conroy your influence of spiritual rebirth, so that she may purely and honorably engage your powers for the purpose of ancestral afterlife, with utmost earnestness and commitment."*

And again, upon concluding the spell, the bells rang. Immediately thereafter, Benjamin dropped a candle's flame onto the parchment containing the sigil of Osiris, along with the blackbird's feather. The parchment burst into flames, viscous black smoke rising to the ceiling. The three of them held their hands over the flame, the smoke seeping through their fingers, and intoned in unison, *"To your service we dedicate earth and roses to strengthen your spirit, oh infinitely powerful Osiris, in hope that you may find this an acceptable offering for your bounteousness."*

They broke their grasp, Elizabeth at once placing her hands, palms up, back upon her knees. Faith grabbed the chalice of roses and Benjamin the mud.

They upturned their gifts onto the flame, smothering it. A thick sizzle emerged from the filthy mound. They opened their eyes. Benjamin and Faith gazed at their daughter in all her glistening nakedness.

"Do you feel Osiris's spirit within you?" Benjamin asked his daughter.

Elizabeth nodded.

A bell tolled, triggering the next phase of the ritual. Benjamin and Faith rubbed their index fingers into the pile of mud and ash between them. Elizabeth closed her eyes and offered her scar to them.

At the same time, Benjamin and Faith pressed their fingers against Elizabeth's sternum, on opposite ends of her scar. Slowly, they traced the shape, looping upward and meeting at the apex of the curve just below her throat, a trail of wet ash layering the damaged flesh like sandy earth on a stream bank.

"Osiris is with you, Elizabeth," both mother and father pronounced.

She nodded, then quietly stood and shrugged into her black knit robe, which had been folded in thirds upon her nightstand.

The bell tolled.

Joining hands, father, mother, and daughter, all clad in black hooded robes, left the room.

CHAPTER SIX

September 6, 2005
4:19 P.M.

It had been a perfect day outside. Summer had refused
to surrender its pleasures to fall. The trees lining the
sidewalks on 88th Street still held on to their green,
proudly displaying their leaves as they did in June. It
was seventy-three degrees according to the circular
thermometer on the fire escape; pigeons came and
went and did their pigeon business on the black grates,
something Johnny would be made to scrub away over
the weekend.

Johnny Petrie, who all his life had felt weak and
timid and unsure of himself, had in the past ten minutes shed all his insecurities now that he might be a
rich man. Who said that money didn't buy happiness?
He didn't have it yet, but the prospect of being rich and
eighteen and able to flee the prison that was his home

gave him a sense of freedom. He would no longer have to play slave to Mary's quirks, would no longer have to abide by her stringent rules, something previously unimaginable in his controlled life. Now it was all potentially within a hand's grasp of the telephone.

The telephone.

Should it not be real, should the letter turn out to be a sham or a mistake, he would have to settle back down to the miserable earth and move on with his measly existence. *God forbid*, as Mary liked to say.

Holding the letter in his left hand, he scooped up the telephone handset from its cradle, tucked it into the crook of his neck, and dialed the number. He could hear the beeps sounding out from the earpiece like little bells tolling . . .

. . . *bells tolling* . . .

. . . his eyes catching a dusty web dangling from the corner of the ceiling like a tiny vine.

The phone rang.

Someone picked up on the first ring. Johnny shuddered at the millisecond of silence between the click of the phone and the husky voice of the woman who answered: "Andrew Judson's office."

The first thing Johnny did was sit at the small dinette table in the kitchen. His heart thudded in his chest, his feet suddenly numb, his tongue dry as parchment. His voice was weak and uneasy: "Mr. Judson, please."

"May I tell him who's calling?" she inquired brusquely.

"My name is . . ."

He stopped.

"Sir?" the woman asked.

"My name is Johnny Petrie. *John* Petrie."

There was a slight hesitation on the line, followed by

what sounded like a gasp of unanticipated surprise. "I'll tell him you're on, Mr. Petrie. Please hold."

Mr. Petrie? That's a new one. A title of respect . . . especially for people who have money.

The next instant he was listening to a canned version of "Angel" by Jimi Hendrix. He smiled, wondering, *What are the odds?* While the tinny music filtered into his head, he looked around at the painful familiarity of his home: the small two-bedroom Upper East Side apartment that boasted a fine neighborhood, but pitiful walls adorned with a helter-skelter collection of religious motifs and statuary, needlepoint canvases depicting snow-covered farmhouses, and a few dust-coated prints of Norman Rockwell paintings. All the furniture was old and beginning to wear, as were the appliances. An ancient rolltop desk sat in the corner, opened to display an old office model typewriter.

A man's voice broke onto the line. There was no introduction, no formal pleasantry exchange. He cut right to the chase, perhaps making an attempt to capture his prey before it made an escape.

"Is this John Petrie?"

Johnny was caught off guard. He straightened up on the chair, not even realizing that he'd crouched down so low. "Y-yes."

"Of 479 East 88th Street, New York, New York?"

"Yes, that's where I live."

"My . . ." was the reply, followed by a gush a heavy breathing. "It is you."

How to respond to that? Johnny had no clue. He shook his head, his mind a blank.

In search of something to say, he quickly looked out the window. At that instant, a large blackbird landed on the fire escape. Johnny watched it as it hopped around on the rusted grates, then came to the window, cocked its head, and aimed its beady little eyes at him.

The lawyer's voice broke the silence and Johnny jolted upright. "I trust you've read the letter I sent to you, then?"

"I did," Johnny answered, pulling his gaze away from the bird. It had had him strangely distracted, almost to the point that, within seconds, he nearly forgot who he was on the phone with.

"And you understand everything?"

"Well, actually . . . this is Mr. Judson, right?" Dumb question, but the surreality of the phone call, along with the sudden distraction of the blackbird, had left him feeling confused, and he had to make certain that he had all his cards straight.

"Yes, Johnny."

"I . . . I'm not really sure what to make of this. Really, I mean, this is some kind of joke, right?" He looked back at the bird. It'd hopped up on the edge of the ladder and was skittering across the step.

"No, Johnny, it's not." Suddenly, Judson's voice sounded calm, reserved, the initial excitement of hearing from Johnny perhaps thinning out some. "Johnny, I know quite well that this sounds crazy. It's not every day this type of thing happens to anyone. But . . . I've been waiting until you turned eighteen to contact you. If I'm not mistaken, you turned eighteen on August 24th, correct?"

Johnny felt a prickle of gooseflesh at that. "Yes," he answered, his voice a weak whisper.

"There are many legalities to discuss regarding this situation, but I assure you that the estate of Benjamin Conroy has been willed to you."

Benjamin Conroy . . .

"Mr. Judson," Johnny said, shaking his head. "I want to believe you, I mean, who wouldn't want to believe that they've just fallen into some big load of money . . . but really, there must be some kind of mistake here. I don't know anyone named Benjamin Conroy."

Or, do I? Again he looked outside. The bird was gone. On the balcony was a single black feather flapping in the breeze, its root caught in the steel grates.

There was a brief silence on the phone, then a shuffle of papers. "In a few days John, you will know *much* about Benjamin Conroy." He paused, then added, "And in due time, you will learn much about yourself."

CHAPTER SEVEN

August 24, 1988
5:58 A.M.

He hadn't slept much at all, mostly fitful naps and sheet-twisting twitches. There were a few jaunts into the world of his dreams, but even they were short and aggressive and menacing. He dreamed of things coming to get him in the night: dead things, with their arms outstretched and mouths gaping, toothless and rotting, waking him the moment they pounced. After each dream, he would lie awake, dry-eyed and cotton-mouthed, hands on his heaving stomach, sheathed in cold sweat.

After what seemed an eternity, the first of the bells eventually tolled, and he'd performed exactly as he had been instructed, as he had rehearsed time and time again until he and his whole family—excepting the baby, of course—got it right. It had all been scrawled—in a thick loopy script in black ink—in his father's preparation handbook: the odd pacing at the tolling of the thirteenth bell, the lighting of the candles and incense at the thirtieth. The prayers, the sigils, the odd symbols and pentagrams and triangles meticulously painted on the ground. It had all been committed to memory, burned into his mind like a brand.

His thirteen-year-old mind had never really been able to grasp the entire premise behind what his father attempted to accomplish. It was, in some odd way, all about "seeking a closer bond with Jesus Christ," that much he knew. It was *always* about coming into contact with the messages in the Bible. When your father was a minister and governed the household with such an impassioned spiritualism, it was always best to follow his guiding principles, lest you find yourself on the receiving end of his God-driven punishment.

So he'd adhered to his father's most recent set of rules, following precisely the stages of the ritual until he found himself naked and sweating in the center of the candlelit circle he had prepared two weeks prior. He repeated the prayer to the God Osiris,

"I beseech thee, O Spirit Osiris from the vast astral plane, by the supreme majesty of God, to allow the child Bryan Conroy an association to our purpose, so that he too may benefit from your empowering gift."

Between the tolling of the bells, he speculated as to who this God Osiris was, and whether or not he was written about in the New Testament. One time, he'd questioned his father as to Osiris's role in the Bible,

and immediately found himself bruised and fat-lipped
with a lengthy list of chores.

"*Listen to me, Daniel, and you shall be saved from the
wrath of evil. We have summoned Osiris to save us from
the ambiguity of the afterlife and keep us together as a family so that we may walk together for eternity. Jesus Christ
once rose from the dead as a savior of the people of
Jerusalem. It was the holiest of all occurrences in the history
of mankind, an event even more sacred than the creation of
Adam and Eve. We, as a family, will work together as sav-
iors in the afterlife, just as Jesus Christ did nearly two
thousand years ago. But . . . beware my son, evil aims to
stop us. You must be strong and follow my lead, so we can be
eternally saved by God.*"

"*But Father, which God do we worship? Is it Jesus, or this
Osiris?*"

"*Jesus and Osiris shall work together to bring us everlasting life.*"

"*Father—is this written about in the Bible?*"

And that was when the strong hand of Benjamin
Conroy came down on Daniel Conroy over and over
again, the minister's greasy hair hanging in strings over
his fierce blue eyes, as he shouted piously, "*Thou shalt
not question the will of God! Evil is working its way into
your soul. Do not let it, my son. Shout at the devil!*"

It had been too much to handle for the thirteen-
year-old. He'd seen no choice but to abide by the stringent rules his father had set in place, just as his mother
and sister had done. But then what of baby Bryan, cel-
ebrating his first birthday today? Twelve years ago,
Daniel had been in the same helpless situation. Obvi-
ously, he didn't remember any of it. But now, he would
be forced to witness the baby—his brother—suffering

the pain and agony of the event that was going to leave him scarred for the remainder of his life.

Daniel remained in place as the bells continued to toll throughout the house. His father had instructed him to repeat the prayer to Osiris over and over again to himself, to clear his mind of extraneous thought and seek the golden light that would open the doorway to the astral plane. Instead, his mind wandered toward the bells—the bells that at five this morning had awakened the entire family and would continue to toll for a total of one hour and thirty-three minutes. Where were they hidden? And how did Father rig them about the house?

Suddenly, he was aware of something moving. He found his gaze drawn toward the window, where he saw a single black feather on the windowsill, its quill buried deep into the split wood, its soft trimmings waving gently in the mild wind.

He stared at the feather until his attention was distracted by the toll of another bell, then scrutinized his naked body with bitter distaste: his plump midsection, white thighs and stomach pressed together in a mass of dips and rolls; his skin, sallow and afire with raised patches of prickly-heat; his feet cramped beneath his weight, ankle bones buried beneath a smooth layer of fat, rubbing painfully against the wood floor.

He made every effort to keep his wandering gaze *(Important—you must keep your eyes closed until we arrive)* away from his stomach, which sweated and pinched and begged to be itched. His hands wandered down, somewhere in the nether-regions below his girth. He adjusted his aching genitals, spreading his legs and alternating between kneeling and sitting cross-legged in an effort to relieve the pain.

He knew that he was going to have to wait the longest (except for the baby, who still slept soundly) for his father to arrive. He'd been instructed to count the bells and perform the exercises and prayers, and had given it quite a stab but ended up losing track about twenty *dongs* ago. So he squirmed and moved and fingered the scar upon his sternum, saying prayers for his baby brother, who would be punished for the rest of his life because of his father's convictions.

As a child, Daniel had been told that accepting the faith of his parents would be the only way to gain protection, the only way to grow up self-confident, with food on the table and a home to sleep in. *It's the same reason little Orthodox children wear yarmulkes, and the Amish wear capes and aprons and drive horses and buggies. They know no other way, no other lifestyle. It is quite simply the way of their people. We, the Conroy family, have our own principles as well.*

But now all that was beginning to change. He could see it, *feel* it. His parents had trusted him, were wholly confident that their thirteen-year-old son had seen no other means of existence other than the Conroy way. They entrusted him enough to allow him out of the house for short walks to D'Agostino's Drug Store on Main Street to buy diapers for Bryan or menthol rub for Mother's arthritis.

Go directly to the store. Buy only the things on this list. Do not speak to anyone on the way there or on the way back.

As always, his mother and father were always busy with the crucial undertaking of *something*, whether preparing Father's weekly sermon or deciding which tea to brew for dinner. There were the fields of corn and wheat that ran east of the house for a quarter mile, and the barn out back where bales of hay were prepared for sale to the locals. Mother and Father worked endlessly, running crops back and forth, handing out chores to Daniel and Elizabeth, who toiled together under Benjamin's strict guidance.

Just recently, Daniel had seen some of the other children from town on the playground at the public school on King Street. His mother had taken him into town to purchase spices for a new recipe of corn chowder. The Conroy's were committed vegetarians, and Faith Conroy experimented with a variety of new-fangled herbs in an effort to "spice up" their dinners; Daniel thought the chowder she made had tasted much like mud despite its yellow appearance. They'd walked passed the Wellfield Public School, and he'd asked his mother about all the other children who were racing about playing kickball and jumping rope and climbing on jungle gyms, and he was told that these were the devil's children, saturated with immorality and foul influence, and should be ignored at all costs.

"This is why your father and I tutor you every night at home, so that you won't be influenced by such evils."

"But Mother, I recognize some of these children from church. They attend Father's masses."

"It is because they seek salvation from their sins. We must remain sin free, for we . . . we have a special purpose, one more divine than the birth of Jesus Christ himself."

"What is it, Mother? What is our purpose?"

"In due time, my son, you shall find out."

He'd continually wondered about the special purpose of the Conroy family, wondering what could possibly be more divine than the birth of Jesus Christ. His father had told him that the most sacred event in all of mankind was Jesus's rising from the dead. The prayers Father had taught him referred to ancestral afterlife. Did their purpose have something to do with that?

There was a noise outside his room, something other than the incessant bells that were starting to give Daniel quite a headache. He immediately felt an odd disquiet, a sensation he hadn't once felt during their dry runs, and the sharp reality came to him: This was no dress rehearsal. Whatever his father's intentions were . . . the ritual would either happen to his satisfaction, or it wouldn't. And regardless, Daniel had a dreadful notion that something terrible would occur.

The floors in the hallway creaked, and then there was a clicking sound: the doorknob to his room being turned. A sudden disquiet struck him, like the time he'd gone swimming at Capson's Lake and the bottom fell out from beneath his feet. The warm water had swallowed him up and dragged him down where it was as cold as ice. When he finally made it back to the surface, and then to dry land, he vomited lake water and shivered uncontrollably, gripping his pained chest as though he'd been stabbed through the heart. This was how he felt now: terrified, with no control of the situation, feeling as though he'd been slashed with an icy-cold knife.

There came a muted padding of footsteps. He closed his eyes, hoping his family would not see that he had not kept to the ritual. He placed his hands upon his knees and moved his lips, feigning prayer. He felt the heat of his family—Father, Mother, and Elizabeth— encircle him like a blanket of hot air.

His heart rose in his chest. It beat in his throat, making it difficult to breathe. He heard the bells toll and then his father's voice as he commenced with the sigil of Osiris. As the ritual resumed at the tolling of the next bell, Daniel followed every last detail as he'd been taught, imagining that he were running the entire performance himself.

CHAPTER EIGHT

September 6, 2005
5:11 P.M.

Johnny Petrie's jubilation upon speaking to Andrew
Judson and coming to the sobering conclusion that this
inheritance was indeed *for real* now faded into thin air
as he considered his next move. His mind wandered in
circles, thoughts running amok and making no sense
other than replacing his jubilation with worry and ill-
defined fear.

After hanging up the phone, he marched into the
bathroom and looked at himself in the mirror. His
face, although still pale and zitty and drawn, wore an
unfamiliar expression; one that was focused and alert
and wholly prepared for whatever lay ahead.

The conversation between Judson and Johnny had
gone on to detail the course of action he would need to
take. Judson had explained that Johnny's silence would

be of the utmost importance, and he strongly requested that Johnny not mention the letter or their
conversation with anyone, including his parents.
When Johnny had asked why, Judson said that everything would be made clear upon his arrival in Wellfield. Johnny had argued that he couldn't just pull some
sort of vanishing act, that his parents would have his
face broadcast on the five o'clock news if he didn't
show up for dinner. But he did promise that in a few
days he'd travel up to Maine to meet with the lawyer,
once he was able to gather some things, including a bit
of cash.

My God, am I really going to do this?

Johnny returned to the kitchen, reading the letter
again and again. Despite Judson's reassurances, the
whole thing still seemed too good to be true. But he
also told himself that the regrets of not investigating it
would fill a list a mile long and would never answer
who Benjamin Conroy was and why this so-called relative he'd never heard of had left him a fortune.

*Maybe I do know someone named Benjamin Conroy.
Somehow, I feel as though I do now. Think, think . . .*

For the next half hour he paced about the apartment
like a caged tiger, sweating away his tentativeness and
building up a life's worth of courage to confront his
parents and gather the truth of the situation. His skin
rolled with goose bumps. He could feel his heart jack-
hammering against his ribs. He felt the need to get this
all out into the open, with no beating around the bush.
He would have to catch his mother off guard, as soon
as she walked through the door and before his father
came home so she couldn't ask him for help.

Eventually, after wearing out a path between the
kitchen and his bedroom, Johnny sat at the kitchen

table and stared at the St. Luke calendar on the door, restlessly waiting for his mother to return home.

Jesus, this is going to be one helluva confrontation.

He remained quiet, listening to the ticking of the clock in the kitchen as it drove itself like a nail, deep into his head. He thought of the faceless man named Benjamin Conroy, wondering who he was, what he might have looked like, how he died, why he left his fortune to Johnny. Then it occurred to him: *Judson waited until I turned eighteen to contact me. Is it possible that Benjamin Conroy died some time ago and had left instructions in his will to wait until I turned eighteen?*

Or did he just drop dead last week?

In between these meandering thoughts, a childhood memory filtered back to him in blinding detail: what he called "the golden pain."

He could recall lying on his back, helpless as though drugged. There had been the sound of a bell tolling, and then a golden light floated over him, and from out of that light emerged the indistinct figure of a person, head tilted, arms outstretched. The figure was flanked by a small group of faceless people he would years later describe as "witnesses." As the central figure emerged from the light and drew closer to him, the witnesses crowded around Johnny's body and latched on to his arms and legs. He could recall the pain of struggling to get away from these dark people, his muscles straining, his biceps and thighs burning beneath their determined grips.

And that was where his memories ended; the proverbial blackout had taken effect, as if he had awakened from a nightmare only to find himself lying atop damp sheets in a cold sweat. But the images had stayed with him, in his memories, and then again in his dreams, where at least once a month the dark, faceless man and his witnesses would visit him while he slept.

Once, after an extremely colorful recurrence of the dream, he'd drummed up the courage to discuss it all with Mother, but she acted as expected: with utter indifference. *This is exactly why we don't want you reading those trashy science-fiction novels. . . . Next thing you'll be telling us is that you were abducted by aliens!*

But now . . . the name of one Benjamin Conroy was in his head, super-glued to his brain and functioning like a hypnotist drawing out suppressed memories. Along with the memories of the golden pain, new memories began flooding his mind—of the events that occurred *after* the witnesses grabbed his arms, *after* the blackout. The recollection of the golden pain, plus the presence of the name Benjamin Conroy, now together in his mind for the very first time, seemed to work hand-in-hand in reclaiming lost memories. He could see it all now, playing out on the walls of his mind as though a motion-picture projector had been turned on. And it made him realize that the dream of the golden pain was not a dream after all. *It'd really happened!*

He could see the events playing out in vivid color: the central figure looming over him, features hidden in a veil of suffocating smoke. There was a moment's hesitation as a voice of protest filtered in from somewhere close by. Johnny saw the central figure kicking away one of the faceless witnesses, then kneel down before his prone body. There was a glow of golden light, sharp and concentrated, followed by a quick, hot searing agony upon his chest.

Johnny could feel the pain upon his chest now.

My God . . . it is real. It really happened.

Johnny himself had thought the incident too fanciful to be true, and he'd made a keen attempt to write it all off as a dream. But now, with the rest of the memories present in his mind, he couldn't do that. As surreal and painful as it was, it carried an undeniable realism that couldn't be ignored—it could only be described as a memory.

Because, despite it seeming like some weird faraway dream, Johnny Petrie had unequivocal proof that the event had actually occurred—that at some point, years ago in his past, when he was just a baby, it really happened.

He opened the collar of his shirt and placed a hand against his chest.

"It's a birthmark, Johnny. It was there when you emerged from my womb . . . I should know, I'm your mother. . . ."

He ran his index finger against the scar on his sternum.

"Mother, if it's a birthmark, then why is it so . . . perfect?"

The central figure leaned down over him and delivered a blow of hot searing agony upon his chest. . . .

His mother would grin away his queries, looking slightly concerned but maintaining her composure nonetheless. Perhaps she had known quite well that at some point her son would ask about the strange scar on his chest . . . the wrinkled purple blemish that was in the perfect shape of an ankh.

Johnny sat steadfastly at the table, body stiff with tension. He shifted in his chair, stood and paced back and forth, checking the facts over and over again. He took a few long deep breaths, then sat back down. *It's falling into place. Yes, I can see it now, it's as clear as black and white.* If there had been any doubt about confronting his parents with the letter or traveling up to see Andrew Judson in Wellfield, Maine, it was now as dead as Benjamin Conroy.

The mark on his chest was *not* a birthmark, as his parents had always insisted. It was a scar after all, a piece of a bigger puzzle.

The ankh on his chest.

The memory of the golden pain and the central figure looming over him, delivering unendurable agony.

And now, the name of Benjamin Conroy, triggering additional memories.

It's all a part of my past, something my mother probably knows about, and has kept a secret from me my entire life. I will find out. I will . . .

In the hallway outside the door, footsteps approached.

He heard a key enter the lock.

Mother was home.

CHAPTER NINE

August 24, 1988
6:23 A.M.

They moved down the hall in a procession: Benjamin in the lead, holding a white candle as a guiding light. Faith followed close behind, clinging to a censer's thin chain and rocking it back and forth as pungent smoke puffed out. Elizabeth and Daniel trailed their mother's elongated shadow, heads bowed slightly, hands folded in prayer.

At the tolling of the next bell, Benjamin entered the last bedroom on the left, everyone else falling in behind his lead. The wood floor settled beneath their gentle footsteps, the aroma of sandalwood from the censer immediately filling the air. The room was stark, adorned with only the necessary ingredients: the painted circle; the pentagrams, unlit candles at their cruxes; the triangle and associated hexagrams. The blinds were drawn, coating the room in welcoming darkness.

Beneath the lone window stood a wooden crib. Inside, Bryan Conroy rested peacefully upon a plain white mattress, his tiny chest slowly going up and down, naked as the day he was born.

Benjamin stepped to the crib and peered down into it. He uttered the preliminary prayer to Osiris, adding, "It is time, Bryan Conroy, for you to join us in our quest for ancestral afterlife. As Jesus once rose from the dead to deliver his miracle to the people of Jerusalem and then ascended into heaven to be seated at the right hand of God, we shall live together infinitely, beyond the confines of our graves. Upon the deaths of our physical existences, our souls shall be gathered up by the hand of Osiris and be granted eternal afterlife, bound by love and commitment."

The bells sounded. Benjamin waited until the resonance faded, then leaned into the crib and picked up the baby. Holding his son close, he felt a wave of elation. The time—Bryan's time—had finally arrived.

Benjamin turned and faced his family. He held the naked baby out like an offering and said, "Here, on his first birthday, the last of the Conroys will pledge his allegiance to Osiris and request the gift of ancestral afterlife."

"Praise the Lord Osiris," the family said in unison.

Benjamin asked his wife, "Do you, Faith Conroy, elect to share your gift of the afterlife with Bryan Conroy?"

Faith nodded and revealed her scar. "Yes."

"Do you, Elizabeth Conroy, elect to share your gift of the afterlife with Bryan Conroy?"

She too showed her scar. "Yes."

"Do you, Daniel Conroy, elect to share your gift of the afterlife with Bryan Conroy?"

Daniel hesitated, earning him a concerned gaze from his father. He shifted uncomfortably, eyes peering downward, then opened his robe and replied, "Yes," his tone slightly off.

The bells rang. Benjamin waited in silence, eyes shut in supplication, lips trembling as the baby began to stir. The toll's reverberation faded. Thirteen seconds passed, and instead of another bell, silence dominated the entire house.

Benjamin's smile was immediate. The first half of the ritual had played out perfectly: Exactly one hour and thirty-three minutes had elapsed since he rose from bed to initiate Bryan's allegiance to Osiris. And now, here he was, standing with his entire family at the correct point in the ritual he'd spent months meticulously plotting.

"Osiris is with us now," he finally said. "Jesus has been with us since we opened our eyes to the light of the earth. Both the Lord Osiris and the Lord Jesus Christ will now work in concert to ensure us the miracle of everlasting togetherness, now and beyond the scope of our present lives."

When Benjamin looked down at his infant son, he saw that Bryan's eyes were wide and alert. He was looking up at his father. Smiling.

And the Conroy family said in unison: "Amen."

CHAPTER TEN

September 6, 2005
5:48 P.M.

Mary Petrie stepped into the apartment, not even noticing her son sitting at the kitchen table with his arms folded, staring at her. Her keys jingled from a loop ornamented with rosary beads and a silver crucifix, one key still inserted into the bolt lock. She yanked it out and draped the ornamental loop over the wooden cross mounted on the wall beside the door.

She turned and caught her son's penetrating gaze. Johnny could plainly see that whatever false sense of security she'd gathered from either the doctor's office or the confessional that afternoon was now gone.

Undoubtedly foreseeing a grave situation with her son, Mary looked down and promptly walked past him, into the living room.

Johnny stayed glued to his seat, shaking his head

with disappointment. His mother, despite all her insecurities and her will to dominate every aspect of his life, had never shown any outright concern for her son when something visibly bothered him. Her priorities lay solely within herself, and if his issues didn't directly affect her, she would simply carry on with her routine. And that was what she was doing now: ignoring her son at a time when he needed her most.

Mary placed her faux-leather pocketbook on the sofa. She peered at her son, but when Johnny returned her uncertain gaze, she looked away and took off her polyester blazer, clearly uncomfortable with what she saw.

Head down, she darted off into the bathroom without a word being exchanged between them. Johnny heard the toilet flush, and then the water running, and it was at this moment he realized that Andrew Judson's letter was still in his hands. He folded it in thirds, wiped his sweaty palms on his jeans, then folded the letter in half again. He slid it into his back pocket, thinking that over his dead body would he let his mother get her claws on it.

He closed his eyes and rehearsed his delivery: *I'm leaving you, Mother. Dad too. And there's nothing you can do about it. I know you're going to be disappointed, but I'm eighteen now, and of legal age to go out on my own. I really should be going to college this September like all the other graduates, but instead you have me living here like a slave, doing chores, praising God and all that jazz. You can't really expect me to study the Bible and do the dishes for the rest of my life. . . .*

For the first time, Johnny Petrie could see a pinpoint of light at the end of the gloomy tunnel he'd been traveling through all his life. And it was within reaching distance too, the payment for the toll sitting right in his back pocket.

"What . . . is . . . this?" Her voice came out strongly and suddenly, with no question or concern for his apparent worries.

He flinched guiltily, and the first thought to cross his mind was indeed filled with guilt: *She knows about Andrew Judson and the letter, and somehow she'd reached her hand into my back pocket and pulled it out and read it without me knowing it, and now she wants to know every last detail!* But when he looked up at her, he saw that this wasn't the case at all.

Mary was standing in the doorway leading into his bedroom. As she did nearly every day, she'd changed into her sleeveless blue floral housedress, topped off with a matching headband that pulled her mostly gray hair back into a short, flat wave. In her hand was the book he'd taken out of the library, H.G. Wells's *War of the Worlds*.

Upon arriving home, he'd taken it out of his knapsack and tossed it on the bed. He'd left it there because his attention had been diverted by Judson's letter. *Damn.*

He smiled at her thinly, partly out of blame, partly out of indifference.

"What have I told you about reading this . . . this *trash*?" She was holding the book out like a preacher would a Bible. "If you read this, your mind will turn to rot, and your soul will carry the taint of the devil!"

"We need to talk, Mom."

He thought it was possible, noticing the sudden redness of her skin, that the blood rushing to her head had blocked her ears from hearing what he'd just said.

"This is going where it belongs," she pronounced, then marched defiantly into the kitchen and pitched the book into the garbage pail. "Utter trash, read by those whose tickets to hell are already paid for."

Now Johnny wondered if all that redness in her face had been caused by a broken blood vessel in her brain—clearly she knew a fine would be assessed if the book wasn't returned. And Johnny didn't have a dime to his name.

Or did he?

There are many legalities to discuss regarding this situation, but I assure you that the estate of Benjamin Conroy has been willed to you . . .

She took a step toward the kitchen table, placing a wrinkled hand upon the chipped wood, as if trying to maintain her balance. To Johnny, she appeared strangely tentative despite her anger.

Johnny stared her down, and was about to speak when Mary shifted her body and dropped into the kitchen chair opposite him. She looked at her hands and said briskly, "I saw Dr. Webster today, and he told me that I'm making some improvements. Helen Sampson, you know her from church, right? She told me that her daughter also suffers from generalized anxiety disorder and mild depression, and that she just started taking this new drug on the market, so Dr. Webster prescribed for me—"

"Mom . . ."

She stopped talking and stared at him. The string of silence between them was bitter and tense.

"We need to talk."

She cocked her head and squinted. "Johnny . . . are you listening to me? Your mother hasn't been feeling well, and now I might be going to a—"

"I'm leaving here," he said, the words coming out with no doubt or uncertainty in them.

She kept her gaze on him. "To church, I presume? Well, as long as you're back for dinner. I'm anxious to tell you all about Helen's daughter. She's a member of the choir at St. Anthony's."

And then an incredible thing happened. Johnny felt his blood rush, as though all his pent-up emotions had finally been released after eighteen years of mental incarceration. His eyes began to tear and his jaw clenched. And his scar was *tingling*. All these feelings coalesced to form a brewing wrath inside him that he'd never sensed before. And damn, it felt *good*.

And as good as it felt for Johnny, he could see an equal amount of fear rising in his mother's eyes. She plucked a string of rosaries from her housedress pocket and began to nervously toy with it, apparently convinced that something hideous and evil had suddenly possessed her son.

"Mom . . . I said I'm leaving here."

Keeping her tear-filled eyes on the rosary, she replied angrily, "You stop this nonsense at once."

"I'm not kidding. I'm packing my things, and I'm leaving."

"Johnny, are you feeling well? Perhaps I should call Dr. Cutler. It's been a few months since your last checkup."

"I am not sick," he answered in that same unambiguous voice. He was making every effort to keep his cool, difficult as it was. He *did* still love her despite her craziness, and that was the only thing stopping him from cranking everything up a few decibels. "Listen, Mom, I have someplace I need to go. It might be for a few days, or it might be for a few weeks. It might be forever. I'm not sure yet. All I do know for certain is that I need to leave here."

The redness flushed back into Mary's face; this time, it was out of anger. She cracked her chin up like a whip, the rosary slapping against the table, gripped defiantly in her fist. "I beg your pardon, young man . . . I'm your mother! And I make the rules around here! You, my dear boy, are not going anywhere! So you drop this nonsense at once before I summon the wrath of Jesus upon you, you *sinner*." Tiny droplets of spittle flew from her lips. One alit on Johnny's cheek.

Johnny stood, fists immediately coming down hard upon the table. The drug store circular fluttered to the floor like a falling leaf. "I am no sinner," he said, voice firm and domineering. "I have obeyed your demands all my life, and now . . . now . . . I'm done with it." He paused, swallowed a dry lump in his throat, then added, "If you want to see a sinner, then look no further than Dad, with his smoking and his drinking and his carousing. C'mon, do you really think he gives a damn about the Bible and Jesus? Huh? All he cares about is staying away from you as much as possible."

Oh, the horror. Mary's face blanched. Her entire body trembled. Her mouth fell open, as big as a mountain cave. Her hands were massaging the rosary hard, as if it might bring about some magical peace. Then the tears came, flowing down her cheeks and carving wet lines into her foundation. "Bite . . . your . . . t-tongue," she stammered through her sobs.

Johnny stood over his cowering mother. "I'm giving you the courtesy of telling you what I plan to do. You can't stop me, Mom. You can't."

"Your father—" she cried.

"He can't stop me either."

"He can."

Johnny shook his head and stepped into the living room.

"*You get back here at once!*" Her voice held the rage of a tiger. Unruly. Defensive. Tears streamed down her face. She was so sad and angry, disappointed and betrayed—it showed in her features, the flood of tears, the trembling scowl, the gasping and the sniveling.

What did I expect? I'm not sure if this is it. She came in, looked at me once, and knew, just knew *that something was wrong. It was almost as if . . . as if she were expecting this to happen.*

He stayed in the center of the living room. He felt for the letter in his back pocket, and it was still there, of course. He looked at his mother and shook his head slightly. "It doesn't have to be like this, Mom."

She shook her head. She moved to speak, but sobs stifled her words. With all her crying, a lull was created. Johnny felt a flutter of anxiety tickle the walls of his stomach—the adrenaline had stopped pumping and was leaving him with a weak, hollow feeling. It was because he was disappointing her—was breaking away from her personal plan for him. And in a way, he felt bad for her. But . . .

. . . you, Mr. John Petrie, are to receive the entire estate bequeathed to me as executor. The value of the inheritance is estimated at two million dollars . . .

"Mom . . . I'm sorry . . . but there's something I really need to do."

She kept her gaze down, unanswering for a minute or more. A fresh flood of tears filled her eyes. "You're hurting me," she finally whispered. "More than you know."

"I'm sorry, but—"

"Why are you doing this, Johnny?" She asked the question almost as if she *knew* exactly what he was doing and why.

"I can't say."

And then the anger returned. She stood up quickly and pointed at him, shouting in a frenzy, "Like hell you can't! You'll tell me, and then you'll tell your father, and then we must exorcise this evil that has taken hold of you!"

Jesus Christ, he thought. *She's completely lost her mind*. "Mom . . . please—"

"Who's putting you up to this?" she demanded. "I know you're not acting alone. And whoever it is, you believe me when I tell you that they will bring you nothing but misfortune. Pain and misfortune! Tell me, Johnny! Tell me!"

He shook his head. "No." He felt a sudden need to end this insane conversation, because crazily, she was beginning to make him think that maybe, just maybe, he might be making some grave mistake after all.

"Who, Johnny?" she asked, leaning forward with her fists on the table, voice deep and intense. "I can see it in your eyes, there's something you're not telling me. Who's making you act this way?"

And then he said it. It charged out of his mouth unbridled, loudly and clearly.

"Benjamin Conroy."

And at this moment, Judson's voice filtered back into his mind: *Silence is of the utmost importance. I strongly request that you not mention the letter or this conversation with anyone, including your parents*. As this thought filled his head, Mary's mouth fell open and she dropped back down into the chair. The chair toppled over, taking her with it. There was a loud crack against the kitchen floor, either wood or skull meeting the vinyl tiles. Her arms flailed and her hands groped the air, and Johnny raced into the kitchen, instantly regretting his hasty decision to mention Conroy's name. But a thought had crossed his mind as to whether Benjamin Conroy was indeed a relative, and if he was, then his mother would've known about him, despite her telling him in the past that the only Petrie family members in existence were the three of them. She coughed heaving chokes, the words following unintelligible garbles.

"Mom!" He kneeled alongside her and grabbed her hand. It was cold. Her fingers were locked around the rosary like chain links.

Her bulging eyes turned on him, ablaze with terror. Her mouth opened . . . but no words came out. Smatters of white foam coated her lips.

"Mom, are you okay?" When she didn't answer, he jumped up, grabbed the telephone and dialed 911. Then he gazed back at her.

Her arm was raised, the rosary still gripped from her hand, the tiny cross dangling between two fingers. She pointed it at Johnny pathetically.

Suddenly, his scar felt hot and itchy.

"Jesus, Mom, are you okay?" he asked nervously, clutching at his chest.

She squinted. Her lips parted, and in a voice that was barely recognizable as hers, shouted: *"No power to the enemy! I implore you, Dear God of heaven, God of earth, God of all creation, save him . . . save him . . ."*

CHAPTER ELEVEN

August 24, 1988
6:43 A.M.

The Conroy family left the house, Benjamin in the lead, followed by Faith, Elizabeth, then Daniel. Bryan, now wrapped in a gray blanket, lay calmly in Benjamin's arms. Pilate, the family dog—a black lab—was leashed to the basement well outside the house. He was lying down on his side, tongue lolling, staring at them inquisitively.

The family walked about a hundred feet to the center of the backyard. When Benjamin stopped, everyone spread out alongside him and faced the barn, which loomed in the near distance.

Benjamin stared at the old wooden structure, its once red surface faded to a shoddy pink, peeling away in unsightly patches. He smiled. *My sanctuary. It is . . . changing. . . .*

And so it appeared. The low-lying eastern sun splayed its golden rays across the entire backyard, capturing the barn beneath its brilliance. Now the ramshackle structure appeared to take on a newfound potency, its ugliness beaming heartily in the day's fresh light. Everything around them—the overgrown grass, the wandering weeds, the dandelions—appeared savagely rich and lush, highly aromatic.

The morning was very hot and humid, more so than it had been all summer long. *Perfect conditions for the ritual*, Benjamin thought. Beneath his robe, his skin felt clammy, sticking to the hot black fabric in damp patches. Behind the barn, from the woods that ran nearly twenty miles all the way to the outskirts of Skowhegan, tendrils of smoky mist crawled in, low-lying and dense. It seeped around the barn, seizing the entire perimeter like an oncoming tide. It carried with it an acrid odor of burning timber that filled Benjamin's nose instantly.

"The Lord Jesus Christ has given us a glorious day so that we may commence with Bryan's allegiance to Osiris." The air seemed to absorb Benjamin's words, and he noticed that there were no sounds at all on the farm: no birds chirping, no roosters crowing, none of the penned goats or pigs bleating for their meals. Even Bryan remained silent in his father's arms. All Benjamin could hear was the static rustle of the hot summer wind as it carried through the distant wheat fields.

Moments passed as Benjamin prepared his mind for the ritual. He could hear the metallic clanging of a cowbell breaking up the brooding silence. It seemed to come from inside the barn. He stood motionless and listened. It struck thirteen times, then stopped.

"The bell has tolled. It is time," he said.

Without saying another word, Benjamin stepped toward the barn, his feet kicking through patches of crabgrass and dew-soaked dandelion clusters. Even the sounds of their footsteps were muted.

He reached the door to the barn, which was padlocked. He looked left, and then right, surveying his surroundings. They were familiar, of course . . . but had taken on an unusually exotic appearance, as though he'd stepped into an old sepia-toned photograph—the vibrant colors of the previous moment had mysteriously vanished, and when he looked overhead, he saw peculiar tan-shaded clouds impregnating the sky.

Before Benjamin could consider the abrupt change in the atmosphere, a flapping noise overhead fell into the eerie silence. He saw a lone blackbird settling down on the pointed peak of the barn. The bird jigged in its effort to find a solid landing position, then pointed its tiny eyes downward, ruffling its feathers as if to acknowledge Benjamin's presence and the event about to take place.

"Osiris's messenger is here," Benjamin uttered, feeling strangely intimidated. *It has delivered the perfect setting for the spirit's arrival,* he speculated as something heavy turned over in his midsection. The bird cawed, and in this instant some of its feathers fell out into the gutter, leaving behind a bare patch of pink hide on its body. The bird poked its beak deep into the raw skin and resurfaced with a fat, buzzing horsefly.

The ground mist continued to spill from the woods. It made its way across the high grass in the backyard—rising as high as their knees—all the way to the rear of the house. Benjamin took a step forward; without the sound of his footsteps, he was unable to tell if his feet were actually touching the ground.

It feels as though I'm floating. . . .

He turned and handed the baby to Faith, then removed a key from his robe pocket and unlocked the padlock. Despite the visible pop of the latch, there was absolutely no sound at all. He removed the lock, and in that instant the bird dropped the horsefly at Benjamin's feet, its falling weight parting the mist like a rock in a pond. Benjamin could see the plump insect fidgeting frantically amidst the blades of tall grass. He pocketed the key and lock, then pulled open the large wooden doors to the barn, whose hinges had lost their loud rusting screech.

The wind gusted, blowing across the mouth of the barn and sending in rolling pillows of fog. It crawled along the hard soil, seeping toward the bales of hay piled beneath the fifteen-foot loft. He could hear a high-pitched whistling sound, the result of a warm breeze whipping in through gaps in the wooden beams; apparently, the strange silence did not to exist in here.

Benjamin bent down and picked up the horsefly, which he gingerly placed into his pocket. *For Bryan, a special gift from the messenger.* He then crossed the threshold into the barn, leaving room for Faith, Elizabeth, and Daniel to settle in behind him. He looked at the gloom-filled store, the hay bales stacked high beneath the loft, blocking the way to the rear of the barn; straw was spread out amidst hunks of wood and pieces of rusted tractor parts. Flattened tires leaned drunkenly against the right wall. Clutter existed nearly everywhere, except at the very center of the barn, where Benjamin had put everything in order for the ritual.

The first thing he noticed was the heat, dense and oppressive. It could've been a hundred degrees in here, maybe more. Sweat poured down his back in quick rivulets, and a warning voice inside his head told him that he would need to commence the ritual quickly and efficiently—that the infant would not be able to withstand the extreme temperature for too long.

Slowly and soberly, he stepped toward the center of the barn, where two four-by-eight slabs of black-primed wood were lodged flatly into the soil. Painted in white on the wood was the magic circle, its circumference exactly eight feet. Benjamin stepped into the circle and the hairs on the back of his neck immediately shifted. On the ground outside of the circle were the four pentagrams, plus the north-facing triangle of the gift; each held white candles at its point. He removed a box of wooden matches from his pocket, then kneeled before each figure and lit the candles, first at the pentagrams, and then the triangle. Scrawled in white paint along the edges of the triangle was the Seal of Osiris, the inch-high words now aglow beneath the bask of motionless candlelight. Once the candles were lit, Benjamin nodded to Elizabeth, who, as directed, closed the doors to the barn.

He immediately paced to the rear of the barn, to a point near the bales of hay, where a black silk sheet had been draped. He removed the sheet to reveal the consecrated mirror, frameless, supported only by black-painted plywood wedged between the bales. The mirror was six feet tall and two feet wide, and various symbols adorned the edges of its surface: six triangles, running along the top with the name of OSIRIS split up, one letter at each peak; down the sides ran the symbolic representations of air, earth, fire, water, and spirit.

Benjamin returned to the center of the eight-foot circle. He nodded to the others, who slowly walked over and stood just beyond the circle's circumference, alongside the pentagrams. He closed his eyes and pledged: "Here I stand at the center of the magic circle, where I shall act with the authority of the divine spirits of Jesus Christ and Osiris. I respect you both, my Gods, and shall act in accordance to your divine rule. We pray to the Lords."

And the family replied in unison: "Lords, hear our prayer."

He opened his eyes and gazed at his family. Their eyes were closed, but their faces still reflected the candlelight in a sheen of golden sweat, wet and glistening. For a stretch of twenty seconds, only silence existed. Then, a sudden rumble of far-off thunder pervaded the air, hanging in the distance like an ominous charm. Odd yellow light seeped in through the clouded window at the peak of the barn, carrying with it a thick tangy aroma that smelled like battery acid. Outside, Pilate began to bark.

Benjamin kneeled down and retrieved the magician's wand that he'd placed in the triangle days earlier. As if trying to attract lightning, he stood and aimed the wand over his head, using the molded end to trace an ankh in the air. He visualized the shape in his head in the color of gold, saying, "The time has come for Bryan Conroy to pledge his allegiance to the Lord Osiris, as we already have, so that we may as a family remain in togetherness for all of eternity. I thereby consecrate thee, implement of the afterlife, by celestial power, that thou may be used as the divining tool in our quest to beseech the all-empowering Osiris."

Elizabeth kneeled down and picked up the black silk cloth from the center of the pentagram before her. Inside the cloth was the Sigil of Osiris; like the others, this too was drawn out on a leather parchment. She removed the parchment, unfolded it, then stepped forward through the circle and placed it in the center of the triangle. Benjamin lowered the wand, plucked the horsefly from his pocket, and placed it on top of the parchment. Removing the candle from the outermost point of the painted triangle, he prayed to Osiris: "*I summon and beseech thee, O Spirit Osiris from the vast astral plane, by the supreme majesty of God, to allow the child Bryan Conroy an association to our purpose, so that he too may benefit from your empowering gift. . . .*

He struck a match and placed it to the parchment. Both the scrawled prayer and the horsefly disintegrated beneath the mounting flame.

Benjamin stepped back and watched the flames rise, his eyes following the pillar of smoke winding its way toward the vaulted ceiling of the barn. While doing this, he imagined himself as a soaring figure, with the earth a tiny sphere below him spinning on its axis. He felt a sudden flood of all-powerfulness, as though he were standing at the center of the universe, surrounded by the galaxies and stars. At the very top of the pillar of smoke, a glowing sphere of white brilliance formed. The sphere expanded and soon began to descend, forcing down the smoke and emitting a loud windlike sound that nearly deafened him. Using the wand, he reached up and pulled the white light down into his body, saying the word *"Matah"* as he did so.

He moved the wand over his torso, focusing it upon

his heart. The light thinned into a beam and connected to him, first at his heart, and then as he moved the wand, his groin. He uttered, *"Alkuth,"* his voice a monotone of prayer. He touched each shoulder, the beam of light following the end of the wand. He could see the shape it formed in the gloom: an ankh, softly aglow with the Lord Osiris's light. He held his hands together, keeping the wand tightly secured between his palms. The ankh grew brighter. Benjamin pronounced, "Here I am, standing at the cross of light that reaches deep into the astral plane where the Lord Osiris resides. Within me shines the five-point star, and with it I beseech Osiris to give the gift of eternal afterlife to the child Bryan Conroy on this, the first anniversary of his birth."

The smoky fire burned brightly, despite a lack of kindling. Benjamin took small, shallow breaths, keeping his gaze upon the glowing beam of light, now wholly absorbed by the ankh at the end of the wand. He realized quite suddenly that he possessed no sense of any time passing, feeling only the stifling heat and thick, hazy smoke. His eyes began to burn, tears forming.

The light from the wand fanned out like a spill of water, traveling slowly through the air, over the triangle where the fire still burned.

It is time!

"Osiris is coming to bring his gift of afterlife!" he shouted. "Place the baby in the circle. Now!" Holding the wand over the fire, Benjamin quickly stepped around to the pointed tip of the triangle and faced his family. Faith removed the blanket from around Bryan and moved forward into the circle. Her face, still framed in the black hood, was deadly pale, nose running, eyes puffy and tearing. Both Elizabeth and

Daniel were hunched forward, chests wrenching up and down in quick, shallow spasms. The baby, closer to the biting smoke, began to cough.

Faith placed baby Bryan down into the circle, then made her way back to her position outside the perimeter.

Using the wand, its end aglow with the heat of the fire, Benjamin traced an ankh shape in the air over Bryan, all the while staring into the mirror.

Through the heaving cries of baby Bryan, Benjamin stated the Conjuration of God, as memorized from the *Grimoire of Honorious*:

"I, Benjamin Conroy, do evoke thee, O Spirit of the God Osiris, by the living God, by the true God, by the holy and all-ruling God, who created from nothingness the heaven, the earth, the sea, and all things that are therein, in virtue of the most holy sacrament of Jesus Christ, and by the power of this Almighty Son of God, who for us and our redemption, was crucified, suffered death, and was buried; who rose again on the third day by the power of the spirit of the God Osiris, and is now seated on the right hand of the creator of the world, from whence he will bear consent for Osiris to judge the living and the dead."

Faith, Elizabeth, and Daniel all responded weakly: "Amen."

Benjamin placed the end of the wand back into the fire, then repeated thirteen times, "Before me, Osiris. Before me, Osiris. Before me . . ."

Upon completion of the summons, the surface of the mirror became fluid, moving inwardly in a spiral and quickly forming a silver vortex. The swirling vortex grew as large as the entire surface of the mirror, generating a sound like that of a roaring ocean. Benjamin stared at it. Watching. Listening. As the seconds passed, it grew darker in nature, the edges turning nearly black, glowing like onyx. In the center, a point of golden light formed, growing larger as the vortex became more turbulent.

In Benjamin's mind: *Before me, Osiris. Before me, Osiris.* He felt his body begin to rise in the air, and yet, when he looked down, he could see that his feet were still touching the ground. He could no longer feel the wand in his hand, but its handle was still tightly clenched in his fist, the steel end glowing red beneath the sparking flames. *The energy of the Divine Providence is with me. . . . I am floating. . . .*

He gazed back at the mirror, his eyes immediately glued to the widening point of light. From within the light, the sound of a ticking grandfather clock surfaced, muting all the other sounds in the room: Bryan's persistent wails and coughs, the nervous shuffling of feet behind him.

Benjamin shouted, *"Before me, Osiris!"*

The expanding golden light at once swallowed up the silver and black vortex, consuming the entire surface of the mirror. Benjamin was momentarily blinded by the glare. He diverted his gaze downward, where he could see baby Bryan shutting his tear-filled eyes against the bright light.

Thunder struck harshly overhead, shaking the beams and drowning out the loud ticking of the clock. Dust and straw blew off the rafters and rained down on the miraculous scene. Pilate was howling outside.

From within the powerful golden glow, the spirit of the Lord Osiris appeared.

At first the spirit's form was just a shadow, distant but moving forward quickly until it ultimately obstructed much of the light. Once the spirit gathered its true form, it stepped forward out of the light—out of the astral plane—into the barn, where it stood before the Conroy family in all its spiritual grandeur, framed by a golden aura.

Benjamin let out a sharp, sudden breath and had to tighten his throat against the gasp that wanted to come out. He was terrified—such a menacing figure had never appeared during the four other summoning rituals, those pledging familial afterlife for himself, Faith, Elizabeth, and Daniel. In the past Osiris always appeared as a shimmer of light and a voice. Why was he showing himself now?

Benjamin noticed that the spirit's entrance onto the physical plane had restored all the silenced sounds: the wind, whistling through the gaps, grabbing the smoke and spreading it throughout the barn; Bryan's panic-stricken cries; the coughs of Faith, Elizabeth, and Daniel.

Plus, the heavy pounding of his own heart.

"It is you," Benjamin finally uttered, his body frozen with fear.

Osiris appeared as a tall bearded man, wearing a long black robe of watered silk that nearly touched the ground. He wore a black Egyptian nemyss on his head, with long drifts of dark hair pouring down over his shoulders. Around his neck was a chain that held an ankh-shaped amulet made of gold. He carried a dark rod in his right hand, this too was fitted with a golden ankh. In his left hand was a glowing chalice, a portrait of a bull with a ring through its nose etched onto its surface. Without moving his body, the spirit at once spread out a pair of black feathered wings that appeared almost metallic, their span perhaps ten feet from tip to tip.

The spirit pinned Benjamin with ringed eyes as black as fresh, hot tar, and Benjamin could see his own frightened face reflected in them. "Perform your deed," the spirit of Osiris said, its voice many octaves lower than any human could possibly reach. To Benjamin, it sounded robotic.

Benjamin pulled the wand out of the fire; sparks flew up like a swarm of flies. Staring at the great black entity before him, he stated: "All-powerful Lord Osiris, who exists amongst the Gods in the astral plane and governs the Realm of Resurrection and Everlasting Life, we have bestowed upon you the gifts of the earth so that Bryan Conroy may purely and honorably engage your powers of spiritual rebirth for the purpose of ancestral afterlife, with utmost earnestness and commitment."

The spirit stood motionless, then gently nodded, his moving face leaving a shadowy trail that faded in seconds.

"Come, my family," Benjamin said. "Faith, Elizabeth, Daniel, join me in furnishing Bryan Conroy with the gift of the afterlife, so that we as a family may remain together for all of eternity . . . so that upon our deaths we may return to our bodies and advance together to the astral plane and exist together in the afterlife as venerated spirits. It is the judgment of Osiris that we hand our fates to."

As Benjamin called their names, each family member stepped into the circle and kneeled before the bawling baby. They all had sallow faces and smoke-reddened eyes. One by one, they grabbed the baby's limbs, Faith and Elizabeth holding Bryan's arms, Benjamin and Daniel his legs. The baby twisted in their commanding grips, bawling, his voice thick with phlegm.

"It is now that I, Benjamin Conroy, conclude this lifelong ritual by imparting upon Bryan Conroy the gift of everlasting life."

Everything happened so fast . . . but to Benjamin it all seemed to unfold slowly, like a movie running at quarter-speed. Daniel let go of Bryan, his arms falling away slow and stiff. He yelled, "*No!*" in a strangely deep voice. Coughing, he turned his head and spit a wad of ashy phleghm onto the wood, just beyond the perimeter of the magic circle.

My God, no! Benjamin thought as Daniel leapt back into his place and tried to tear the baby away from his family. Benjamin jerked his head up and saw that amidst the sudden disruption, the spirit of Osiris had vanished, leaving behind a very mundane looking mirror. *No!* Using the same hand that still held the wand, Benjamin shoved Daniel aside in a fluster, then raised the fiery end of the wand over the baby. . . .

He hesitated, staring through the smokescreen, into Bryan's eyes. His heart sank like a lead weight against his ribs; his mind seemed to melt away.

He could hear Daniel crying and choking and babbling, "No, Dad, d-don't hurt the baby. . . ." The boy's eyes were wide and staring, filled with terror, looking not at his father, but *through* him.

Faith released her grip, and Elizabeth immediately followed, pale faces drawn with consternation, staring up at Benjamin.

Benjamin loosened his grip on the wand; its glowing

end had begun to fade, its heat breaking up in the early morning air.

He stared at the mirror, at its utter normalcy, and thought of the spirit that had shown itself. *Perform your deed.* . . .

Benjamin Conroy took a deep lungful of searing hot air, coughed, then brought the fiery hot wand down upon the baby's exposed sternum.

CHAPTER TWELVE

September 7, 2005
1:48 P.M.

The rain continued to pound against the windows, slowing the bus to the interstate minimum of forty-five miles per hour. Thoughts of his mother and father stirred Johnny's emotions into a frenzied mess. The outside world, muddied from the rain and his tear-filled eyes, looked unreal, as transient as some fleeting dream. The bus drove into a passage cut into a channeled cliff. He stared at the nondescript rock face and the metal mesh fencing closing out the falling debris, and thought: *Bad memories may come and go, but the emotions that come with them remain.* Tears filled his eyes, and he had to turn his head so no one on the bus would see. *It didn't have to be this way*, he thought.

It was all beginning to take its toll on him; his heart surged in his chest; his eyelids struggled to stay open as he watched the muted landscape break apart around the bus. He peered down at his watch and saw that given the weather and the bus's sluggish pace, it would take another three hours to get to Wellfield. It didn't matter. He wasn't expected to meet with Andrew Judson until tomorrow morning.

He leaned his head against the rain-streaked window, closed his eyes and thought of his mother, lying there in her hospital bed. He shivered, wondering if she'd realized that he'd left Manhattan for the mystery that awaited in New England. He imagined her with her sallow cheek pressed against the thin Tempur-Pedic pillow, eyes glued to the door, waiting for her husband and son to come waltzing in with smiles on their faces and flowers in their hands, showing to her that it had all been a cruel dream and that everything was going to be all right. And as he drifted off to sleep, Johnny knew that there would only be the dreadful certainty that Mary Petrie would soon be discharged from the hospital, never to see her son or husband again. . . .

September 6, 2005
9:53 P.M.

Johnny sat in the hospital waiting room, staring at the cover of the *Cosmopolitan* magazine in the hand of an attractive woman seated across from him; the teenage girl on the cover had the whitest teeth Johnny had ever seen. There were two other people in the corral of orange vinyl seats, both of them with absolutely nothing to do: an unsmiling elderly man with a herd of pockmarks on his face, and a balding man of about forty reading a Preston and Childs paperback.

A young nurse with a red-striped uniform bustled by, and everyone waiting looked up at her in the hope that she would take them to visit their loved ones. She passed by and everyone went back to their routine. Johnny sipped at the stale coffee he bought for fifty cents at the cafeteria upon arriving at St. Michael's Presbyterian Hospital. He had killed nearly three hours here, waiting for some word on Mary, keeping his eyes on the main entrance with hope that his father had arrived home and seen the note Johnny had left for him on the kitchen table.

Eventually a nurse did approach, but kept a safe distance, as if those in the waiting room had also come down with some communicable illness. She called, "John Petrie?" Johnny stood and followed her as she immediately darted across the lobby without him, the eyes of his waiting-room comrades pinned to him as he disappeared though a pair of swinging doors adorned with big red letters that said INPATIENT.

"You are Mrs. Petrie's son?" she asked as he caught up with her. She was young and attractive, with shoulder-length blond hair and rather large breasts pushing out against her uniform. All his life, Mary had vehemently instilled in Johnny the evils of sex, and how the strong arm of God would punish him should his mind stray from a life of wholesome decency. He'd always done his damnedness to avoid lascivious thoughts such as this, but now . . . feeling attracted to a woman as pretty as this seemed more natural than dirty and unquestionably sanctioned by whatever higher authority might be looking down upon him at the moment.

Eyes still on her breasts (her name tag said MELANIE), he nodded. "Yes, I am."

Melanie was holding a clipboard with a number of papers attached to it. She lifted the first sheet and said, "Your mother seems to be fine. All the preliminary exams have been completed, blood tests, MRIs, nothing wrong was detected. No heart attack, no stroke. Of course she'll remain on bed rest for a few days, which will give us enough time to find out what actually happened to her."

Johnny didn't know what to make of the news. Had he caused his mother to have some sort of mental breakdown? Or was it something physical that had been lingering at the threshold, waiting to kick down the door? They turned left and went down another hall lined with glossy wooden doors. Down the hall, inside one of the rooms, Johnny heard a woman sobbing lightly; the sound of a television emerged from another: someone was watching the ten o'clock news. An intermittent beeping filled the room.

"Your mother is in room 107. Down the hall on your left."

"Thank you," Johnny said, watching Melanie as she scooted away at the call of another nurse seeking assistance in the reception area. He walked slowly down the hall to room 107. He peeked inside and saw his mother's bare feet jutting out from behind a cloth partition. He entered the room, circled around the partition, and stood at the foot of the bed.

His first thought was how different she looked from just hours earlier, when she arrived home from work. She was asleep on her back with the sheets pulled aside, her exposed legs pale and trunklike. Her hands were upturned alongside her, an IV tube snaking out from the crook of her arm. Her face was pale with a peculiar blotch on her forehead. Her hair was all flattened out on one side.

As he gazed at her, Johnny began to feel his breath shorten. He'd never seen her in such a terrible state. Waves of guilt hit him hard, and when he tried to say something, he couldn't. His throat was parched.

At that moment, a doctor walked in. He was a heavy-set man with a full beard that made his face look even fatter. He wore glasses, which he immediately removed to reveal two red spots on the bridge of his nose. He offered a hand to Johnny. "Hi, I'm Dr. Hanson."

"Johnny," his voice managed as he accepted the man's plump hand. "I'm Mary's son."

Dr. Hanson nodded, then slipped his glasses into his shirt pocket. "It's my understanding that your mother fell."

"Yes, that's right."

"She has a small laceration on her head, but it should heal over in a week or so." Hanson hesitated, then asked, "You saw her fall?"

Johnny nodded gently. "Yes . . . we were talking, and she got angry about something, and I guess she just fainted, because next thing I knew, she was on the ground."

Hanson nodded. "Well, other than the cut on her scalp, we couldn't find anything wrong with her. All her MRIs have come back negative, blood tests normal, white blood count is fine. Probably had the wind knocked out of her when she hit the floor." Hanson put his glasses back on and opened the folder clipped to the edge of the bed. "We'd still like to find out why she fainted, of course. Judging from your mother's medical records, it's safe to assume that she might've forgotten to take her anti-depressants, which in effect can cause terrible withdrawal symptoms, including dizziness and even fainting. I'm guessing that it's either that, or she had an anxiety attack, which could also bring about similar symptoms. But we need to rule out anything else before we can make that determination."

Yeah, she had a major-league anxiety attack all right, right after I mentioned Benjamin Conroy's name. Clearly, she knew the man, because right after that she threw some desperate prayer at the Lord to save my soul from eternal damnation.

"How long is she going to be here?" Johnny asked. "The nurse mentioned something about her staying for a few days."

"We'll give her a more complete examination tomorrow, make certain that she takes her medication and gets enough liquids. She's been rather groggy since coming in." He paced along the bed and adjusted the flow on her IV drip. "Probably the day after tomorrow, but I'd like to wait until the morning before we come to any conclusions."

"Okay, thank you."

Dr. Hanson returned the file back to the foot of the bed. "Is your mother still married?"

"Yes," Johnny responded quickly, feeling somewhat guilty that his father had not yet arrived. "My dad works late," he lied, knowing that his father was probably out at some watering hole down at the docks. "He's probably on his way."

"At this point I think it's best that we let Mary sleep for the night. It's late, and she needs her rest. Try to get a hold of your father. You can both come back in the morning, around eight."

"That'll be fine," Johnny answered blankly, wondering if he would even see his father before the morning. Hanson grinned politely and walked out of the room. Johnny turned back to gaze at his mother's sleeping face. The corners of her mouth were twitching, as were her hands, and Johnny could see her eyes shifting beneath her lids. *I'm sorry this had to happen, Mom. I'm sorry I disappointed you.*

Johnny stepped around the side of the bed and placed a gentle kiss on her forehead, catching a whiff of her bitter, stale hair. He was about to say something to her, but realized that waking her would be a grave mistake. He walked around to the foot of the bed when a thought crossed his mind . . . something instinctual.

Feeling strangely uneasy, he grabbed the patient info folder clipped on the bedrail.

The first page was a medical history record, which included all Mary's personal information.

Her name.

Her date of birth.

Her social security number.

The names of her family members—only two answers here.

And then, her . . . *oh my God* . . .

When he looked back at his mother, she appeared even more different, not his mother at all but some stranger he'd never met, and he realized at this moment that he needed to be away from her, not just now but forever and ever, because part of the mystery that she'd kept bottled up inside her all these years had finally escaped by chance from the sheet of paper he gripped in his trembling hand.

He closed the folder and clipped it back onto the bedrail, the image of line five on the medical history sheet bound to stay with him until his dying day.

Maiden name: Conroy.

CHAPTER THIRTEEN

August 24, 1988
9:17 A.M.

Benjamin Conroy was sitting in a chair before an open window in his office, staring unblinkingly at the notebook in his lap as he scrawled his thoughts about the morning's events. The baby had stopped crying about an hour ago, thank God, and now the wind provided a fairly soothing backdrop as it bustled across the wheat fields a hundred yards away. He'd been in this position for over two hours, a copy of *The Egyptian Book of the Dead* on the desk beside him to provide moral support.

No matter how much he prayed, how much he wrote down, he knew it would not reverse the blunder that had ruined the ritual.

Amazingly, things had gone entirely as planned up to that point. But then something had gotten into Daniel. *Damn him, doesn't he appreciate what I'm doing for him?* And all that had been worked on was flushed to hell when the spirit of Osiris vanished. *He'd never appeared before!* Countless times Benjamin had explained to everyone that all conditions had to be perfect for the ritual to succeed, and they *had* been perfect, and things had gone off as planned, better than he could have ever hoped for. Even the timing of the bells had worked properly! But then the boy had decided to pull his stunt—had tried to spare his little brother a moment's pain, and in turn may have destroyed a lifetime's worth of effort and planning. *Didn't he see the spirit?*

The spirit must be angry.

Angry at me, for failing him. For my sins . . .

In between his prayers and thoughts of failure, Benjamin reflected upon his years of preparation and his lifelong obsession with the biblical history relating to Jesus's rise from the dead; how he became convinced that the Son of God could not have relied on his Father's unseen inspiration alone; how fifteen hundred years earlier, in the mid-fifteenth century BCE, Egyptians had left behind what would later be interpreted as *The Book of the Dead*, a series of mortuary spells written on sheets of papyrus covered with magical texts and accompanying illustrations. Thousands of these exhaustive passages had been found in coffins, detailing prayers addressed to the god Osiris, who carried with him the power of the afterlife. Those worshipping Osiris's power could call upon him to lift the spirits from the passed-on bodies of kings and princes, so that their souls could be reunited with their loved ones in the underworld, or what modern occultists now called the "astral plane." Here the souls of the deceased would make their ultimate decision: remain as spirits for eternity in the astral plane, or choose to return to their own bodies so their kingdoms could be protected by their divine rule. Many would place this ultimate decision in the hands of the Egyptian god himself. Jesus had chosen the latter, according to the code Benjamin found in the Bible, while Benjamin elected to pursue an eternity with his family in the spirit world. *It is my only chance for salvation. . . .*

Benjamin had divided his life's work equally between his Christian beliefs and his clandestine occult practices. He'd inherited the farm from his father— Wellfield's previous minister, Anton Conroy—who'd died of a heart attack when he was forty-three. Benjamin had been eighteen at the time, with plans to marry Faith two months later; the wedding had commenced as planned. Additionally, Benjamin had inherited the church that his father built in 1956, and without hesitation had stepped into his father's shoes to perform Sunday services himself. At the time, the church had had about 200 devout parishioners, most of them from Wellfield, although perhaps two dozen people would make the trip in from Skowhegan to sit in on the elder Conroy's services. As the years passed, and as Benjamin's obsession with the occult grew, he would focus his sermons more upon the darker writings of the Old Testament, which eventually disenchanted many of the parishioners. Still, today, there were about 100 faithful followers of the assembly, and Benjamin would perform two masses every Sunday, collecting more than enough in donations to keep the farm running smoothly.

Sundays had been reserved for his Christian practices. The other six days of the week would go toward tending the farm, with the evenings spent practicing the rituals as demonstrated in *The Book of the Dead*, and then, in an effort to expand his powers as a magician, from the *Goetia* and the *Grimoire of Honorious*. He'd never felt a conflict of interest, wholly convinced through years of exhaustive research that Jesus had known all along he would be crucified and had performed a spell from *The Book of the Dead* prior to his death with intentions to come back as a savior. A synchronous fate existed amongst the two gods. Benjamin had proof of it . . . He had cracked a code in the Bible that revealed Jesus's use of Osiris's name in the Old Testament. It was proof that Jesus himself had studied portions of *The Book of the Dead* prior to his fall. Jesus rose from the dead because he evoked the spirit of Osiris!

Benjamin loved his family, and had made every effort to keep them close to him, re-creating a lifestyle as evidenced by the chronological accounts in the Bible. They lived and worked and studied at home, remaining solely amongst each other and making every last effort to keep themselves free of the evil influences of the outside world—to maintain lives consisting only of purity and sinlessness. *It is the way of God*, Benjamin would say. *And the demand of the Lord Osiris. If we seek his support, then we must conform to his conditions.*

It had made no sense for Benjamin to perform the ancient rituals solely upon himself—who else would ultimately crucify him? To Benjamin, there would be no place on this earth for him without the worship of his family. Upon completion of the ritual, he would die for their sins . . . and they would die for his. And as always, upon envisioning how they would all remain together for eternity, he recalled his very first evocation of the Lord Osiris, and how he dedicated his life to the ritual of ancestral afterlife . . .

. . . and a sharp, needling pain struck his chest, and then his head; it had come without warning, pulling a fearful cry from him. And then the golden light appeared . . . at first it was just a pinpoint, but it soon expanded to an orb the size of his head, maybe bigger, and from within he could hear the winds gliding across the surface of the astral plane, he could see the starlight within . . . starlight that in some mystical way carried the voice of the spirit he'd spent years trying to summon: "Commence with the ritual." The small fire before him rose, and he clapped his hands to his eyes before reaching down and groping for the wand. He grabbed it and shoved the molded end roughly into the flames. He held it there for a minute, taking deep breaths as his heart ran fast in his chest, and when the heat from the wand rose to his face, he opened his eyes and thought he saw for the briefest instant the embodiment of a million unrealized fears . . . and it had a voice . . . and it told him to make the sacrifice . . . and Benjamin had listened to it, bringing the fiery end of the wand down against his own sternum . . .

"Benjamin?"

The voice shook him from his musings. He opened his eyes and saw *The Book of the Dead* sitting on his desk, its tattered leather cover seeming to undulate. He shook his head and rubbed his tired eyes, unsure if he'd fallen asleep. The scar on his chest tingled, and he touched it tenderly with trembling fingers.

There was a gentle knock on the door.

He cocked his head and looked at the book again. It was *not* moving. *A trick of the light, is all.* "Enter," he said, his thoughts far away, charged with the past—a hopeless distraction from the morning's fiasco.

Faith entered the room, her face pale and solemn, a frozen mask of fatigue and sickness. Like a schoolgirl called to the front of the class, she stood before Benjamin, hands folded compliantly before her. "The baby is asleep," she whispered.

"We've failed," Benjamin stated, ignoring her. "The damn boy . . ."

"I've spoken with Daniel. He feels terrible for what he did. Please, Benjamin, he needs no further punishment."

"Did you not see the spirit?" he asked, teeth clenched, voice low but filled with fury.

She took a deep breath, then asked, "Aren't you worried about your baby?"

"He's experienced a pain no different from the rest of us." He paused, then added, "He'll live . . . for an eternity now." *I hope and pray . . .*

Faith looked at him, surprised. She ran a hand over her stomach and grimaced. "So then . . . we haven't failed?"

For a moment he did not reply. He wasn't certain if he could answer that question truthfully. He did his best to hide it. "I shall not steer my beliefs toward failure. I am convinced only of success. Only success."

I'm fooling myself. There was something else at play there today. Some sort of outside interference. The boy could not have been that stupid.

She sighed, seemingly relieved, and her blue eyes, still bloodshot from the smoke, glossed over with tears. "I love you, Benjamin. And I *will* follow you to the end."

She walked to him and hugged him, and Benjamin accepted her comforting embrace with open arms, feeling kind despite the morning's bitter disappointment. She pressed against him and it made Benjamin realize that no matter what the future held, a never-ending happiness would always exist in her, and that was something he was so very grateful for. *She is my strength, my power. I love her and all that she has done for me. And she loves me, and our children, more than the sun and stars. And that's why I have chosen to assure an ever-lasting afterlife together. For all of us. So we can remain together long after we grow old and die. Forever.*

He whispered in her ear: "We shall go together, as a family. And then, a family we shall remain."

Faith released him, nodded, then grabbed her stomach again and frowned.

"Faith?"

"I'm not feeling well. My stomach's hurting me."

"It's from the smoke," Benjamin answered hastily, unconvinced of his diagnosis.

She nodded again, then turned and paced silently from the room. Benjamin watched her suspiciously as she closed the door behind her.

Yes, Benjamin thought, shuddering as the baby began to cry again. *When one goes, then we all shall go.* He closed his eyes, said a prayer to Osiris, then attempted to clear his mind to prepare for the final stage of the ritual.

CHAPTER FOURTEEN

September 7, 2005
12:08 A.M.

Johnny returned to the apartment feeling tired and hungry. The first thing he saw was the note he'd left for his father, still on the table. The apartment lay in unfamiliar silence except for the ticking of the kitchen clock, and Johnny assumed that his father was probably riding the subway, either en route to the hospital, or on his way back.

After a drink of milk and a handful of shortbread cookies, he went to his bedroom and closed out the rest of the world, realizing that this would be the first time in his life that he'd gone to bed all alone in the apartment. It unnerved him slightly. But after he changed into his red plaid pajama bottoms and a T-shirt, and got into bed, fatigue beat back the nerves, and he fell asleep.

He dreamed of the golden pain, of the hooded witnesses crowded around him, grabbing him . . . of how one of the shrouded figures let go of him and made a vain attempt to save him from the pain soon to be delivered: a sharp, burning agony seared upon his chest . . . he screamed, and then complete darkness followed, and he dreamed of another previously lost memory where he saw himself as a baby again, completely naked, and he was being carried by a young man, a teenage boy perhaps, and he could clearly see the boy with his keen features and blond hair and intense gray eyes . . . this boy . . . someone Johnny didn't recognize, and Johnny shuddered because he looked terribly frightened . . . he was running, crying, clutching Johnny close to his chest . . . they were in a house, somewhere dark and musty with the smell of mud and rain and of things thick with mildew, and the young man in sheer panic wrapped Johnny up in burlap and slid him into a cool dark space, then turned and disappeared into the shadows, where he screamed and screamed and screamed . . .

Johnny awoke with his own scream.

He shivered in a cold sweat, curling himself into a fetal position, arms wrapped protectively around his knees. He opened his eyes, and when he looked down he saw that, as in his dream, he was naked. He shivered uncontrollably, terrified, not because he'd undressed himself while sleeping, but because he was lying outside on the fire escape with the cold steel grating carving indentations into his goose-fleshed skin. Nearby, a siren ripped through the night. He startled, wholly confused, looking toward the lighted window, which was wide open, Mother's beige linen curtain billowing in the gentle breeze. He clambered up and groped for the sill. And that was when he saw the feather clutched tightly in his hand.

The bird I saw earlier today . . .

He stared uncomprehendingly at the large black feather. He squeezed it tightly between two fingers, guessing it had some vital significance and that he needed to hold on to it. *Jesus, what am I doing out here?* He lifted his heavy eyes toward the partial moon, then crawled back into the apartment, careful not to trip on the window frame.

Once inside, Johnny got his balance, then looked up and nearly screamed.

His father was sitting at the kitchen table.

A wave of embarrassment hit Johnny like a gale-force wind, and it wasn't until he was halfway into the living room that he realized his father hadn't yet noticed him. Ed Petrie's eyes were closed, brow furrowed as though he were examining some sort of problem, one that he, despite his efforts, had no idea how to solve.

From the corner of his eye, Johnny could see his pajamas crumpled on the floor at the foot of the sofa. He immediately sneaked over and slid back into them, careful not to damage the feather. He made just enough noise for his father to hear him, but his dad, probably drunk, remained silent with his elbows on the table.

Johnny placed the feather down on the end table next to the sofa, then went into the kitchen, where he quietly waited for his father to open his swollen eyes. It took a few moments, but eventually he acknowledged Johnny's presence, looking up with eyes that were wet and red and weary.

Ed Petrie had been crying.

"Dad?"

"Hmmmm?" He looked at Johnny, and Johnny thought he recognized a kind of pale distraction in his

Dead Souls

99

features that might have been the result of a few too many. He shifted his hands, and Johnny noticed the note he'd left earlier crumpled in his father's right fist. Johnny took a deep, nervous breath, then turned his attention back to his father's face; it now seemed to suggest fear settling in.

"Are you all right, Dad?"

His father grunted and looked toward some nondescript point in the kitchen between the refrigerator and stove. A frown line dipped between his eyebrows when he said, "Just spoke with your mother." Johnny could smell the sour stench of alcohol on his breath.

"You did? Just now?"

His father stood up, hesitated, then paced unevenly across the living room, stopping halfway between the kitchen and his bedroom. After a long pause, he said, "I called the hospital. They put me through to her room."

Johnny swallowed something hard in his throat, thinking, *He must have seen the fire escape window open. He must have seen me crawl in without my clothes on. So why didn't he say anything?* He wanted to ask his father what was wrong, but was quickly able to put some of the pieces into place: Mother had shared her secret fear with Dad, and Dad, like Mother, had spent his entire life being terrified of it as well . . .

Benjamin Conroy

. . . and now here he was attempting to cope, but he was having a real tough go at it because he was completely smashed and his sanity was systematically disconnecting itself from his brain, one plug at a time.

"What did she say, Dad?"

He looked through Johnny with glassy eyes and said, "I'm going to bed, now." He turned and left the living room, gently shutting the door behind him.

Johnny remained standing in the kitchen, fully mystified, staring at the closed door. He stepped quietly into the living room and picked up the feather from the end table. He gazed at it curiously, thinking inexplicably, *This is some kind of gift*, then went back into his bedroom, clutching it close to his heart as if it were a security blanket.

CHAPTER FIFTEEN

August 24, 1988
11:11 A.M.

Pilate lay next to Daniel, tongue lolling, pleased with the attention he was getting from his thirteen-year-old master. Daniel scratched behind the lab's ears, digging deeply with his fingers all the way down to the hide, reaching every last spot the dog positioned his head for.

What a perfect day this would have been had it not been for his father's utter foolishness this morning. The sky was a bright crisp blue, the climbing sun beaming proudly. A temperate breeze kept the flies at bay, and the birds were out in full chorus. In the distance, the goats nagged loudly.

The storm door behind him screeched, and Elizabeth appeared carrying a plate of buttermilk muffins and a pitcher of milk. She was wearing a pair of blue jeans and a plain white tee, her hair tied back into a ponytail. "Cooked them myself." She came down the wooden steps and sat in the grass alongside Daniel, where they ate and drank in silence, shooing Pilate away as he made his bid for a muffin.

"Lizzie?" Daniel asked, taking a small bite; his throat still stung from inhaling all the smoke in the barn, and he grimaced with every swallow.

"Yeah?"

"Can I ask you something?"

"Of course."

He hesitated, peering toward the door to make sure neither of his parents was listening. Finally he whispered, "What's wrong with Dad? I mean, what's the real story behind this ritual thing?"

A long moment of silence followed. Elizabeth seemed to have a few thoughts rolling around in her head as well, and as a big sister who appeared as sane as he, her opinions carried a lot of weight. "He's a man of conviction. He believes that our business here on earth is a stepping-stone into a much bigger and better place. He's just trying to make certain that we reach this better place together, as a family."

"But . . . do you believe it?" Daniel asked mildly, hoping she'd say no.

Elizabeth picked a buttercup from the grass and held it under his chin. "Do you?"

"No . . . not really."

"The reflection on your skin says you're lying."

"I'm not!"

She giggled. The wind picked up and Daniel caught the clean scent of strawberries rising from her damp hair. His own hair still carried the acrid stench of smoke.

"I believe in God, and I believe in heaven," she finally answered.

Daniel felt a familiar weight settle around his heart, a weight he continually carried around with him. "And so do I. I really, really do . . . but this other stuff, Osiris, and the astral plane. I mean, I don't remember reading about *any* of this in the Bible. Do you?"

Elizabeth shook her head sympathetically, and picked at the corner of a muffin. "Dad seems to believe it's in there. It's a code of some sort."

Daniel felt as though he were suddenly treading in deep water. "Well, I don't," he blurted, then added, "and I didn't see any of those things Dad was talking about this morning. Did you?"

"You mean—"

"The spirit, the mist, the bird, the cowbell. And I remember him saying that he had a gift in his hand . . . but his hand was *empty*, Lizzie."

"Yeah . . . I didn't see any of those things either."

He found himself thinking of his father, surrounded by the smoke, staring at his reflection in the "magic mirror" saying, *It is you*. It'd really seemed so *odd*—all Daniel had been able to see was his father's image staring out from the mirror.

Elizabeth added, "I think I saw Dad put the feather on my windowsill last night."

"You did?"

She nodded. "It was late, probably around midnight. I'd heard something. I woke up and it was dark, but I saw someone outside my window." She paused and peered over Daniel's shoulder. "Look over there." She pointed and Daniel looked to the corner of the house where an extension ladder leaned up against the shingles. "I think he set them up ahead of time, just like he did with the bells and all the props."

"So then it's not real. None of it."

She paused, then asked, "You believe in God, right?"

"Of course."

"But . . . have you ever wondered if God really does exist? I mean, is He this omnipotent being with a beard and long flowing robe who looks over His creation and checks His naughty and nice list to see who deserves a pass into heaven? Or . . . is God just a concept? An image of goodness to fall back on when we're feeling down—when we need a shoulder to lean on?"

Daniel shrugged. Inside the house, baby Bryan began to wail. Pilate picked up his head, but quickly settled back down again.

"Well," she continued, "it seems to me that God doesn't plan on coming down from heaven anytime soon to shake hands with the people of Wellfield."

Daniel shrugged again. Pilate shifted his body closer to him. Daniel obliged with smooth, even strokes across his furry back.

"Daniel, we as God-fearing Christians must assume that He's watching over us, and we have to follow our hearts toward a path of acceptance. And that, my little brother, is exactly what Dad is doing. He feels he has no choice but to pursue his beliefs, to make certain he protects himself—and us, too—from what he fears."

"And what exactly does Dad fear?"

"Who knows," she answered quickly, brows drawn tightly together. "I do think that Dad is a bit off his rocker, but I also respect his beliefs, even though I don't have much faith in them."

"Gosh Lizzie, why didn't you just say that at the beginning?"

"Because I want you to realize that it's important to give Dad the benefit of the doubt."

Daniel nodded in silent understanding, watching her as the smile slowly faded from her face. This was her way of protecting him, by offering some big-sisterly advice. Like Daniel, Elizabeth had also disobeyed their father's demands in the past, and in turn had suffered the consequences. What these consequences were, Daniel could only guess—Benjamin had always meted out his punishments behind closed doors. Like last Tuesday when Daniel had arrived to the dinner table seven minutes late and was immediately forced into the walk-in pantry. Benjamin pulled a piece of flat cardboard down from between the shelves, put it on the floor, and spread an even layer of raw white rice on it. Grabbing the boy by the neck, he shoved Daniel down to his knees, and Daniel remembered looking up at his father, how crazed he looked with his skin flushed and his eyes dilated. The elder Conroy demanded of Daniel, "Hands down," and Daniel obliged, pressing his palms into grains of rice. Benjamin then stood on his hands, forcing his body weight down and shouting, "May the Lord cleanse your soul, sinner!" Daniel had screamed and cried, and although the entire punishment had lasted only a minute, the deep, purple impressions the rice had made in his palms had lasted nearly three days.

Elizabeth never had any battle scars to show for her transgressions, except for the dark circles sometimes under her eyes, and this led Daniel to believe that her wounds bled below the skin, where they hurt the most.

The baby's wails increased in volume; their mother had carried him into the kitchen, and the window was open directly above their heads.

"I feel so bad for Bryan," Daniel said.

Elizabeth leaned forward and whispered, "You really shouldn't have interrupted Dad this morning."

Daniel nodded and wiped a tear from his face. "Lizzie . . . I-I don't remember doing it. It was like . . . like I blacked out or something. Like I didn't have any control of myself. Next thing I knew, Dad was yelling and then I saw him burn the baby. Somehow, I guess I knew what I did, but I don't remember doing it. All I know was that I didn't want him to hurt the baby."

"Dad would have never let that happen. He's a meticulous planner."

Daniel nodded soberly, realizing that Elizabeth, as the older and wiser sibling, knew much more about life, about their father, than he. Perhaps he *had* been wrong. After all, Bryan still ended up getting his wound, and now Daniel was going to get the worst of all punishments from their father.

The baby's wails reached a horrific crescendo, and their mother suddenly appeared at the door. She looked awful, her face pale with dark puffy half-moons beneath her bloodshot eyes. The baby writhed in her arms, and she seemed to be having trouble simply holding on to him. "Elizabeth, I need your help with the baby."

"Thanks, Lizzie," Daniel said, not really feeling any better about the situation. He stood up and gave her an enthusiastic hug.

She released Daniel, smiled, and placed a finger across her lips. Then she turned and followed their mother into the kitchen.

Seconds later, after Daniel decided that a shower was first in order, their mother reappeared at the door, this time without the baby. She came outside, stood on the top step of the porch, and took a deep, nervous breath. She peered over her shoulder into the house, then looked at Daniel and said, "I need you to go into town, to the drug store to pick up another tube of Bacitracin for your brother. His injury's bad, so we're going to need it."

"Mom . . . you told me we had enough—"

"Quickly," she said, "before your father comes downstairs."

And it was then that he felt truly scared for the first time. Scared for what he did that morning. Scared of his father's possible reaction. His father had remained out of sight following the ritual, and what Daniel hadn't seen or heard didn't trouble him any. But now . . . he knew his mother had spoken to his father, and was more than concerned with what she'd heard and saw. She probably thought it would be best to let the dust settle as much as possible and send Daniel into town for a trip that really didn't have to be made. Let time soothe the wound, so to speak.

"Okay." He peered up at his mother as she peeked back into the house. She looked exhausted.

She handed him a five-dollar bill. "Bacitracin. Got it?"

He nodded, then asked, "You okay, Mom?"

She shook her head, clearly unsettled. "The smoke . . . it made me sick." Just saying the words caused her to cough. "You better go now, and come right back home."

"Okay," he answered, folding the five-dollar bill and placing it in his pocket. He was about to say "thank you," but his mother wasn't there to hear him.

She was inside, throwing up in the sink.

CHAPTER SIXTEEN

September 7, 2005
7:15 A.M.

Again Johnny dreamed of the golden pain, the searing heat strong against his chest and the masked man who delivered it, pulling his hood back to reveal a featureless face, no eyes, no nose or mouth, just knotted pink flesh that beat at the same slow rhythm of his heart.

Thump . . . thump . . . thump.

Johnny tried to move, but couldn't avoid the inevitable: the pain against his chest that worked its way deep into his heart. The shrouded figure at his side did not attempt this time to interrupt the ritual. Instead he slowly stepped back into the golden light, and from out of the light emerged the young man with the blond hair and sharp features. Moving faster than anyone else in the room, he picked up Johnny and whisked him away, running from one dark place to another—from a very hot room to a much colder one. He

was gasping with terror, looking down at Johnny, eyes thick
with tears. He placed a finger across Johnny's lips and said,
"I'm sorry . . . I'm sorry . . ."
Thump . . . thump . . . thump . . .

Johnny awoke, sheathed in hot sweat. His heart was
pounding. His scar itched, nearly burned, and when he
pulled the collar of his T-shirt down, he could see that
it blazed beet-red, as though he'd been clawing at it all
night.

Lying across his scar was the black feather he took
to bed with him last night—the feather he'd found on
the fire escape.

Thump . . . thump . . . thump . . .

What's that noise? He grabbed the feather, then
shifted up on his elbows and looked around, first at the
window—*might be a black-feathered bird poking at the*
windowsill—then into the living room.

Johnny knew you never second-guess any odd noises
when living in an apartment building in Manhattan;
they either came from the apartment next door, or
from the streets, where anything was possible.

Thump . . . thump . . . thump . . .

He turned and kneeled up in bed, then cocked his
head, listening even more closely.

Thump . . . thump . . . thump . . .

He placed an ear against the wall.

Thump . . . thump . . . thump . . .

The sound was coming from his father's room.

It sounded like the gentle rap of a fist, as if his father
were taking out his frustration on the wall. It was much
too soft to be made by a hammer, and besides, his father was never one to fix anything around the house,
especially this early in the morning.

Johnny decided to ignore it, figuring it was his father's arm or knee hitting the wall.

But its persistence soon had Johnny sitting on the edge of the bed, covering his ears with his hands.

Thump . . . thump . . . thump . . .

It went on and on, three or four seconds of dead silence between each beat.

A strong wind swept across the window in Johnny's room, vibrating the panes. The thumpings in his father's room grew suddenly louder.

Twirling the feather in his hand, Johnny looked at the clock. 7:27 A.M. His father didn't go to work until noon, so there was no need for him to be awake now, particularly after being up so late last night. The noise was still there, like the deliberate drip of a leaky faucet.

It's too . . . even.

Johnny placed the feather on his nightstand, next to the framed photo of his parents, then crawled out of bed and staggered from the bedroom, the wood floor warm against his feet. He went into the kitchen, fought back a bad case of cotton-mouth with a tall glass of water, then turned and saw that the door to his parents' bedroom was shut.

He walked across the living room and stood in front of the bedroom door, gazing groggily at the worn wooden grain. An individual in a normal frame of mind could explain the thumping rationally: a water pipe in need of repair or a laboring air-conditioner in another apartment.

He knocked on the bedroom door. First lightly, then a bit heavier. He realized that he'd never had to knock on his parents' door before, primarily because it had never been closed. His mother and father were never ones to seek privacy from Johnny. He really couldn't imagine them needing it, *good God!*

A rapid uneasiness rose in him, and he took a few deep breaths.

"Dad?"

No answer. He tried the knob. Locked.

Locked? Is there even a lock on this door?

He pushed against the door, but it didn't budge. He knocked again, then slapped against the frame with his open palm. "Dad? You all right?"

No answer.

Johnny pounded on the door, making a racket that might've stirred the neighbors.

"Dad! Dad!"

Heart slamming, blood racing, he pressed an ear against the door, and he could hear the steady thumping against the wall.

Thump . . . thump . . . thump . . .

His mind desperately tried to drum up the source. He grabbed the faux brass doorknob and twisted it hard. Indeed, the door *was* locked. He shouted again but there was still no answer. Only that damned *thump*, drilling into his mind.

Johnny closed his eyes and took a huge breath, trying to beat back the building panic.

He peered down at the doorknob and saw the keyhole. Of course, if his parents actually had a key to a door they hadn't locked for fifteen years, he wouldn't know where on earth to begin looking for it.

Thump . . . thump . . . thump.

The noise maintained its steady cadence but grew suddenly louder. He took another deep breath and called his father again: "Dad?", retrying the doorknob at the same time. He didn't really want to kick down the door because that seemed so final.

Again he banged on the door. But his only reply:

Thump . . .

His entire body was shaking now, and he felt the fear mounting in his heart.

He stepped back, squeezed his fists, hoping that when the door came crashing in, he wouldn't scare the living bejesus out of his sleeping father. Raising his right leg, he kicked hard against the door, just to the left of the doorknob. As he did, he realized he would've been much better off putting on a pair of shoes or sneakers first. But his barefoot kick still proved productive, and the hollow door broke away from the jamb in a shower of splinters.

The door creaked noisily as a few strips of wood fell to the floor, and Johnny entered the room.

The bedroom was cool, almost cold. Only later would he notice that both windows had been left open, their curtains fluttering in the morning breeze.

He saw the queen-sized bed had been moved to the center of the room. He gazed to his left and could do nothing but stare . . . stare straight at the source of the thumping against the wall.

The bedroom's lights were on. All of them. The overhead fixture, plus the two bedside lamps. It was very bright in here, showing everything in crisp detail, the only visible shadow that of his father's lifeless body hanging from the jagged hole that had been cut into the plaster ceiling. He'd adeptly tied one of his size-46 belts over an exposed steel beam above where the bed had been. The other end was buckled tightly around his swollen neck, which was twisted into an impossible angle, eyes bulging from their sockets, tongue swollen and protruding from his open mouth. His skin looked soft and pulpy with a milky tone that reminded Johnny of a fish's belly. The skin on his neck had split open from his weight. Rivulets of blood, both wet and dry, tracked down over his shirtless girth like pinstripes.

The body swayed in the wind gusting through the open window, stopped, then swung back.

And hit against the wall.

Thump.

Johnny gripped the edge of the open door for support and stared at his father. Ed's face was dead and staring; arms, white and swollen; pants bunched down around his ankles, soiled with feces and urine. In his hand was a crumpled piece of paper, the note Johnny had left for him, his cold, stiff fingers curled lifelessly around it. Johnny could see a dark, lurching line across the thin penciled words he'd written a little over twelve hours earlier.

Thump . . .

On damp, numb feet, Johnny walked over to his father's swaying body—three small steps was all it took—the wind gathering up the body's deathly odor. Johnny gagged. He turned his head, thinking he was about to vomit, but instead was able to beat it back.

Thump . . .

Sour tears filled his eyes. With his head turned, he used a single finger to poke at the piece of paper, but not without touching his father's cold, purple, clammy hand. He shivered, gagged again, and watched the crumpled paper fall silently to the blood-spotted mattress.

Thump . . .

He allowed the body one more sway in the breeze, then hurriedly leaned in and retrieved the paper, and staggered from the tainted room.

He immediately collapsed heavily on the living room couch, hands trembling, eyes stinging with tears. He'd never felt so scared. Scared for his father. Scared for his mother, who had just lost a husband . . . and was now going to lose a son.

Only a fleeting moment passed before he uncrumpled the notebook paper and flattened out the creases, the wavering line now coming together to disclose Ed Petrie's final, dark imprint upon the world. The single word, repeatedly scribbled in a thick line, shouted out to Johnny:

OSIRIS OSIRIS OSIRIS OSIRIS OSIRIS OSIRIS

It frightened him, the mere sight of it drawing tears from his eyes. He stared at the word, and decided to flee this life for good, now and forever.

Thump . . .

CHAPTER SEVENTEEN

August 24, 1988
12:03 P.M.

Wellfield, Maine, was a town that grew by default. The original builders settled it with intention of using the Tennebec River for trading with Canada, and for years it had seemed to work grandly—until the rains of 1908 flooded the valley and nearly drove the entire population north to Bangor. That was when the canal was built. Nearly three miles long, it passed beneath the center of town all the way to the township-owned fields in the north, where it eventually turned back into a river. This resulted in the building of affordable homes and the addition of many new families seeking work beyond the city's limits.

The northern region, a sore spot for most of the entrepreneurs in Wellfield and beyond, remained locally owned to this day, empty and devoid of anything more than shallow water, weeds, and litter. The roads that led to this messy part of Wellfield gave way to what eventually became low-income housing. In the center of it all was the town dump, a junkyard, and the municipal sewage mill, where nearly thirty percent of the area's male population was employed.

Capson State Park, all fifteen acres of it, eventually mated this part of town with downtown; it was a gradual fade-in that would creep up on you if your mind wandered too much while you were out for a leisurely stroll.

The business district had thrived over the years, yet still managed to retain its small-town glory. Outside of an Ames Supermarket, chain stores had yet to bleed their way in, thanks to the town's organizers who, favoring local entrepreneurs, refused to sell off the fields in the north to corporate America.

Downtown Wellfield meshed quite favorably with the finer homes to the south, owned by white-collar workers who commuted on the cross-town buses into Skowhegan and Orono every day. Here also lived the local business owners who just got by on their profits.

Most of the remaining lands were Wellfield's farms, the town's bread and butter, hundreds of acres of privately owned properties that kept up with the colonial spirit of New England's forefathers, generating nearly forty percent of the area's commerce. Seven families owned working farms within the city limits of Wellfield, each cooperating with one another to keep their crops unique.

Thirteen-year-old Daniel Conroy didn't know much of Wellfield beyond his father's property. The road he walked today was one of the few familiar ones, Breton Road, with its winding curves and whitewashed fences penning in the homes of the mostly faceless neighbors. Mailboxes gathered at the street corners like loiterers, weeds and vines choking their bases in thick, unruly patches.

Daniel reached the corner and headed left over the wooden bridge that cut into Rollingwood. Both sides of the bridge were lined with rickety weather-beaten railings. Below, ankle-deep water trickled faintly over a streambed of rocks, a relaxing backdrop to Daniel's harried thoughts.

To his left, at the corner of Rollingwood and Center Street, was the Wellfield Public School. Built of cement and bricks, it sat in an open field north of the railroad tracks. Somewhere between Wellfield and Skowhegan was a rail station. Daniel had never seen it, although he knew it was there because the freight engines would blow their whistles upon their approach.

About fifty kids were lined up on the edge of the playground's basketball court, waiting for a freight train to pass. Daniel watched them, and when the train vanished, they dispersed and went back to playing their games. *Friends*, Daniel thought. *This is what it's like to have friends.*

A large man wearing a blue nylon running suit appeared from the side doors of the school. He blew a whistle hanging from a string around his neck. It made Daniel flinch, and he took a few steps back along the side of the road. The kids queued up to go back inside, and Daniel immediately hated himself for being so jumpy. *What am I scared of anyway? There's nothing to be scared of.*

Except my father.

After the kids filed back inside the school, Daniel bitterly turned and continued on his way into town, fingering the five-dollar bill in his pocket every so often to make certain it was still there. Above, a flock of circling sparrows dipped and dived in formation, seeming to be taunting him. *Hey, look at the fat kid. His mommy and daddy finally let him out of the house!*

He reached the end of street, then turned left onto Main. Here there were stores as far as he could see. He saw the large cement fountain at the center of Main, its three stout bears spilling water from cupped palms. The marquee for the Wellfield Town Theater bore its display in large red letters: DIRTY DANCING. SHOW-TIMES: 5:30, 7:30, 9:30. Although the Conroy home didn't have any televisions—*a waste of valuable mind-space that could be used for prayer* Benjamin would say—Daniel figured that this was exactly the type of movie that fueled his father's holy-than-thou fire. Televisions were the devil's prop, the theater, his stage.

At the yellow-painted crosswalk, Daniel crossed the street, noticing a small group of older kids wearing worn jeans and white T-shirts. They appeared to be giving him the once-over as they leaned into one another and shared some sort of burning secret. Daniel grew suddenly hot. His T-shirt, gripping every roll of flesh on his torso, was damp with sweat. The smell of smoke was still on him, like rot on a dead fish, mixing with his perspiration. He looked away from the kids and made his way into the cool interior of D'Agostino's Drugs.

At once Daniel saw the comic book rack on the left alongside the window, and he licked his lips with excitement. This was his third trip into town (all to D'Agostino's Drugs), fourth if you counted the first time he came with his mother. Each time he'd beelined for the rack with the colorful thin magazines that cost twenty-five cents. Now here he was again, spinning the rack leisurely, checking out the covers and once again wondering if he was allowed to pick them up and look inside. Superman. Spiderman. Tarzan. Who were these mysterious characters? Daniel considered buying one. After all, it was only a quarter, and would his mother really notice twenty-five cents missing from the change?

He backed away from the rack and walked down the aisle with a sign overhead that said FIRST AID. Here he nosed through a variety of bandages and balms, looking for the specific ointment his mother had asked for: Bacitracin. He eventually located it, taking his time plucking it off the shelf—he really wanted this journey to last! After all, God knew what fate awaited him upon his return home to Benjamin's stewing rage.

He went slowly up to the counter. There was an elderly woman there wearing polyester from head to toe, with scuffed penny-loafers and gray hair permed into a standing beehive. She was engaged in conversation with the person behind the counter, a middle-aged, nearly overweight man whose name tag said TED. She was droning on about "Anna," who was heading off to college in Bangor next week. Probably her daughter. She turned, looked at Daniel, and said, "Well, Mr. Pharmacist, you have another customer, so I'll be on my way!" She smiled, then marched down the aisle marked SCHOOL SUPPLIES.

Ted smiled at Daniel. "You saved the day."

"Pardon?"

"Mrs. Darmody talks too much."

Daniel grinned, unsure if he was supposed to laugh at that revealing little tidbit. He placed the tube of ointment on the counter.

"Is that all?"

Daniel hesitated, then asked, "How much is it?"

Ted turned the tube over and displayed the price tag to Daniel. "Two forty-nine."

In a spontaneous move, Daniel said, "No, wait," then hurried briskly to the front of the store and grabbed the first comic he saw: *Superman*. He ran back to the counter, overcome with excitement, little shivers racing down his spine. "I hope this doesn't get me into trouble." He placed the comic on the counter, figuring he had a good deal of punishment in store for him anyway.

Ted grinned and raised an eyebrow. "You're the Conroy boy, right?"

Daniel nodded.

Ted leaned forward, elbows on the counter. He gripped the comic between his fingers. "It's my suggestion that you don't let either of your parents see this."

Eyes wide and alert, Daniel nodded again. "Okay." He saw a glimmer of knowledge in Ted's eyes—apparently the pharmacist had heard stories about his family. *Did he know about Osiris and his father's obsession?*

Ted slid the comic into a separate bag, then reached down behind the counter and grabbed another one: *The Incredible Hulk*. He slid that into the bag, too. "No charge for these, son." His eyes twinkled.

Daniel was speechless. He'd never received a gift before, except at Christmastime, and even those—a new Bible, a polished cross, an incense burner—were things he couldn't actually enjoy.

Ted smiled grimly, as though feeling sorry for Daniel, then slid his gold wire-rimmed glasses up the bridge of his nose. "I've attended your father's services in the past. I've seen you perform altar duties."

Daniel smiled back, hands gripping the paper bag. His palms left wet irregular patches on the dry brown surface. They resembled the sweat stains on his shirt.

Ted placed the ointment in another, smaller bag and handed that to Daniel. "Here ya go, young man."

"Are you sure?"

"Of course I'm sure."

"Gee, thanks, Ted . . . uh, Mr. Pharmacist." Daniel moved to leave, then turned around and said, "Sir . . . can I ask you a question?"

Ted nodded, eyebrows arched. "Sure."

"My mother told me once that school was always closed for the summer. So . . . why are those kids up there?" Daniel felt a tightness in his chest, as though he might've just brought up a subject that wasn't his business.

"Probably summer school for those who didn't make the grade. Although, now that I think about it, school does start next week. Could be that some of the kids are starting a week early to try out for the football team."

Daniel didn't quite understand all of Ted's explanation. He replied, "Thanks," then quickly retreated toward the front door. He could sense Ted watching his lumbering departure. Without stopping, he peeked at the spinrack with the comics one last time, then left the store.

When he came out onto Main Street with both bags in his right hand, he saw the three big kids from before standing near the curb to the right of the drugstore. They were laughing and smoking cigarettes, something he'd only seen adults do in the parking lot outside his father's church. Common sense told him to retrace his steps back into the cool, comfortable shelter of the store, but he ignored his voice of reason and continued along the curb, gripping the two bags tighter in his sweaty hand.

One of the kids looked up and saw Daniel. He elbowed the biggest kid, who immediately glared at Daniel with a pair of piercing blue eyes. The third kid took a few more seconds to realize that the moment they'd been waiting for had finally arrived.

The kid in the front, the leader it seemed, to Daniel, said "Hey fatso . . . watchya got in the bag?"

"Git 'im, Mack!" the third boy yelled. *Mack*. A suitable name for a fifteen- or sixteen-year-old boy who was almost as big as a truck. His arms and legs were thick with farmboy muscles. His hair was long and straight and straggly, reaching down over his shoulders like vines. His T-shirt had a variety of stains on it, and he retained the collective odor of most of them.

Daniel made a valiant attempt to walk by the trio, pretending not to see them at all, which was kind of silly because as soon as Mack asked about the bag, he hid it behind his back.

A calloused hand grabbed Daniel's arm roughly, and he screamed.

Immediate laughter followed. Daniel twisted around and shrank back against the hot brick facing of Goodman's Cleaners, next to D'Agostino's Drugs. The three big kids, now looking even bigger, dragged him a few feet into the alley between the two stores. They slammed him against the wall alongside a small green Dumpster and formed a impenetrable semi-circle around him.

Mack, hair hanging in his eyes, said, "You got fat in your ears, too? I said . . . what's in the bag?" His lips thinned and Daniel could see a layer of spit coating them like varnish.

"Nothing," Daniel replied mousily, tears welling in his eyes, and his fingers loosened on the bags.

"You know," Mack said, "if there's one thing I hate, it's a liar." His face contorted into something that matched the insanity in his eyes.

He looks like my father. . . .

Mack reached quickly for the bags. Daniel ducked and flinched away.

"Grab hold of him, guys."

The two kids in the back, near mirror images of Mack, leaped forward and latched on to Daniel's arms. Daniel howled in fear, and in a bit of pain too, realizing that despite all Benjamin's punishments and the pain and heartache that came with them, he had always emerged from them safe and sound.

But here and now? This was something entirely different. These strange kids were fueled by a different fire. The outcome of *this* situation was completely unknown.

The tears welled even further in Daniel's eyes, and he prayed that the kids didn't see them.

"Hey, fatso," Mack said. "You sound just like the puppy we drowned last week." The kid gripping his right arm laughed and gave it a sharp twist. The pain ran all the way to Daniel's shoulder, and he howled again, the bag nearly slipping free of his grasp. He tried to break away, but the two kids gripped him even tighter. They pushed him hard against the brick wall and his breath fled his lungs in a painful rush.

Mack reached forward and grabbed the collar of Daniel's shirt. He pulled down, ripping the thin cotton tee in half. Daniel's belly and chest, blindingly white, were completely revealed.

"Holy moly!" Mack shouted, eyes wide with disbelief. "What in the hell is *that?*" He pointed to Daniel's chest.

His two accomplices, keeping Daniel pinned against the wall, twisted around to see. Daniel craned his neck and looked out of the alley for help. He saw some people on the sidewalk across the street, but they were at least a hundred feet away. They might as well have been a light-year away. He shouted, "Leave . . . me . . . alone!"

"What *is* that, fatboy?"

"Leave me alone!"

"Answer my fucking question!" Mack threw a swift jab into Daniel's stomach. A knifing pain stabbed Daniel's lungs as the wind was again knocked out of them. He wondered how Superman or the Incredible Hulk might have handled the situation. He didn't know much about the superheroes, but he guessed they would have found some way to fix the bad guys real good. They certainly wouldn't have started bawling uncontrollably, which was what he was doing right now.

The kid holding his right arm teased him in falsetto: "Aw . . . the baby's got a fucking boo-boo!" He howled in laughter, and the kid on the left joined in.

But not Mack. He was holding his gaze on Daniel's scar . . . which frightened Daniel real bad.

Mack pressed his index finger against Daniel's scar. "That hurt, fatboy?"

Daniel shook his head.

Mack pressed it harder, digging a dirty fingernail into the gnarled skin. "How about now?"

Daniel grimaced. Despite the thick appearance of

his scar, it had a few clusters of nerves that when touched sent a jolt of pain across his chest. Mack had managed to ferret one out, and it nearly made Daniel pass out.

Mack reached into his back pocket and brought out what looked like a knife handle without a blade. When he pressed the small silver button on top, a blade shot out.

The fear in Daniel erupted. His heart leaped about in his chest like a monkey in a cage. He began to rock frantically back and forth in a fruitless attempt to escape, and at one point almost managed to tear an arm away, but the boys were too big and too strong for him and slammed him back against the brick wall.

His spine and skull collided with the hard surface. A hostile blackness filled his sight, and this time it felt as though the air in his lungs had him left for good. The D'Agostino's Drugs bags fell from his hand to the ground and were quickly retrieved by Mack.

"Don't let him do that again!" Mack yelled, ripping open the bigger bag. He removed the comics and hurled them to the ground. He plucked the ointment from the second bag and peered at it like an entomologist might a rare insect.

Daniel tried to wrestle free. Mack lunged forward. He pressed the blade of the knife against Daniel's scar. It felt hot, like a brand.

"*This* hurt?" Mack asked, grinning.

Daniel froze. He gasped for air, trying to suck his chest away from it. The blood pounded frantically through his veins. A thin line of spit dripped from his mouth.

"Answer me!" Mack yelled, pressing harder.

"Ahhh! It hurts!" Daniel shouted, hopefully loud

enough so Ted the pharmacist would come to his rescue. The point of the knife punctured his skin and a
thin line of blood trickled down his chest. The rolling
blackness in his eyes cleared to gray and filled his head
with something almost tangible, as if he really did have
fat between his ears.

"So . . . answer me, fatboy. What *is* it?"

"It's . . . a . . . birthmark," he cried.

"Bullshit!" Mack's voice penetrated Daniel like a
spear. The two kids holding him loosened their grips,
perhaps fearing that Mack would come after *them*.
Daniel sobbed uncontrollably, belly heaving up and
down. He looked down and saw his comics lying on
the gritty cement under Mack's feet, and that made
him even more distraught.

Suddenly, two boys riding bicycles turned the corner
and rode into the alley. They were about Daniel's age,
smiling . . . until they spotted Mack and his gang.
Mack spun toward them. "Get out of here!" The boys
hit their brakes, screeched on the gravel, then quickly
U-turned and rode off the edge of the curb. Daniel
could see them speeding away across the street like rac-
ers eyeing the finish line. They disappeared behind a
large blue car that rolled by, its driver oblivious to what
was happening in the alley.

Daniel managed to work his right arm free. Mack
yelled, "Jeezus, Butch! Hold him! And don't let go."

Butch grabbed Daniel's arm and said, "Hey, man, I
thought we was just gonna give him a scare."

"You better fuckin' hold 'im, or I'll cut you up, too."
Mack's face had evolved into the mask of a demon, red
and twisted and maniacal.

Butch and his partner didn't seem too intent on con-
tinuing this sadistic game—their grips on Daniel were

now loose and uninspired. Mack, using one deft hand, popped the top of the Bacitracin tube off. He squeezed out half the greasy contents, which purled over his fist like lava from a volcano.

While Daniel watched the erupting medicine, Mack jerked the switchblade across Daniel's midsection and sliced into him like a hunter might a fresh kill. Blood spurted across his skin in a parade of red that ran from his scar all the way down to his beltline.

Shocked, Daniel could only stare down at the blood oozing from the long cut. *Oh my God, if I don't get out of here, I'm going to die!* In this moment of do-or-die, he realized that both Butch and his accomplice had released him, most likely out of fear and uncertainty about Mack's fury.

Mack held the knife up like a trophy, admiring the blood jeweling on the blade. "Got yourself a fuck of a boo-boo, kid," he said. He then took the blob of Bacitracin on his other hand and wiped it forcefully over Daniel's oozing wound. "There . . . that oughtta help."

Mack leaned back to admire his handiwork, and it was then that Daniel, decided to make a run for it.

He pitched forward. Mack responded by pushing him back against the wall. With no clear plan other than to survive, Daniel planted a swift kick into Mack's groin. An unmistakable look of shock appeared on Mack's face—mouth agape, eyes wide and disbelieving—and this brought about a glint of hope in Daniel. He lunged past Mack, who'd dropped the knife in favor of his balls. Butch, staggering after Daniel, tripped over Mack, and his partner in crime slammed into him. They both fell on top of Mack, who was howling now, not unlike Daniel had only moments earlier.

Daniel fled out onto the sidewalk, looking back only once as he lumbered across the street. He saw a man and a woman getting out of a parked car. The woman pointed into the alley, and the man, hands on his hips, shouted something. Another man walked out of the drugstore and looked toward Daniel. He yelled "Hey, are you okay?" but Daniel ignored him, running as fast as he could—which wasn't very fast at all—down Main, his torn tee fluttering behind him like a cape.

Superman's cape!

When he reached the corner, he turned and looked back one last time, just to make sure he wasn't being followed. If Mack and his boys had decided to chase him, they would be on him faster than yellow on bees—and if that were the case, he would need to take refuge inside the corner service station. A cop jogged across the street toward the alley, and that was the last thing Daniel saw before racing up Center Street, his portly legs managing to carry him far away from yet another chapter of hell in his life.

CHAPTER EIGHTEEN

September 7, 2005
3:22 P.M.

My father is dead. . . .

It was the first thought to enter Johnny Petrie's mind as he left his life behind, and he quickly followed this harsh reality with a daunting contemplation: *And my mother is as good as dead, too.*

He sat up straight in his seat and used a thumb to loosen the knot of tension in his neck. He'd spent the better part of the last hour falling in and out of sleep, mostly five-minute catnaps, and during his semi-lucid states his mind tossed about myriad thoughts. Like who was Benjamin Conroy? And how did this man fit into his life? The revelation that his mother shared a family name with Conroy led Johnny to think Benjamin Conroy was either an uncle or a cousin or . . . his mother's first husband? Was it possible that Ed Petrie wasn't really his father? His brain ached as he considered the possibilities, and he struggled to shove them all aside until tomorrow, when Andrew Judson promised to unveil the truth of the matter to him.

He cracked one eye open and peered out the window. It was still splattered with raindrops, and the landscape looked pretty much the same: mountainous and muddy. The bus still crawled along the interstate, hunting for its turn-off, and he could hear the swish of cars as they passed by on the left. The wipers on the front windshield cleared the view to a dismal scene, cool and gray . . . and yet, so new and inviting. Johnny welcomed it, and he closed his eyes again, thinking of his last waking minutes at 479 East 88th Street in Manhattan. . . .

September 7
8:35 A.M.

Thump . . . thump . . . thump . . .

Still holding the yellow piece of paper with the odd message from his father, Johnny staggered back into his room. He slid into the first pair of jeans he could find, on the floor next to the closet, then opened the top drawer to his armoire and put on a white knit golf shirt. From his closet he retrieved the blue tote bag he'd used once to lug home a stack of Bibles from the church book sale. Mary had purchased them to donate to the local YMCA, and all Johnny could wonder at the time was what the heck the YMCA needed Bibles for.

He set the bag on the floor. With trembling hands, he began rummaging through his drawers, all the while listening to . . .

. . . thump . . . thump . . . thump . . .

. . . the horrible noise of his father's lifeless body hitting against the wall in the adjoining room. He haphazardly stuffed the bag with clothes, underwear, T-shirts, and socks. From the closet he retrieved a pair of loafers and a belt, and shoved them on top. From the bathroom, he gathered all his toiletries and a bottle of aspirin. He gazed at his mother's vast collection of pill bottles, and without even thinking, knocked them all onto the floor with a few vicious sweeps of his arm.

Nearly hyperventilating, Johnny looked at his handiwork: pill bottles, everywhere. Some of the bottles had opened, their colorful contents scattered on the tiles like candy from a piñata. He knelt down and searched through them until he located one marked Xanax. He gripped it in his fist, then slid it into his pocket. *I'll probably need these.*

Sudden dizziness threatened his balance. He grabbed hold of the edge of the sink and took a series of long, deep breaths. Catching a glimpse of himself in the mirror of the medicine cabinet, he was startled to see how sickly white and terribly frightened he looked.

He reeled out of the bathroom and leaned listlessly against the mattress of his bed. Breathing heavily, he scanned the room one last time.

He saw the black feather sitting on his nightstand. It struck him with a strange, undeniable force. He immediately circled the bed and retrieved it. He studied it curiously. It seemed to demand that he hold on to it forever.

With his other hand, he picked up the photo of his parents. *God, what happened to them?* He gazed at the portrait of Jesus above his bed. *All your prayers, Mom . . . lots of good they did you.*

He felt sick to his stomach. Shouldering his bag, he

tucked the frame inside, then fled the room, his heart clamoring loudly for him to flee this place once and for all. In the kitchen, he set the bag on the table. He could hear his father's body thumping against the wall—the pounding of blood in his head filled in the dreadful silent gaps between thumps as he visualized the bloodstain on the wall growing larger and larger. He leaned down, pulled open the bottom kitchen drawer, which always got stuck halfway, and removed two small plastic bags. In one, he gently inserted the feather. In the other, the yellow sheet of paper with his father's scrawled note.

He placed both in the side pocket of the tote bag, then headed for the door, purposely leaving his keys behind. The bag swung at his side, and as he grabbed the doorknob, he remembered something very important.

He tucked a hand into his back pocket, realizing that the jeans he put on were the same ones he wore yesterday. And the lawyer's letter, with the phone number and address of the firm, was still in the back pocket. He heaved a deep sigh of relief, knowing that he didn't have to venture back into his room—into what was quickly becoming a dark hole into his past—to retrieve it.

Then he caught sight of something else—something that might do him some good on the ride up to Maine.

In the trash can, where his mother had tossed it yesterday, was the library's copy of *The War of the Worlds*. He leaned down and retrieved it, feeling a wave of light-headedness as he did so, sensing that his bold decision to borrow this book had triggered his newfound life of independence. He tucked the book under his arm, then took one last look around before finally leaving his old, dead life behind.

CHAPTER NINETEEN

August 24, 1988
2:18 P.M.

Chaos had erupted in the Conroy house.

Bryan was in his crib, wailing inconsolably. Faith was vomiting in the upstairs bathroom, and although Benjamin had lost count, he'd figured this to be her sixth or seventh round. Pilate, still leashed in the backyard, had been barking up a relentless storm since Daniel left for the store at noon. And, in the pens at the perimeter of the wheat fields, the pigs and goats bleated incessantly for their grain.

Chaos had also erupted in Benjamin Conroy's mind. Still sitting in the chair in the corner of his office, he attempted yet another sequence of prayers—*forgive my sins, forgive my sins*—despite having found it increasingly impossible to maintain his concentration. His eyes kept moving toward the closed door, over and

over again, in desperate search for a respite that would
never arrive.

Something is very wrong. . . .

He peered up at the small speaker anchored into the
ceiling alongside the door, a pair of thin white wires
running like snakes into the walk-in closet where the
stereo system was located. He stood up and opened the
closet's twin doors, the dry cedar smell within tickling
his nostrils. He reached for the recorder on the shelf
and removed the reel-to-reel tape that contained two
hours worth of tolling bells . . . bells that struck at exactly thirteen-second intervals. Carefully, he returned
the plastic reel to its box, peering toward the rear of
the closet where a roadmap of wires snaked along the
wall en route to seven different rooms in the house. He
reached up and tucked the box away on a shelf at the
top of the closet where no one could get to it.

He stood there for a moment, listening to the noises
in the house, the *goddamned noises*, feeling his head
throbbing painfully. He could still taste the smoke on
his tongue, and welcomed it as though it were a gift
from Osiris, despite the dull rage rising in him.

The baby continued to cry.

Faith vomited again.

The damn dog was still barking.

The pigs and goats bleated endlessly.

And it all drove into Benjamin's head like darts from
a blowgun, each maddening noise a shot of deadly poi-
son to his brain. Nothing, not even a gift from the
spirit, could alleviate the agony.

He rubbed his temples with his palms—the pain in
his head was excruciating. And now the prayers
wouldn't come at all, and he knew he needed to escape
the insanity of his home before he exploded.

In the closet, on the shelf, Benjamin grabbed the bottle of bourbon he kept there: a vice he'd stopped hiding from Faith a few years ago. He removed the top and swigged a mouthful, pacing back and forth about the room, trying to make sense of all the madness as the liquid burned its way into his stomach. Simple logic told him that things were amiss because the ritual had gone awry. *Because the damn boy interfered! Or . . . is it because of my sins?* His copy of *The Book of the Dead* (now on the floor next to the desk, hurled there out of frustration) warned that misjudgments made during the evocation of spirits into the physical world might prompt the evoked spirit to cast a spell of retribution upon the conjurer. *And that*, Benjamin assumed, *is what's happening now.* He and his family were paying for their carelessness, *his* carelessness. *How could I let the boy do that?*

You know it's not entirely the boy's doing, Benjamin.

No!

He took another swig of bourbon, then, still holding the bottle, left the office and went into the bathroom. When he opened the door, he saw Faith hunched over the toilet. Her eyes were wet and red, her skin ashen. Her hair was plastered across her face in fever-soaked strands, hands gripping the sides of the toilet as though trying to steer it away.

In between heaves, Faith cried, "Benjamin . . . something's wrong with me . . ." Her voice was strange and jagged.

He gazed down at her, feeling no pity whatsoever. He took another swig, swished it around like mouthwash, then swallowed it down. "Smoke inhalation is all," he replied, unimpressed with his own lie.

She shook her head violently. "No . . . I need . . . I

need to go to the hospital. This is not right!" She
heaved loudly. It sounded amplified. Nothing came out.

Anger swelled in him. The pain in his head screamed.
His heart started pounding more forcefully. He could
feel it pushing its painful beat into his ears, his hands,
his chest. His head grew hot, and he tried to cool it by
swilling from the bottle. It didn't work.

"Move out of the way," he demanded. "I have to use
the toilet." He didn't want any part of Faith's misfortune, which wasn't from smoke inhalation, not at all. It
was from his own failure to complete the ritual. *Osiris's
retribution.*

"C-can't you use the other bathroom?" she coughed.

"Puke in the bathtub. I gotta go." His words and his
pity were both slurred by his intoxication. *That, and so
much more.*

She crawled backwards and leaned over the edge of
the bathtub. He caught sight of her face, pale and scared
and restless. "Benjamin . . . I can barely get up. Please,
something's wrong. I have a fever. I need to go to the
hospital. . . ." She coughed and gagged, but again, nothing came up.

There is nothing I can do for you, Faith.

Ignoring her, Benjamin urinated, flushed, then
zipped up and leaned down alongside her. With the
bottle in his right hand, he grabbed her hair and pulled
her head back, until her face was within inches of his
own. She smelled like vomit. "Now listen to me and listen good. If you go to the hospital, they're gonna ask
you what happened, and if you tell them that your husband was burning a fire in the barn, they'll ask you why,
and in your state you'd probably tell them that it was in
an attempt to summon a spirit from the astral plane,

and let me tell *you*, that'll really stir up the fires of hell. And even if you *don't* tell them, they're still gonna send the police out to investigate, because as you know, there are people in this town that would love to see me fall, and believe me when I tell you this, they will see me— *us*—crumble if anyone sees what I have in that barn. So, you hear me, Faith? *You are not going anywhere!*"

She flinched and began to cry hysterically, gagging as she did so.

"Do you hear me?" he asked again, his voice now chillingly composed.

She nodded, but only because Benjamin was still holding her hair and jerking her head up and down.

"Good," he said, letting go. Her head fell against the side of the bathtub, and she grunted in pain. He stood up, drank the rest of the bottle, then belched and threw the bottle into the tub, where it shattered into amber pieces. Faith jolted. Benjamin leaned down and grabbed her face with one hand, squeezing her damp cheeks roughly. Her eyes rolled toward his, wet with distrust.

"Please, Benjamin . . . leave me alone." She looked shocked and frightened.

Benjamin shook his head, and his eyes filled with tears. He felt an odd flux of emotions racing through his mind, as though the spirit had eased up on him, relieving him of his anger—and his pain—for a moment. "This . . . this isn't my fault. I meant well. . . . I did it all . . . all for *us*." He grunted as his anger instantly returned. Then he released her and fled the bathroom before he did something he would later regret.

He hesitated just beyond the threshold of the door, leaning against the doorframe and rubbing the moisture from his eyes. He listened to Faith as she commenced another round of dry heaves. A wave of dizziness hit him. The alcohol had taken full effect now—it'd numbed his senses, but also exacerbated his anger, his pain, his confusion. He called out for Daniel, forgetting briefly that Faith had sent the boy to the store.

The pain swelled in his head again. In the room down the hall, he listened as baby Bryan's cries tapered off, and he realized suddenly that had the infant not stopped his damn wailing, he might've been forced to punish him.

He pitched forward and thumped against the wall across the hall. His eyesight blurred as he fumbled with the doorknob to Elizabeth's room, then burst inside.

When his sight finally came into focus, he saw his sixteen-year-old daughter lying on the bed, her robe molded to her freshly showered body, partially opened with one firm breast peeking out from beneath the pink terry fabric. On the floor, beside the bed, he saw the painted circle, its candles left untended. Quickly, he turned back toward her.

Her legs and hips fidgeted, hands gripping the sheets in bunches. Her hair was mussed. Blond strands splayed out like straw. Instinctively, she pulled her robe over her breast, keeping her gaze away from Benjamin as he continued to stare.

To Benjamin, she was beautiful. But she was also weak and naïve, a prime target for temptation. This had become a constant worry for him; evil could very easily lure a curious teenager away from God's righteous path. Thankfully, he'd always been able to keep tabs on her; she'd never been able to hide her emotions when she felt guilty.

Like now.

Slowly, Benjamin paced across the room, struggling to keep his balance. He gripped the footboard of the bed and leaned down. He could smell her sex, tart and pungent. He forced a grin, her guilt giving his anger pause. "What have you been up to?"

She kept her gaze away. "Praying," she answered calmly.

He knew better. He swallowed his gorge, feeling suddenly sick despite being aroused by what she'd been doing. Seething with newfound anger, he clenched his fists, having to control himself from beating her for her sins—for making him feel like he did. "The animals," he finally said, teeth clenched. "They need to be fed."

She nodded compliantly. "Then I'll tend to them."

He leaned back up and nodded, doing his damnedest to ignore his suspicions, his urges, his anger. "My dear Elizabeth," he said. "You did well at the ritual this morning."

"Thank you, Father."

He grinned, then turned and fled the room, shutting the door quickly behind him as though closing out a demon. He stopped and leaned back against the doorframe, breath escaping his lungs in nervous bursts. Slowly, he turned and cocked a curious ear against the paneled wood.

From inside, only silence. He performed the sign of the cross, then staggered down the hall. He stopped at the door to Daniel's room.

Wiping the sweat from his brow, he opened the door and poked his head inside. The room was empty—the boy had yet to return from the store. With his son's absence, Benjamin's anger instantly returned, devouring all other invading emotions. *The boy is going to need a great deal of grace from God by the time I'm through with him*. The recurring image of his son leaping into the circle and interrupting the ritual tortured his fragile state of mind. The boy had always been so attentive to instruction, had always been so compliant to his demands. What could have made him pull this stunt? *It's his fault my wife is sick, the dog is barking, my daughter is committing sins in her room. Not mine. Hear my prayer, Osiris. I'll fix the boy good. Real good, just for you. I know it's what you want.*

Leaving the door open, Benjamin plodded down the hall. He paused, then turned and stood before the door to Bryan's room.

He went inside.

He tottered unevenly across the wood floor, stepping over the painted circle as he approached the crib.

Hands on the edge of the crib, he peered down, that damn image of Daniel interrupting the ritual feeding his anger. Sweat jeweled on his brow. His head pounded furiously.

Wearing only a diaper, the baby slept in fitful silence, fingers clawing at the gauze wrapped tightly around his chest.

Benjamin whispered, "What is your real purpose?" He reached into the crib and put a trembling hand around the infant's neck.

And began to squeeze.

Instinctively, the baby reached up and caressed the hand grasping him.

The soft, innocent touch of his sleeping son's hand seemed to cure Benjamin of his pain, his anger, his confusion; they dissolved from his body like a patch of soil beneath a stream of hot water. He loosened his grip, instantly aghast at his actions. Gently, he ran his hand across the gauze wrapped around Bryan's chest.

Faith had tended to him appropriately, for the good of the ritual, and for the good of Bryan. Benjamin was instantly grateful. He took a deep breath, his anger now restrained. He backed away from the crib, said a prayer, then quickly fled the room.

What now, Osiris?

He staggered downstairs and called for Daniel again. With no answer, he ran through the kitchen, knocking over a chair as he grabbed his keys from the table and bounded out the back door.

The sun hit him hard in the face—about as hard as the screen door slamming against the side of the house—blinding him as he tripped down the five porch steps. Head pounding again, Benjamin brought his hands up and shielded his eyes from the glare, seeing Pilate's dark form pulling hard against his leash, barking and growling ferociously. The dog, enraged since noon, was only inches away from Benjamin, paws digging trenches into the soft earth, jaws snapping up and down, eager for a piece of his leg. Benjamin gazed fearfully at the once gentle, loving black lab, its eyes now wet and ablaze with mad fury.

In a panic, Benjamin backed away, tripping over a shovel that had been left out. *Damn that boy!* He landed solidly on his rear, breath escaping his lungs in a solid *umph*. Wild rage immediately erupted in him. He scrambled to his knees. His mind barked crazy orders at him, and he listened intently to its demands.

The dog strained, growling, eyes red and bulging.

Benjamin stood.

He shoved the keys into his pocket, then grabbed the soiled wooden handle of the shovel.

He firmed it up good and tight in his grip.

The dog leaped crazily, pulling ferociously on its

tether, the rusted handle to the basement well screeching as the screws holding it in place began to loosen.

Benjamin raised the shovel back over his shoulder. He ran at Pilate, head down, the shovel blindly cutting through the air. The flat of the blade connected with the dog's shoulder, driving it away from the steps. The dog yelped, turned half-heartedly, and growled.

Benjamin raised the shovel again and hit the dog in the ribs. Raised the shovel and hit the dog on the tail. Raised the shovel and hit the dog on the back.

Like a rabbit, Pilate cowered against the foundation of the house, whimpering, paws groping the earth, its head lowered to the ground in an ineffective attempt to avoid its attacker. A puddle of urine seeped out from below its hunkering torso.

The anger in Benjamin begged him to rain more blows down upon the dog. He stood in position, breathing heavily, waiting for Pilate to come at him, the shovel poised for another strike. But the dog remained motionless, wheezing raspily, a deep, bloody slash in its midsection.

Benjamin stopped. He grinned, absorbed with triumph and wallowing in his victory. He dropped the shovel and walked away, deciding to let the dog die slowly and painfully.

Benjamin circled around the side of the house, stopping only to momentarily gaze down at his hands and clothes, now spattered with the dog's blood. He wiped his hands on his shirt, admiring the dark splotches they made. He then approached the front of the '73 red Ford pickup parked in the gravel driveway. He opened the driver's door and slid in behind the wheel, his palms sticky on the hard plastic. This reminded him of the special event that had just transpired. He took a series of deep, calculated breaths, his anger toward the dog subsiding now—not fading away completely. A surge of euphoria washed over him, and he felt the urgent need to press on.

He started the truck and turned on the radio. From the speaker, riding a wave of static, the message from Osiris came, the voice distant and tinny, but recognizable: *Benjamin Conroy . . . do not let anyone hinder your attempt to complete the ritual.* A loud squelch followed, and then country music filled the pickup's hot, rank interior.

Benjamin grinned. He closed the door and backed the truck out of the driveway, feeling calm and unafraid now that he knew Osiris was offering guidance and forgiveness. The tires kicked up a shower of gravel as he pulled out onto the road and sped away en route to the only place he knew he could pray peacefully to God—to Osiris—for salvation.

Daniel rounded the corner of the street where he lived, guided only by his instincts and his will to live. He'd lost a good deal of blood from the knife wound in his belly, the waistline of his pants soaked deep red. The entire way home, he kept looking over his shoulder, looking for Mack and his gang, but he didn't see anyone. Now, as he lumbered toward the house, he saw his father driving away in the opposite direction, the tires of the pickup kicking up a hurricane of dirt and dust. Lightheaded and foggy, Daniel reeled down the driveway and into the backyard—where he collapsed in agony alongside Pilate. He wrapped his blood-stained arms around the dog's trembling body, searching for comfort. But fatigue quickly claimed him, and he leaned back down against the dog and closed his eyes, allowing darkness to take over.

* * *

Faith pulled herself up to the toilet and vomited again.
Crying. Spitting. She prayed to God that it would end
soon, and thought it might for a moment. But then she
heaved again, and something big and solid came up out
of her.

Something red, and wet, and organic that made a
loud plop as it fell into the toilet.

Elizabeth took great pains to wait until her father had
gone downstairs before masturbating again. All morning, following the ritual, inexplicable urges overwhelmed her. No matter how many times she brought
herself to orgasm, she felt an all-consuming need to
continue. On and on she went, like a machine on an assembly line, alternating fingers and palms and even using her wrists to massage her breasts, her vagina. The
moment her father had entered the room, she managed to cover herself before he caught sight of her in
the act, and the entire time she felt as though she
would implode from not being able to touch herself;
he'd been in there for about six minutes (she'd counted
the seconds in an effort to distract herself), making
this the longest she'd gone that morning without an
orgasm.

But now all the masturbation had lost its glamour. It
had stopped fulfilling its promise.

Like a junkie in need of a fix, her mind demanded
that she find another means of gratification. Fast. And
she felt no choice but to comply, lest she explode with
frustration and . . . withdrawal.

Wearing only her robe and slippers, Elizabeth hurried downstairs and fled the house through the back
door, so blinded by a need for pleasure that she never

saw her brother and her dog lying in a pool of blood alongside the basement doors.

Bryan Conroy dreamed, and although his one-year-old mind didn't truly comprehend much of what he'd experienced, he knew that he was in pain, and that the pain had triggered something in him, and it made him see. And what he saw was a large individual, just like those who fed him and bathed him. And this individual was looking down at him. But . . . it looked different than the others. This one didn't move, didn't talk or even breathe. No. It swung. Back and forth. And it made a noise that created a dull, hard pain inside his head.

Thump . . . thump . . . thump . . .

CHAPTER TWENTY

September 7, 2005
6:13 P.M.

The bus finally pulled off the interstate. The rain had lessened to a drizzle, and through the drops on the front windshield Johnny could see the sign at the end of the turnoff: WELLFIELD—12 M. The bus turned right, and Johnny shifted left into the empty seat next to him.

Hours earlier, when the bus had left Port Authority, it had been filled to capacity. But after stopping in Boston, it'd dropped off about eighty percent of its passengers—college students, most of them, lugging knapsacks. Had his mother and father gone the route of most other parents, he too would have been off to school now.

The air in the bus was thick with one-dimensional conversations, about who fooled around with whom, what classes were being offered, etc., etc. Johnny had been fortunate enough to have a quiet, unassuming man in the seat next to him who was as uninterested in striking up a conversation with Johnny as Johnny was with him. The man, after a two-hour nap, had gotten off in Boston with all the college kids. The bus sat for about fifteen minutes, giving Johnny enough time to stretch his muscles and take a leak in the terminal rest-room. Eight passengers got on the bus in Boston, joining Johnny and four others. Then the bus was back on the road, driving through the rain on its way toward Skowhegan, Maine, with a couple of pit stops in small towns on the way.

The bus rode the winding country road slowly, and Johnny was grateful to be taking in the natural scenery at this snail's pace, despite the shadows of rain and gathering darkness. It did a decent job of distracting him from the horrible truth that had become his life.

Despite their idiosyncrasies—his mother's strict method of childrearing and her God-driven principles, his father's uncaring attitude toward him—he still loved them. They were his parents, and they'd raised him to adulthood, always making certain that he had food on the table and a roof over his head.

But now he realized that none of it seemed to matter anymore. No question about it. The past had become history. Dead and buried. Now he was well on his way to beginning a bold new life, one without Ed and Mary Petrie.

Johnny gathered his single piece of luggage from the overhead rack as the bus pulled into the parking lot of the Wellfield Inn, on Farland Avenue. He tucked a thumb into his back pocket—a procedure that had become an obsessive habit—and felt Judson's letter, his

Get out of Jail Free card. After fleeing the apartment he'd caught the subway to Port Authority. Once there, he'd placed a collect call to Andrew Judson from a pay phone. Johnny had to conserve the forty-three dollars he pinched from his father's wallet, which had been left out on the kitchen table. Judson had told Johnny to go to the Greyhound terminal in ten minutes, where a ticket would be waiting for him. Johnny had located the bus in the terminal, and had been pleased to discover that Wellfield was on the list of as-needed stops en route to Skowhegan.

Now he got off the bus, thanked the driver—an elderly bald man he never really took a look at until this moment—and stepped across the lot toward the motel's entrance. The bus hissed loudly, then shut its doors and pulled away, leaving Johnny alone and feeling vulnerable. He took a deep, nervous breath, looking up at the sky, which had just begun to turn dark. In the lot next to the hotel was a Pizza Hut, which he decided to immediately visit.

His food was quickly served, and he managed a few bites, but soon felt full—the restaurant was as loud as the bus had been on its way to Boston, packed with screaming toddlers and their frustrated parents. He asked the waitress to wrap the rest of his dinner to go, then headed across the parking lot to the Wellfield Inn. The girl behind the desk informed him that his room had already been paid in full. Judson had fronted the bill.

Alone in his room at last and nursing an awful headache, Johnny fell asleep on his side. His dreams were filled with images of his mysterious past, of the golden pain, sharp lights, and ghostly human figures trying desperately to draw him closer into what appeared to be a huge white circle painted on the floor.

CHAPTER TWENTY-ONE

August 24, 1988
3:25 P.M.

At the same time Elizabeth Conroy fled nearly naked through the cornfields alongside her home, at the same time Faith Conroy stuck her fingers into the toilet to retrieve what appeared to be an human organ floating in the water, at the same time Daniel Conroy lay barely breathing alongside his dying dog, and at the same time Bryan Conroy dreamed in his crib, Benjamin Conroy pulled his pickup truck into the small dirt lot outside his church, The Organization of God.

The lot was empty, of course, as was the church. He kept the doors locked at all times, except on Sundays when performing the two scheduled morning masses, or the night before, for confessions. Every now and then he'd hear a good piece of Wellfield gossip, but for the most part it was the same old trivial concerns over nothing.

There really wasn't much of value inside the small church, outside of a few porcelain statues or some brass plates . . . but wouldn't some of the damn local politicians love to find a way to close his doors for good so the faithful parishioners could line their pockets instead? God forbid if they ever broke into his office and unlocked his desk drawers, where they would unearth the ammunition needed to bring him down.

He stopped the truck right up front, setting the tires into a tall patch of witchgrass. His back cracked as he got out, the sharp pain traveling up his spine into his head. He rubbed his temples, an action quickly growing into habit, then slowly climbed the four wooden steps to the entrance of his church.

A padlock hung from a clasp on the wooden door. He shuddered as he slid the key into the lock. He turned it, then yanked it down. The clasp tore away from the wood of the door. He paused, gripping the clasp and lock in his hand, realizing with dismay that someone must've unscrewed it in an effort to break in. Could they still be inside? He didn't think so. They wouldn't have been able to replace the clasp with the doors closed.

Benjamin's guard rose up, disquiet racing through him like steam from an engine. His head ached furiously, and he moved it from side to side, cracking the bones in his neck.

Recognizing that he may very well have another complicated situation on his hands, he threw the lock and clasp to the ground, then pulled open the twin doors. Their rusty hinges screeched like ghosts in a haunted house. Above, a bird fluttered, and when he looked up, he saw a blackbird flying away over the roof of the church.

As he entered the church, a palpable wave of heat hit him. The interior of the church offered nothing more than welcoming solace, four wood-slatted walls painted white, exposed beams in the ceiling, polished pews, and an intricately painted crucifix hanging on the wall behind the altar. Over the years, Benjamin had used only a small percentage of the weekly mass collections toward the upkeep of the structure, and it showed with the remainder going toward the preservation of the Conroy house. *Thank the Good Lord. Thank you, Osiris.*

He walked down the center aisle, the ranks of pews on each side deadly silent. He peeked behind each one, making certain that no one was hiding, awaiting the perfect moment to jump out at him.

He felt a sudden weight against his chest. His hands and feet tingled. *Osiris? Is it you? Is this your presence I feel?*

Upon reaching the front of the church, he stepped up to the altar, and after making a quick survey and concluding that nothing was amiss, he walked to his office, located just below the crucifix.

He ferreted out the key. A sharp pain filled his head, and he interpreted it as a warning to danger. Instead of inserting the key, he simply turned the knob and realized with sudden panic that his instinct had been correct.

The doorknob, usually locked, turned freely.

The clasp clicked, and another jutting pain lanced through his head; this time it felt like a splash of hot liquid. He grimaced, fighting against it, hesitating with the door open only a few inches.

Then he pushed it open all the way.

At once he heard a woman's voice.

"Benjamin . . ."

He opened his eyes wide, feeling the pain, the *pain*, and he stopped in the doorway, in utter fury at the sight before him. His keys fell from his hand to the ground.

Damn you!

She was sitting behind his desk, hands resting on the ink-stained blotter. Her hair was a store-bought blond that flowed over her floral Sunday dress in curly tresses, down to her protruding breasts. Her eyes, buried in thick eyeliner—harlot's makeup, Benjamin would say—regarded him with utter contempt. Tears painted thick gray lines of streaky makeup down her cheeks.

Ignoring her and the beating ache in his head, he looked over to the glassed-in shelf on the right side of the room, right below the two-foot crucifix on the wall. He walked to it silently, opened the doors, and removed a bottle of Wild Turkey. He unscrewed the top and sucked down a mouthful in one quick movement. He then stepped back in front of the desk and stared at the woman with unfaltering scorn.

"What are you doing here?" he asked. He used the mouth of the bottle to scratch a sudden itch on his scar.

"We need to talk," the woman replied, her eyes flitting down to the bloodstains on his shirt.

Damn you, he thought again, feeling the rage swarming inside. He had to take a few long deep breaths to keep it at bay.

Her name was Helen Mackey, and she was a parishioner of The Organization of God. He'd met her after a service about a year ago, but had noticed her much earlier than that. She'd always sat in the front row, alongside her husband and thirteen-year-old son. Benjamin would stare into her unwavering eyes, which later became harlot's eyes, and pick up silent messages from her in his head. A gentle wink, a slight smile, and he'd stammer his way through the hour-long service, considering the implications behind her gestures and wondering how far he could take them. When the final prayers were said and done, he would quickly bow to the congregation and escape into his office, thinking only of her eyes, her smile, and the young supple skin that peeked out from the plunging cut of her Sunday dress.

Then one day she showed up for confession.

I've got a sin, Benjamin Conroy. And it needs confessing. . . .

On Saturdays, Benjamin would sit and listen to what Wellfield's apprehensive folk had to say. The usual suspects would wait in line outside his office, spilling their guts in turn, leaving with pennance of prayers and feelings of forgiveness, courtesy of their faithful minister.

Less than a year ago, after a rather light showing—the Brantley sisters, one right after the other, moaning about their argument the night before over the correct way to mix tapioca, and Calvin Mooney, who had thoughts of coveting his neighbor's wife—Benjamin stood to leave, only to find the door to his office blocked by Ms. Bleach-Blonde-Dark-Eyes, as she leaned seductively against the frame, her dress opening slightly at the sash and her beautiful fall of golden hair slightly mussed.

And she'd said, "I've got a sin, Benjamin Conroy. And it needs confessing. . . ."

A sin . . .

She slammed her hand on his desk, wrenching him

from his memories. He looked at her, fury enveloping him.

"How did you get in here?" he asked.

She leaned forward, picked up a key from his desk, and shook it derisively back and forth.

"Get out of here," he said, thinking, *How in the hell did she get that?*

Because you got careless, Benjamin. She lifted it from your desk after you finished laying her one afternoon. That's how. And God knows what else she got her hands on.

Oh, God. No . . .

Then she held up his diary. She waved it at him like she did the key.

He was instantly petrified, frozen with disbelief at her utter audacity, her *nerve* for breaking in here, into his desk. She stood and his heart lurched, his mind trying hard to come up with a quick solution to this problem. *Osiris, help me!* But there seemed to be no solution.

Their affair had been intense, fiery, undeniably passionate, lasting much longer than Benjamin had ever intended. All his other exploits had ranged from a single afternoon to three months—mere flings. But Helen Mackey lasted a year. And as with all the other women, he fed his swollen ego further by chronicling every sordid detail in his diary, keeping Polaroid photographs of her in provocative poses with each written account. This had been his big secret, this diary—the only secret he'd kept from every other living soul. Even God.

But now . . . here it was, out in the open for the world to see, for God to see, in the hands of the woman he'd been trying to end a year-long affair with.

She came around the side of the desk, stumbling a bit, and sat down on the edge, knocking over a cup of pens and pencils. "This one is really interesting," she said, holding up a photograph of a naked girl. Her words were slurred, and Benjamin could tell that she'd been drinking. "I believe this is Brittany Wellman. Grace Wellman's daughter. Gee, Benjamin, last I heard she just turned sixteen. Hmm . . . and let's not ignore what you wrote about her. Shall I refresh your memory?"

Her cheeks were flushed, eyes wide and sparkling. She seemed to be enjoying this little performance. Impulsively, he lunged for the diary, a half-hearted effort. She flinched away and dropped it to the floor. The photos fell out like confetti.

When he bent down to pick them up, she said, "Don't move."

He didn't like the tone of her voice. He turned his head and looked up at her.

Oh my God, is that a . . . a gun?

He didn't know where she'd had it hidden—in her purse perhaps, which was draped loosely over her shoulder—but here it was, aimed at him. A second round of tears darkened the eyeliner tracks on her face. A gust of late afternoon wind rattled the beams in the church. He held up his hands, feigning innocence, eyes darting from the gun to her face, then to the Polaroids spread out on the floor.

"Helen . . . please, don't . . . ."

"Listen to me, Benjamin . . . we have a problem, and I need you to fix it." Her voice sounded hurt, brimming with uncertainty and pain.

"What is it? Helen?" His eyes moved back toward the gun, slightly loose in her grip.

"I—I'm pregnant." She tried to say something else, but only sobs came out.

And the gun dropped an inch farther.

Benjamin could see he was dealing with a woman who'd never used a gun before. She must've lifted it from her husband's nightstand drawer and tucked it into her purse with no real intention of pulling the trigger. She'd wanted to frighten the man she'd been having an affair with . . . the man who'd presumably gotten her pregnant.

With this in mind, Benjamin said, "Let's talk about this, Helen. Are you certain you're pregnant?"

"*Of course I am!*" she screamed, fixing her aim on him. He inched closer to her, despite the threat, catching a thick reek of alcohol on her breath. *Very nice, mother-to-be.*

"How do you know it's mine?" he asked, inching closer still, looking back and forth between the gun and her messy, muddy eyes. *Harlot's eyes.*

"Damn you, Benjamin," she slurred, eyes drifting in their attempt to focus. "You know me better than anyone, even my husband, even my son. And you know I haven't been with anyone but you." The gun lowered again. Her voice hitched as she said, "Benjamin . . . I . . . I can't handle not being with you." The tears started flowing again, and she blurted angrily, "You told me I was your soul mate! And . . . and I gave myself to you, over and over again, right here on this damn desk! And then . . . you, you refused me! Oh God, you refused me! You just think you can just throw me away like a piece of trash! Well, I can't let you do that." She looked at him scornfully and added in a frighteningly calm voice, "If I can't have you, then . . . no one can."

He remained silent, striving to work his magic on her as he'd done so many times in the past.

Osiris, I beseech your strength to allow me the good fortune of my desires.

"And have me you shall," he said softly. Lovingly.

The emotions on her face changed almost immediately, confusion reflected in her eyes as she attempted to regain her focus.

The gun wavered in her hand, then dropped some more.

He stared at her, fear and anger pooling into a distinctly unique sensation. It was as though he were waiting for a single spark to set him off. He had never seen her like this before, so distraught, so out of control. In the past there *had* been indications of instability, of depression. But she'd always been able to compose herself, despite her lack of confidence, her lack of self-worth—weaknesses he'd always preyed upon to further his own needs. But she'd never gone over the edge like this before.

He stepped closer still, struggling to find an opportunity. She looked at him blankly, then gazed down at the gun in her hand. A scared look crossed her face, cheeks red and glistening beneath the jagged lines of mascara.

The gun!

Benjamin wasted no time. He charged her like a bull, cocking his right fist back and lunging at her with all his body weight behind him. A small grunt escaped his lips, alerting her. She twisted and at the same time raised the gun. His first blow struck the side of her head. A split second later, the gun went off, taking out a large chunk of plaster in the wall behind him.

"You crazy bitch!" he yelled. He grabbed her wrist

and forced her arm away. Their bodies fell back, and her hand struck the wall. The gun fired again, tearing a hole in the ceiling. Plaster rained down on them. As the struggle ensued, he locked eyes with her, saw the fear and terror and shame in them. She forced her arm forward with surprising strength, the barrel of the gun now only inches above his head.

In a do-or-die move, Benjamin whipped his head forward and connected full force with her nose, producing a warm, wet cracking sound.

Helen staggered back against the wall, mouth wide open, eyes wide open. A fountain of blood spewed from her face. Her hands swung blindly through the air, the gun hanging limply from three trembling fingers.

Time seemed to unfold in slow motion. Vicious pain rocketed through Benjamin's head. His vision blurred, obstructing his view of the woman he'd made love to countless times in the past. Her once beautiful face slowly came into focus, revealing a gory mess of a nose. She attempted to scream, but only guttural, throaty gurgles came out.

Benjamin stood trembling at what he'd done, staring as Helen's body stiffened, her eyes fluttering as if struggling to keep free of the squirting blood and mucus. Again she tried to speak. Again a thick gurgling sound came out. She doubled over, gagging, strings of fluid spewing from her mouth.

Benjamin looked at the gun.

It was still in her hand.

And her fingers were tightening around it. Her arm began to slowly rise.

He bellowed and lunged at her, fist held high. He punched her in the bloody meat of her shattered nose. Blood burst out at him, forcing him to close his eyes.

Blindly, he swung again and connected once more with her face. He swung again and hit her on the side of the head. She staggered sideways along the wall, leaving a streak of blood. He continued to punch her, telling himself that it was all self-defense, that she was holding a loaded gun and had fired it at him, leaving him no choice but to protect himself. She raised her hands, not to point the gun—Benjamin guessed that at this point, she didn't even realize it was still in her hand—but to shield herself. It did her little good.

A series of noises emerged from what used to be her lips, but that was all. She fell silent beneath the attack, collapsing to the floor in a dead heap. The gun hit the floor with a loud clunk and fell from her grasp. Beneath her bloody mask, Benjamin could see the whites of her eyes rolling toward the gun. She made a vain attempt to reach for it. Benjamin pounced on her, groping at her face, digging his nails deep into her flesh, clawing at her eyes. She swiped at his chest and managed to rip his shirt and uncover his scar, a single blood-coated nail tearing into the knobby purple flesh. He howled, then gripped her matted hair and began slamming her head hard against the floor, over and over again. He heard her skull shatter, felt it soften beneath his grip. But the adrenaline continued to flow in him, forcing him to continue. Soon, the rear of her skull was nothing more than gritty pulp.

Finally, Benjamin released her. He collapsed back, crawling away. He leaned his head against the wall, dizzy and feeling as though he might black out. Blood dribbled into his eye, stinging and warm. He thumbed it away, then stared at her body, her *corpse*, the dress torn open, her white breasts sagging lifelessly. Her face was unrecognizable, lost beneath a mask of blood.

My God . . . what have I done?

He clambered to his knees, hands folded between his legs, head thrown back, a thin, weak whimper falling from his lips. He mumbled a Hail Mary, then struggled unsteadily to his feet, nearly collapsing back down from dizziness. He backpedaled out of the office in a panic, eyes glued to Helen's motionless body, a single Polaroid of a scantily clad woman stuck to the bottom of his shoe like a piece of chewing gum.

Once out of the office, he spun and staggered past the altar. He continued down the center aisle like a drunk man fleeing an angry mob, eyes trained on the closed doors.

The clasp had been replaced after she closed the door. . . .

He looked down only once to see that the blood-stained photo had come away from his shoe somewhere along the way.

He burst through the doors, out into the cool, late afternoon, the sun now hidden behind a blanket of gray clouds. He stopped to catch his breath and gazed down at his torn shirt, Helen Mackey's blood now mixed in with Pilate's. He tore off the shirt and threw it to the ground. More evidence for the authorities.

Murder. No, she was pregnant. Double *murder . . .*

A bird cawed. He gasped and looked up to the roof of the church, where a large black bird sat perched, staring down at him.

Osiris, still watching over him?

"What shall I do now, my Lord?" he shouted, his voice sounding dull, as though absorbed by the air—just as it had this morning, outside the barn.

The bird took off into the sky, a single black feather coming away, caught in the wind, bouncing lazily along the shingles toward the rear of the church. He followed it around the side of the small structure, tripping and stumbling, keeping his eyes on the feather as it fluttered over the edge of the roof, behind the church. He turned the corner . . . and nearly collided with a small silver sedan parked along the perimeter of thin woodland.

He stopped, slapping his hands down on the trunk, and gazed at the car. *Her* car, hidden back here so he wouldn't know she was waiting for him inside the church. The driver's side door was open and he could see a smear of blood on the inside chrome handle.

With one hand on the car to help keep his balance, he stepped over to the open door, leaned down, and looked into the front seat.

He drew back, then looked again.

Helen Mackey's husband was in the passenger seat. Dead. There was a single bullet hole in the side of his head, a dry line of blood plastered down his colorless face. A host of flies and mosquitoes buzzed noisily around the wound.

Benjamin's body grew cold and he crumpled to his knees in the weeds and soil. Gripping the edge of the door, he stared at the murdered man, thinking crazily, *One good murder deserves another.*

Then he began to laugh. *Really* laugh. A sense of abandon washed over him, and all his rational thoughts drifted away like canoes in a river. *Osiris, thank you for the strength to carry on*, he thought.

Slowly, he climbed to his feet and peeked in the backseat.

And at once realized how the clasp and lock had been put back into place on the church door.

Helen Mackey's thirteen-year-old son was lying across the backseat of the car. He was trembling, a swath of dried blood streaked across his forehead like Indian war paint.

He stared up at Benjamin.

Benjamin smiled at him. Then he laughed even harder.

CHAPTER TWENTY-TWO

September 8, 2005
8:00 A.M.

The ringing telephone pulled Johnny away from his dreams, and into bitter consciousness. Eyes still closed, he groped for the handset, and by the time he plucked it off its cradle, he'd completely forgotten what he'd been dreaming about.

And where he was.

He opened one eye, then the other. He saw ugly green walls, bad flower art, and a stucco ceiling. He felt frightened before recalling that he was about to embark on a new life, and for the very first time in his eighteen years, he had slept someplace other than his room.

He struggled up on one elbow and raised the handset to his ear.

"Hullo?"

"Johnny . . ."

"Yeah."

"Wake you?"

His mind felt totally vacant, and he had to think a moment before remembering the lawyer's name. "No, Mr. Judson."

"Let's set the record straight, Johnny. I won't lie to you about anything, and you don't lie to me. Fair enough?"

Johnny hesitated, already feeling self-conscious and uncomfortable. "Okay." He leaned up and looked at the digital clock. Eight o'clock.

"Sorry it's so early," Judson said, as though able to see Johnny's actions, "but I've set aside the entire day for you."

Johnny sat on the edge of the bed, one leg dangling. "Okay . . ."

"We're going to need it."

"The whole day?"

"That's right, the whole day."

He thought of his mother, her maiden name Conroy, lying alone and afraid in her hospital bed, her long-buried secret suddenly unearthed. "I'm guessing there's more to this than just signing a few papers," he said.

"There is, which is why I need you here at nine. There are others who will be joining us as well."

"Others?" The word died in his mouth, and a sudden fear settled into his gut. It was a feeling he'd gotten so used to since this all began two days earlier, when the letter arrived.

After a moment Judson finally said, "I know this is very hard for you, Johnny."

"Yeah, it is." *How do you know?*

"But the end result is a nice sum of money for you."

Given his mother's family connection to Benjamin

Conroy, Johnny felt that he could trust Judson. However, the lawyer was still just a voice on the phone. And it didn't take a scholar to know that when there was money involved, it was prudent to keep up your guard, especially with an individual who claimed to be devoted to helping you.

"Can you be here by nine?" Judson asked.

"How am I—?"

"There'll be a cab waiting for you outside the motel. You can have breakfast here."

"Thank you," he answered, not feeling very hungry.

"So I guess I'll see you in about an hour."

"Sounds good." He hung up the phone, stared at it for a moment while wondering what to expect from Judson, *the whole day*, then got out of bed and took a shower. While getting dressed, he watched a local newscast about an escaped patient from a neighboring psychiatric institution who was still at large, and was to be considered "armed and dangerous." A photo was broadcast of the man named David Mackey, who had only one eye, and a large dent in his forehead.

In twenty minutes, Johnny was walking out the front door of the motel, his tote bag over his shoulder. A cab waited for him beneath the motel's cement canopy. The driver, a thin man wearing a black polo shirt and a Red Sox cap, leaned out the window.

"You Johnny Petrie?" he asked.

Johnny nodded. His stomach growled, and he realized—despite not having any appetite—that he hadn't eaten much over the last thirty-six hours. He tossed his bag into the backseat and slid in alongside it. He felt for the lawyer's letter in his back pocket, now becoming a security blanket of sorts, then reached into the tote bag and removed the clear plastic bags containing the feather he found on the fire escape back home, and his father's strange suicide note. He placed these into his pocket as well.

Once the door was shut, the driver pulled out of the lot, turned left, and moved slowly down Farland Avenue. Johnny sat quietly behind the driver, taking in the sights, observing the differences between the hustle and bustle of Manhattan and small-town New England. Here, everything was spread out, with small shops and parking lots adorned with flower pots. The city, on the other hand, was Wellfield's polar opposite: crowded with just about everything under the sun; you couldn't see ten feet in front of you because there were so many buildings and people in the way.

The cab reached what appeared to be a busier part of town—the heart of Wellfield, perhaps—and made a right. Johnny saw a diner, a small movie theater, and a bank with a large LED display that showed the temperature to be seventy-four degrees. As the cab idled at a stop light, Johnny noticed a drug store, a toy store, and a stationery store.

"Where are ya from?" the driver asked, breaking the silence.

"New York."

"City boy, eh?"

"Yes, sir."

"Here visiting some relatives?"

"You might say that."

The cab jerked forward as the light turned green. They rode in silence for another half-mile, passing shops, homes, and rows of cars parked with their rear-ends facing into the street. They circled around a fountain with three cement bears, then passed another strip of small retail stores. Perhaps a hundred yards behind these stores, Johnny could see a large stretch of unused land that sloped upward into a knoll. It was surrounded by a rickety-looking wooden fence, weeds and gnarled bushes growing high behind it, packed tightly into the area like subway riders during rush hour. A rusted metal sign warned that it was "Private Property" and that there would be "No Trespassing." To Johnny, the unused land seemed out of place in this built-up area of town. But then again, what did he know? He was a stranger in these parts: a stranger in a strange land.

The driver made a right turn onto Center Street, then pulled over against the curb, about fifty feet up. "Before nine, almost impossible to find a spot on Main. Hope this is okay."

A flutter of nervousness tickled Johnny's gut. He turned around in his seat. "That was Main Street?"

"The one and only in Wellfield. You leave it, and there's not much else to see. The lawyer's office is right there on the corner. Number fourteen." In the distance, Johnny could hear a freight train whistle blowing.

"What do I owe you?"

"It's all paid up."

"Great. Thanks." He grabbed his bag and stepped out onto the sidewalk. The driver yelled, "Have a good day!" then pulled away, leaving Johnny, once again, all alone. He stood there for a moment, feeling the warmth of the sun beating down on him. Even the sun felt different here. Cleaner. More golden. Shouldering the bag, he walked down the street, passing a young mother with a stroller, who smiled and said, "Good morning." He returned the greeting, realizing that there were a good many things he'd have to get used to while here in Wellfield.

Then he wondered with dismay as to how long he would actually get to stay here, knowing that it was only a matter of time before someone eventually tracked him down. Soon enough someone would report a terrible smell coming from his apartment. And they might notice the mail piling up. And his father's employer would start looking for him because he hadn't shown up for work. Eventually, the cops would break into the apartment, and there they would find Ed Petrie, three or four days dead, the cockroaches and waterbugs investigating his remains. They would discover that Johnny was missing, and his face would end up on the five o'clock news.

Needless to say, if his mother got there first, the events would play out differently. A sick feeling settled in Johnny's stomach as he envisioned his mother stumbling upon her dead husband, hanging and swinging and thumping, her son nowhere to be found.

He reached the corner and found himself looking at a white doorway set into a three-story brick building, a brass number 14 at its center. To the side of the door, a matching brass plate indicated three tenants. Andrew Judson's office was on the first level, below a dentist's office and a real estate agency. He took a deep breath, opened the door, and went inside.

He was immediately greeted by the smiling face of a woman in her late forties, sitting at a desk. "Johnny?" she asked warmly.

"Yes, ma'am."

She picked up the phone on her desk and buzzed Judson. Johnny waited about thirty seconds, listening to canned Neil Diamond until a man appeared from an adjoining office.

Judson was pushing sixty, with fair skin and white receding hair. He was neatly dressed, wearing blue trousers, a navy-and-red striped tie, and a pressed white dress shirt. His smile was wide and beaming.

"Johnny," he said, coming around to greet him. He held out his hand, which Johnny accepted. It was warm and clammy. "Such a pleasure to meet you finally."

"Likewise," Johnny answered, thinking, *Finally? It's only been two days.*

"Come with me," Judson said, seemingly ready to get down to business. He escorted Johnny past the secretary, into the office. Johnny had never been in a lawyer's office before, and he gazed at the two built-in bookcases lining the side walls, each jam-packed with legal volumes. On the wall behind Judson's cherry desk hung six fancy frames boasting the lawyer's educational credentials. Just to the left was a window that overlooked Main Street.

Judson said, "Please, take a seat."

There were three chairs arranged in front of Judson's desk. Johnny placed his bag down on a small ottoman to the left of the door and sat in the closest chair. Andrew Judson sat in the large leather swivel chair behind his desk (much plusher than the three Johnny had to choose from), and said, "Welcome to Wellfield, John."

"Thanks." Johnny's heart started pounding. He wondered how long it was going to take for him to walk out of here gripping a big fat check and a new lease on life. *Give me the papers to sign, and let me out of here.*

It isn't going to be that easy.

The whole day . . .

"Sleep okay last night?

"Very well, thank you."

"The Wellfield Inn is pretty much the nicest place in

town. Certainly not as posh as what you're used to, living in Manhattan and all."

"Well, Mr. Judson—"

"Please, call me Andrew."

"Okay, Andrew . . . last night was actually the first time I've ever stayed in a motel."

Judson smiled warmly. "You don't say?" He hesitated a moment, studying Johnny's face, and Johnny imagined the lawyer might be pitying him. "Well, Johnny Petrie, after we're through, you'll be able to stay in the nicest hotel Manhattan has to offer."

That impressed Johnny. It wasn't so much the lawyer's promise of wealth, as much as his ability to instantly mold Johnny into a firm believer—now Johnny felt he could trust him. He also felt that Judson knew a great deal more than he was letting on.

"Mr. Judson . . . Andrew . . . before we get started, I have to tell you something . . . a lot's happened since I received your letter two days ago, and I'm sure it's all related to what you already know . . . and talking about it . . . well, it'll probably make me feel a bit better about this whole situation."

Judson nodded and tilted back in his chair while Johnny spent the next few minutes divulging everything that'd happened, from his receiving the lawyer's letter, to the discovery of his mother's maiden name in the hospital, to his father's suicide. He left out a few details, most notably the note his father had left behind.

When Johnny was finished, Judson asked, "So you just left your father hanging there in the apartment? You never called the police?"

Johnny nodded, using a thumb to feel the folded baggies in his pocket.

Judson rubbed his chin in thought. "Which means

we'll have to move faster than planned. The bus tickets were issued in your name, and once they discover I paid for them, they'll call. May take them a while, but they'll figure it out."

"I didn't do anything wrong." Johnny shifted uncomfortably in his seat, and his breathing became shallow.

"No, you didn't. But there's much to discuss, and now, less time to do it."

Johnny didn't respond; instead, he sat up straight in the chair and folded his hands protectively in his lap.

The intercom buzzed. Judson pressed a button and said, "Yes?"

The secretary's voice spilled into the room from the tinny speaker: "They're here."

"Tell them to wait," he said firmly. "And, Susan . . . could you bring the food in, please?"

"Right away," she answered, and not ten seconds later appeared with a small tray filled with bagels, muffins, and coffee. She offered it to Johnny. He helped himself to a bagel and a cup of black coffee.

"The men waiting for us," Judson said, taking a muffin from the tray, "are the mayor of Wellfield and his lawyer."

"What do they want?"

Judson waited until Susan left the room, then said, "They want your inheritance."

Johnny hesitated for a moment. "What *is* this all about? I mean, why am *I* here? And how is it I'm the one to get this inheritance?"

Judson took a quick sip of coffee, then leaned forward and clasped his hands together. "Johnny . . . this is all going to come as a shock to you, but I feel it's best that I come right out and tell you." He took a deep breath, and Johnny imagined Judson telling him that he was going to die of some form of incurable cancer, and that he had only ten days to spend his newfound fortune before dropping dead. But Judson said instead, "Johnny Petrie is not your birth name. Your real name is Bryan Conroy. Benjamin Conroy was your father. And you are the sole living heir to his estate."

Johnny froze for a moment, then placed his coffee and bagel on the desk. His interest in food had vanished. His hands started shaking, and he could feel his heart rate speeding up. He sat back, feeling as though he were in a dream.

"Johnny, I want you to know that I'm here to help you, that it's my job to see you are rightfully taken care of in the eyes of the law. Benjamin Conroy was my client, and I've been paid to make certain his will is properly executed. I assure you that every last detail will be thoroughly outlined for you so that you may understand everything correctly."

Again Johnny thought of his mother. Mary Petrie. Formerly Mary Conroy. And again he wondered if she was lying in her hospital bed, praying to the good Lord Jesus Christ to heal her, all the while waiting for her husband or Johnny to appear at the door and take her home. Then he thought: *Has she been released? Has she gone to the apartment and found Father's hanging body?*

Ed Petrie: *not* his father.

He looked at Judson and asked, "What about Mary? Is she my real mother?"

"Mary Petrie is your aunt. Benjamin Conroy's sister. Your real mother's name was Faith Conroy."

Johnny clutched his chest, his scar tingling. "No . . . no way. There must be some sort of mistake. I mean . . . I have memories of my parents since I was little, three, maybe four years old."

Judson opened his desk drawer, brought out a photograph and showed it to Johnny. It was a dull color portrait of a man and a woman. They were dressed nicely, standing in a small flower garden in front of a farmhouse.

Johnny noticed the resemblance at once: He looked just like the man in the picture. Additionally, he could see the man's resemblance to Mary. *Which is where,* Johnny realized, *I thought I'd inherited my features from.*

"The resemblance is uncanny," Judson remarked. "Wouldn't you say? I really couldn't believe it when I saw you just now—there was no question in my mind at that point, and there's no doubting it now. Johnny, you are Benjamin Conroy's son, Bryan Conroy."

Johnny leaned forward and took the photo. He stared at the picture, into Conroy's far-away eyes. Their firm dark stare seemed almost accusatory. He could virtually hear the man's deep voice, *What is your real purpose?* The woman, his mother, stood meekly at his side, one limp arm through the crook of his elbow. She'd blinked as the photo was taken, which made her look as though she were wincing in pain.

"These people, they're my real parents. . . ." Johnny stated dully, eyebrows pinched with bewilderment.

Judson nodded.

"So . . . if Mary is really my aunt, then Ed—"

"Ed Petrie is your uncle. Married her right here in Wellfield over thirty years ago."

Shaking his head, Johnny laughed uncomfortably. He placed the photo on Judson's desk, then sat back and looked out the window; Wellfield's locals hustled busily along Main Street. He let a few moments of silence pass.

Johnny pulled his gaze away from the window. His

brain whirled, and he began to feel sick to his stomach. "So, Mr. Judson . . . what is my real purpose?"

Judson grinned and looked at him intently over his folded hands. "Your purpose is to claim your estate. But first . . . you need to know exactly what it is we're dealing with."

"Okay, I'm ready."

"All right then . . . so, in a nutshell, you've inherited Benjamin Conroy's farmhouse, as well as all of his land, which, if you look out the window, down Center Street, you can catch a glimpse of. It used to be a thriving farm, but it's remained untouched since Benjamin's death seventeen years ago."

"Wait . . . seventeen years ago? My real father died seventeen years ago, when . . . when I was one?"

Judson nodded. "As did Faith Conroy, your mother. Benjamin Conroy's will—which I myself prepared many years ago—stated that in the event of Benjamin's and Faith's untimely passing, Ed and Mary Petrie would become the lawful guardians of their children. So they legally adopted you and had your name changed to Johnny Petrie. Soon thereafter, Ed and Mary Petrie moved to Manhattan. Being that I had also been assigned to hand over Benjamin's estate, I had to keep close tabs on Ed and Mary all these years, which really wasn't all that difficult, since they didn't move once they arrived in New York all those years ago."

"Andrew . . . you said his *children*. Does this mean that I have . . . siblings?"

Judson hesitated. Oppressive silence descended upon them. Finally, the lawyer replied, "You had a brother and a sister. They too are dead." Judson tilted his chair back; it made an uncomfortable creaking noise.

Johnny was about to ask *how?* when there was a light knock on the door and Susan poked her head in. "Your guests are getting impatient."

"Perhaps now is not the time to talk about finances, John. If you'd like, I can reschedule them for later today. They've waited seventeen years, they can wait a few more hours."

Judson got up and came around the side of the desk. Standing alongside Johnny, he asked, "You okay?"

Johnny nodded. "I'm a bit overwhelmed, but I'm trying to keep it all in check."

"That's good."

Johnny stood, then walked to the window. He looked out beyond the small drug store across the street, toward the sloping land a hundred yards behind it.

His land.

A single black bird landed on the fence, just above the "No Trespassing" sign. It fluttered its wings once, then quickly flew away in the direction where Johnny imagined his very own abandoned farmhouse to be.

CHAPTER TWENTY-THREE

August 24, 1988
4:13 P.M.

Erotic assault.

It seemed the only way for her to describe the afflic-
tion, which had grown far beyond mere self-
gratification. She needed to satisfy it using any means
necessary. Without question, she felt *chosen*, as if a
higher power looked down upon her and guided her
with its protective hand. Yes, she believed in God and
loved God, but she didn't think He was responsible for
this. No, something else was at work here, something
previously lying dormant within her, now awake and
given free rein. She felt unreservedly alluring: a sexual
creature for whom no rules applied. She retained a
level of urgency that insisted she not waste time ignoring her insatiable desires.

And now, exactly forty-eight minutes after fleeing

her home, she stood between a parked Dodge pickup and a beat-up Harley, outside of the The Bull Pen Tavern, the closest bar to the Conroy house—and one with a notorious reputation that had reached even Benjamin's ears—where she felt she could make her passion known to the world.

Opening her bathrobe, Elizabeth strode across the lot, the gravel crunching lightly under her bare feet. Without being seen, she pushed open the front door and went inside. The interior, dank and dark and stinking of stale beer, was presently home to eight men, all of whom the very type one might find getting soused on a weekday afternoon.

They all stopped what they were doing—throwing darts, shooting pool, snuffing out their Marlboros—and looked at her. The men, with their swollen beer bellies and their tattoos, gazed at her unwaveringly, this pristine teenaged peach.

She dropped her robe to the sticky floor, a move that put wide incredulous grins on the Bull Pen's clientele, all of whom felt as if their lottery ticket had finally been pulled. She sidled up to the closest man, a burly waster stinking of cigarettes and body odor, and grabbed his huge hand. This brought forth guffaws from the others, including the bartender, who, Elizabeth noticed, was already stroking himself through his worn jeans. She led the man to the pool table (but not before he downed the rest of his beer), where she sat, legs spread apart, her wetness glistening in the dim light.

In her mind she saw nothing wrong in her actions. She felt only a need to satisfy her unceasing desires, her unbridled lust.

She said nothing, just stared into the man's thoughtless eyes, knowing he would now never allow her to stop. Keeping her gaze firm, she reached forward and unbuttoned his jeans; out fell his dark, filthy, and more-than-ready manhood, which she expertly led inside her.

At once, Elizabeth drifted into a state of mind she never knew before her fragile virginity shattered, making way for a newfound existence, one she eagerly accepted. The wide-eyed men howled, their tattooed arms raised, cheering on their comrade as he emptied his seed inside the no-longer pristine girl.

With the front door now locked and the windows drawn, Elizabeth offered herself to the next brute willing to come to bat. The shouts and laughs grew, and the beer flowed, free for everyone in celebration of this miraculous event. They took her, and she them, sometimes more than one at a time as they filled her every orifice. An hour passed, after which she lay hoarse and bleeding . . . and even after every man had had his fill, she writhed and thrashed atop the saturated pool table, uncaring of her bruises as she masturbated furiously, stinking of much more than beer and tobacco.

She could hear the men talking now, not laughing anymore, some of them afraid of having to return to the county lock-up, or afraid of contracting the others' diseases. Arguments rose, muscles flexed. Still, they unanimously agreed to keep this event a secret—a pledge soon to be forgotten. The bartender found the common sense to return Elizabeth her robe and send her on her way, out the back door so anyone waiting in the parking lot for the bar to open wouldn't see her.

Tattered, torn, and bloodied, a filthy Elizabeth Conroy, a virgin not an hour before, left The Bull Pen Tavern, finally satisfied.

* * *

"Oh yeah!" he shouted.

The words came out strongly and triumphantly. Eddie Carlson gripped the steering wheel of his father's Mustang convertible with the same vigor he would a football while crossing the goal line of the opposing team. He pressed down on the accelerator, taking it up to sixty despite Mill Pond Road's thirty-mile-an-hour speed limit. He honked the horn playfully while Steve Miller's "The Joker" blasted from the stereo. The wind whistled in his ears. His wavy blond hair blew back in a rippling wave. *First-string quarterback*, Eddie thought happily. He knew that carrying the team to a winning season would propel him into the spotlight. Which in turn meant passing grades, lots of friends, and *girls*. Not to mention the possibility of a scholarship. *Yeah!*

The local farmland sped by in a blur, adding to his rush. The Mustang gripped a tight curve effortlessly, and he cruised by a stop sign that had never been useful in this lightly traveled section of Wellfield. Ahead, a mile of straight, single-lane blacktop met his eyes. In the past he'd taken the car up to eighty here, and for a moment he considered taking a crack at breaking his speed record (the adrenaline pumping through his veins begged him to do so), but he decided to ease up on the gas instead and fire up the congratulatory joint Jimmy Gibson had given him for a "job well done."

That was when he saw the girl.

Head down, arms hanging limply at her sides, she walked out of the wheat fields and into the middle of the road like a zombie in *Night of the Living Dead*. Eddie realized that if he had decided to take the Mustang's speed up instead of down, he wouldn't have had time to stop before he ran her over. Even now, cruising at fifty, the tires screeched and the car spun out when he slammed on the brakes, sending up a thick cloud of dust. His body jerked sideways, one hand slipping from the wheel. There was a heavy jolt, as if a tire had plunged into a deep pothole. After what seemed an eternity but was only a few seconds, the car came to a jarring stop at the side of the road.

He sat motionless, breathing heavily, both hands back on the steering wheel, gripping it tightly. Dust and dirt buried the scene, and he had to wait for it to settle before he could see if he'd hit her or not. Once he could see, he was immediately thankful to have narrowly missed the girl, who stood just feet away in the middle of the road, oblivious to the fact that she'd almost been killed.

He opened the door and got out, coughing away the dust in his lungs. Despite the heat of the day, a shiver marched across his spine. His heart thudded like a drum, and he could only spread his arms in question and study the girl in disbelieving silence.

He was as amazed by her beauty as he was by her condition. The girl remained motionless, staring at the ground, a ghostly figure enveloped by the settling cloud of dust. Eddie glanced left and right to see if any cars were approaching, but the scene was deserted. He came very close to leaping back into the car and hightailing it home, certain the girl, who seemed to be in a blank daze, hadn't even seen him.

Instead, he walked toward her hesitantly, wondering if he should be scared; after all, something *did* this to her. In the distance, a passing diesel engine chugged and blew its whistle. Closer by, a bird cawed loudly.

Moving only her head, the girl looked up at him. Eddie didn't recognize her, but he thought she was about his own age, seventeen, eighteen tops. She wore only a bathrobe, stained with mud and brambles. It hung open, revealing a filthy, naked body, rivulets of dried blood zig-zagging down her trembling legs to her bare feet. Her blond hair was wet, matted and muddy. Her eyes, dark and glazed, were bloodshot.

"Hey," Eddie called to her, waving as if testing her sight. "Hey there . . . you need some help?"

"Yes," she replied feebly. Her voice seemed to come from someplace far away.

Eddie could smell a horrid stench on her, of cigarettes and beer and sweat. He walked up to her and grabbed her arm gently. The terrycloth of her robe felt grimy and stiff. "I think you better come with me. I'll take you to the hospital—"

"No!" The girl jerked back, her face a terrified mask.

Eddie flinched. He held his hand up, trying to calm her. "Hey . . . okay, look, I'm just trying to help you. . . . Good God, what happened to you?"

The girl shook her head gently and closed her eyes tight, as if anticipating a blow. She began to sob. "I . . . I don't know."

Again Eddie looked up and down the road. He shifted uncomfortably from one foot to the other, his eyes returning to her grime-coated breasts, which trembled from her sobs. He noticed an odd scar on her sternum and found himself more conscious of it than her exposed breasts.

He looked away and was immediately drawn to the streaks of blood on her legs. He wished another driver would come along so he wouldn't have to take care of this all by himself. Of course, he'd driven along Mill Pond Road enough times to know that unless you were traveling east to the dairy farms, or were out for a little rubber-burning, you had no reason to be here.

So he motioned for her to follow, making an effort to keep his eyes off her exposed body. "If you don't want to go to the hospital, then maybe you should let me take you home. Do you live around here?"

At last she wrapped the robe tighter around her body, then motioned east, over the wheat fields. "Pine Oak," she whispered huskily.

"Pine Oak Road? Off Breton?"

She nodded.

Holy—! A flash of recognition hit him at once. He knew who this girl was, which made the circumstances even more mysterious—and alluring. "You're the minister's daughter."

She trembled and looked away, her sobs tapering down into whimpers.

She remained silent, staring down at the cracked, weedy road, seemingly unable to help herself at all. Gently, Eddie took her by the arm, and she followed him to the car. Filthy as she was, she would mess up the Mustang's seats, which in turn would piss his father off, and when Harry Carlson got pissed off, it meant no more Mustang privileges for Eddie. So he reached into the backseat and yanked out his football jersey, weighted beneath his helmet so the wind wouldn't take it away. *Damn, I just got it this afternoon too, my name "Carlson" nice and clean across the back.* "Here," he said. He placed it on the front seat and gently guided Elizabeth inside.

Once she was seated, he shut the door, then circled around the front of the car, looking in at her and deciding that his first impression of her had been right: Despite her wretched state, she was beautiful. *Prince Charming rescues the fair maiden*, he thought smugly.

Things have been going my way, he thought. *So why not let them continue?*

He slid into the front seat behind the wheel, then looked over at her. She was trembling. Her feet were curled up under her rear on the seat. "My name's Eddie."

"Eddie . . ." she muttered. "Please, take me home now."

"The Conroy house?"

She nodded.

"I'll have you there in no time. . . ." he said, then added, "Elizabeth."

Everyone in Wellfield knew about the Conroy family. The minister and his wife had educated their kids at home and put them to work on the farm that the local council had fought hard to get its hands on in an attempt to expand downtown. He'd seen the mother and a young boy a number of times, but had only seen Elizabeth once before, and that was from a distance while driving past their house on Pine Oak. Regardless, she'd made a few rare appearances at Ewing's Food Emporium lately, and word had gotten around that she'd grown into quite the beauty—an untouchable one, though, kept under lock and key by her parents.

When she didn't respond to her name, he turned the car around and started back up Mill Pond Road, for the first time in his life keeping the car at the speed limit. They rode in silence, and the wheat fields soon gave way to green pastures. He kept his eyes on the road, wanting to look at her—at her frail, shivering body. The question, *Were you raped?* danced on the tip of his tongue, but he managed to choke it back.

"Here we are," he announced, pulling the car into the long gravel driveway. He came to a stop beside the walkway that surrounded the house. "Are your parents home?" He looked around, but didn't see any other vehicles.

"Pull up," she said. "Front door's always locked."

He nodded, then shifted the car back into drive and went another fifty feet to the rear of the house. The late afternoon sun slouched in the multicolored sky, the house's shadow spread across the overgrown grass in the back; farther along, a lofted barn abutted an expanse of dense woodland, its once-red paint faded to a cracked pink. Five wooden steps led up to a screen door in the house; just beyond that, a rusted basement well lay amid a tangle of goldenrod.

Elizabeth, in a sudden panic, fought with the car door handle before getting it to pop open. She nearly dropped out onto the driveway, but caught her footing and staggered away, her stained robe billowing behind her like a cape.

"Hey, Elizabeth . . . wait . . ." Eddie wanted to just let her be, drive away, and consider his good deed done. But *what if there was no one home to help her?* He got out of the car. Prince Charming would continue to help the injured beauty.

Not once looking back, Elizabeth quickly stumbled up the five steps and disappeared into the house, allowing the door to slam loudly behind her. Eddie raced forward and stopped at the bottom of the steps, uprooting a patch of chickweed with the toe of his left sneaker. Through the screen door he could see a kitchen table behind a veil of near darkness. Heart pounding, he grabbed the iron handrail, the chipped surface of black paint and rust, scraping his palm. He slowly climbed the steps, one at a time, looking back over his shoulder in the process and seeing nothing.

As he reached the landing, he heard a loud buzzing of flies.

He looked around.

And he stopped. All of a sudden he had no strength in his legs. He gripped the handrail bone-tight, fighting panic, his head reeling.

Lying in the dirt against the cement foundation of the house was a young boy and his dog. A puddle of blood seeped out from beneath them like a dark, motionless shadow. The dog, despite its wounds, was still alive, but barely, tongue lolling idly, body heaving. The boy, on the other hand, lay eerily motionless across the dog's front paws, a deep meaty slash running the length of his torso from which blood still oozed. Dust and soil and bits of grass coated his shirtless skin. He probably spent a good deal of time writhing on the ground before succumbing to his injuries.

There were hundreds of horseflies covering them.

Eddie remained petrified and staring. A need to scream clawed at his mind. He opened his mouth, but nothing came out.

From inside the house he heard a woman's terror-filled scream.

Elizabeth!

A split moment passed where he struggled with his choices: help the boy, help Elizabeth . . . or simply get the hell out of there and let the police do their work. Jesus—how long would that take? Elizabeth would be as dead as the boy by then.

Without allowing himself a moment to second-guess his decision, he yanked open the screen door and raced into the house to save Elizabeth Conroy's life.

CHAPTER TWENTY-FOUR

September 8, 2005
9:56 A.M.

"Its location is prime," Judson said, loosening his tie. "The mayor, along with the Wellfield Council, has a number of deep-pocketed Orono businessmen lined up with the blueprints to construct more than a dozen commercial buildings. They're also planning a gated community of homes, which will cater exclusively to those over the age of fifty-five. It's their way of convincing the locals to spend their Social Security checks here instead of sunny Florida, something I plan to do myself in a few years." He paused, then added, "Johnny, it's my duty to tell you that your land is worth a good deal more than what they're planning to offer you."

They turned right off Main and proceeded down Center Street toward an undeveloped area overflowing with four-foot-high grasses and brush.

"This is all mine?" Johnny asked, gazing at the grassy countryside.

"Not all of it. Some of it is owned by the town, but they can't build on it until your land is rightfully obtained."

"Why is that?"

"Well, this area here," he said, pointing to the right, "was originally zoned back in the fifties, and in accordance with the law, must remain multi-jurisdictional. Both your land and the town's property, overlap between commercial and residential zones."

"Which means?"

"Which means that there isn't enough open space for the town to achieve what they want without building on your land. And they can't seek to modify the ordinances, because then it would have to go up for a council vote, which, if approved, would cost the mayor his job—the voting public would *never* endorse such a variance. There would also be a host of other complications, particularly when the construction companies start applying for building permits. It's a big vicious circle, one that can't be broken without your cooperation."

"Sounds complicated."

"And that's just the beginning of it."

Judson reached a four-way stop at which nothing but fenced-in meadows could be seen. He looked both ways, then turned right. After a minute of silence, he said, "Johnny, when you turned eighteen, you became the sole owner of *this* land." He pointed east, out the driver's side window. "It continues northeast along Rollingwood, all the way to Pine Oak, where the house is located. I have it all mapped out—if you like, I can show it to you when we get to the house."

"Andrew . . . how much . . ." Johnny didn't want his

budding anxiety to show, so he coughed, then lowered his voice. "How much are they planning to offer me?"

"About a half million . . . but the house and barn alone have been assessed at nearly half that, and they will be torn down as soon as they secure ownership of your property—*if* they secure ownership." Judson peered into the rear-view mirror, then added, "It's the land that they're after, Johnny. As I mentioned in the letter it's valued at approximately two million dollars, maybe more. Understand, their motivations are purely economic, and yours should be as well."

"Mr. Judson, Andrew . . . why are you going to such lengths for me?"

"Well, frankly, my motivations are financial as well. There's a fair sum of money that Benjamin Conroy placed in escrow for me that's been collecting interest for eighteen years. Once you sign on the dotted line . . ."

Johnny took a deep breath and struggled to keep his cool. He wanted to pump his arms and stomp his feet and scream out loud, *Dear God, I'm going to be rich!*

They passed fields of wheat and corn that looked electric beneath the morning sun. In the distance, Johnny could see smoke rising from the roof of a small factory, its thin dark plume melting into the air. The car jostled over a set of railroad tracks, then moved onto a single-lane highway.

They rode in silence for another minute, and Johnny made a determined attempt to think the way his mother would. He told himself that the Good Lord had willed this fortune, both good and bad, and that all he could do was go along for the ride.

Judson turned right onto Breton, then left onto Pine Oak Road. The house came into view, stark and desolate, crippled by the elements and time. *Looks as though it has quite a story to tell,* Johnny thought.

The car crawled to the side of the road, sand and pebbles crunching noisily beneath its tires. Judson pulled into what years ago might have been a gravel driveway, but was now a tiny farm in and of itself, bringing forth a healthy crop of crabgrass, chickweed, and lamb's quarters. He closed the car's windows, noting that in thirty minutes the bees would have a hive built inside if given the opportunity.

Without saying a word, Johnny got out of the car and looked around. Damselflies the size of hummingbirds hovered about his feet, flitting to and fro, probably sniffing out a potential puddle to plant their eggs. He stepped out of the knee-high weeds, then moved along the cracked cement pathway bordering the house. He could feel the sun beating down on him, the oppressive heat making it difficult to breathe. His chest tightened. The scar on his sternum began to itch, and he gently scratched at it through his shirt. *Just anxiety, nothing more,* he tried to convince himself, and tried to distract himself by imagining the Conroy family—his real parents, his real siblings, himself as a baby—all living here as a happy unit, tending to the farm and the garden, eating home-baked cornbread and apple pie at the kitchen table, playing games and watching television together on rainy nights.

But these memories wouldn't come; instead images on par with the decrepit condition of the house arose, of darkness and dilapidation, of shadows and ruin: wood shingles losing an age-long battle with termites; the windows, blind and boarded with split sheets of plywood; weeds growing wild across the waist-high lawn; in the back, a lofted barn, its red paint long faded to a pallid, splotchy pink, the weathervane on its peak lurching drunkenly, muddy brown and rusted.

And Johnny thought: *When the Conroy family died, so did their home.*

But it's still standing. Yes, its frame is weak and rotting, but it is still alive.

I can feel it . . .

Just as one last Conroy family member stands: still alive. Me.

A breeze swept by, kicking up a cloud of dry dust; in his mind it whispered: *Come to me, boy. I've been waiting for you.* A dreadful shiver raced down Johnny's back, and his scar prickled with pins and needles.

As Judson got out of the car, Johnny walked along the path and surveyed the house. An old iron water pump, its handle splotched with rust, stood just below the lone side window. The wood nailed over it was rotted and practically gone. The pane beneath was still intact, but clouded with grime. In the distance, Johnny could hear a chorus of birds singing; closer by, bees humming. Their collective song sounded slightly muted, as though pressure had plugged his ears.

He stepped around the back of the house, Judson silent at his heels.

In his mind, the hushed message came again: *Come to me, boy. . . .*

"I brought a flashlight," Judson said, and Johnny jumped a little. "In case you want to go inside."

Come to me . . .

"I think I will," he said, crossing the overgrown lawn to the porch. He saw a flicker of movement in his peripheral vision, which made him jump back again, this time bumping into Judson.

"Whoa, Johnny . . . what's the matter?"

"Over there," Johnny said, pointing.

At the left, a rusted cellar well burst through a thick patch of crabgrass, which, approximately two feet farther, lapsed into a small circle of dead grass, brown and flattened along the house's foundation. In this circle droned a swarm of horseflies, hundreds of them, not in flight but crawling within the dead grass as if trying to hide it.

At that moment, while looking at the flies, Johnny understood why Ed had killed himself, why Mary had fainted: It was because there was something terribly *wrong* here, a badness he could smell, not necessarily with his nose, but with his mind. It existed in and around the house, nearly palpable, lurking in the shadows, waiting for someone to come and breathe life back into it. Ed and Mary had known all about it—it had lived on in the memory of Benjamin Conroy and quite likely in their own past experiences. And now it had returned.

It knows I'm here, he thought. *And it's . . . evil.*

A flood of terror stole over Johnny. His scar burned red hot. On the patch of dead grass, the horseflies whispered and droned:

Bryan . . .

"We best either go inside or walk around out back by the barn," Judson said, interrupting Johnny's thoughts. "Those buggers'll bite ya. Don't suppose you got horseflies in the city."

Johnny shook his head. "They're disgusting," he muttered. Still staring at them, he asked, "Why are they all in that one spot?"

From somewhere behind them, a bird cawed.

"Maybe it's mating season." Judson took the porch steps slowly, his speed matching his age. When he reached the porch, he turned and faced Johnny. "C'mon, let's check out your new place." Johnny looked at the lawyer; there was a gritty impatience in his face that hadn't been there before.

About to protest, Johnny said, "Andrew . . ."

But the lawyer was already opening the old door, his bony right hand jiggling the key back and forth. The door screeched as it opened, and Johnny had to practically chase him inside, noticing that at one time there must have been a screen door attached to the frame as well—in his mind he could hear it slamming behind him as he entered the kitchen.

When Johnny went inside, Judson was standing to the left, pointing the flashlight around like a cop in a dark alley. The room was dim, lit vaguely by the light shafting in through the open doorway behind them. A mold-coated butcher-block table stood abandoned in the center of the room, one leg partially broken, barely providing support. As Johnny walked, the lifting linoleum floor popped beneath his weight. He scanned the row of cabinets sitting crookedly against the right wall, their doors falling away from stripped hinges. Beneath the room's only window was a sink, its faucet tarnished green, both handles missing. He stepped around the table. Shards of glass littered the sink's yellow porcelain. Four dead beetles lay on their backs near the drain, legs curled inward. Johnny could smell garbage, dampness, rotting wood . . . and then something else, faint but definite. *Like a dirty, wet animal,* he thought.

Johnny followed Judson into what was probably a living room at one time. Almost immediately he heard a dry rustling sound coming from behind the walls, and soon thereafter, from the ceiling.

"The mice aren't too pleased with our visit," he commented.

"Home sweet home," Judson said, looking a bit uneasy.

"Can I get you something to eat or drink?"

"You're too kind."

They moved out of the living room down the front hall, stepping over a small puddle of water that stunk like sewage. The wallpaper, displaying rows of roses and drooping sunflowers, peeled away from the plaster in curling strips. Judson pointed the flashlight up a set of stairs. Here were the unattractive scents of mildewed plaster and mice droppings. Broken glass lay strewn on the few steps they could see, with the rest rising into the stuffy darkness of the second floor. Tucked against the corner of the second step was a newspaper, damp and swollen, a fat spotted slug crawling along its lower edge.

"There are four bedrooms and a second bath upstairs. Wanna go up?"

Johnny felt cold all over. "Do we have to?"

"I was hoping you'd say no."

"No, then."

Judson sighed with relief. "The steps are secure, but other than bugs and mice, there's nothing else to see up there."

To the right, they went through a pair of twin doors that led into a cryptlike room, vacant except for a stained boxspring leaning against the right wall, its rusty coils bursting through the frayed, gray skin. Hanging loosely from the center of the ceiling was an ancient brass light fixture, swathed in a shroud of cobwebs and dust. A boarded-up fireplace filled half the opposite wall. To the right were twin doors that Johnny presumed led into a sitting room.

"Andrew?"

"Hmm?" Judson was pointing the flashlight up at the brown waterstains on the ceiling. His brows were arched, as if he'd seen something of interest.

"How did my family, the Conroy family I mean, die?" Johnny walked across the room, past a lone scum-coated window, marveling at the decrepit state of the cracked walls, the stained wood floors.

Judson cleared his throat, then looked at Johnny, his lips pressed thin. "Your father, he—"

"*Bryan Conroy . . .*"

The voice. It had returned. Only this time it was louder, higher pitched and nervous. Johnny glanced at Judson. A pale, anxious look washed over the lawyer's wrinkled face.

"You hear that?" Johnny asked.

Judson nodded, which reassured Johnny that the voice had *not* come from inside his head.

Johnny jerked his head around. "Where'd it come from?" His voice rose as he realized with no doubt that this house—and the history of Benjamin Conroy—was indeed *bad*. The room began to spin. His scar itched again. He leaned against the wall for balance.

Judson shouted, "Who's there?"

There was a flicker of unexpected movement, the sound of feet shuffling on the grainy floor. Judson spun toward it, pointing the flashlight at the twin doors next to the fireplace.

The doors burst open, with a harsh screech that echoed throughout the house. Judson immediately drew back. His body seemed to stiffen, and he was unable to avoid the shrouded figure racing out of the sitting room.

Johnny screamed, "Look out!" but his voice died

away, strangely absorbed by the thick air. He backpedaled along the wall, not at all convinced of what he was seeing: a robed person springing across the room, arms raised high, hands clasped together over its head as if in prayer.

Judson tripped over his own feet and lost his footing. His eyes bulged, and he let out a high-pitched bellow that sounded almost like a laugh. The flashlight fell from his hand and dropped to the ground with a dull clunk, the beam cutting across the room. For a moment it flashed into the crazed face of the figure.

Johnny shuddered at the thump of Judson's body slamming against the wood flooring.

The figure stopped. It hulked over Judson, breathing heavily, raspily. It twisted its head, peered at Johnny, then quickly turned back to the old man.

What Johnny saw in the figure's face that instant was terrifying enough to make his own worst nightmare seem like a sweet dream.

Johnny gagged on his own scream as the figure drew a garden spade out from beneath its billowing robe and plunged it into Andrew Judson's stomach.

CHAPTER TWENTY-FIVE

August 24, 1988
5:52 P.M.

"Your name's David? Ain't that right, boy?" Benjamin opened the back door of the car. "I'm a friend of your mom's."

David Mackey shrunk back against the opposite door, keeping as much distance as possible between himself and Benjamin. The shirtless, blood-spattered man was in all likelihood the last person he could trust at the moment.

"What's wrong?" Benjamin asked. "Don't you know it's impolite not to talk to your elders?"

David dropped his eyes and shook his head. His cheeks burned like wildfires. "Where's . . . my . . . mom?"

Benjamin laughed—it came from him like a spill of water from an overturned pail. "Your mom? Your *mom?* Oh, she's in the church having a conversation with God." He peered into the front seat and smiled. "Just like your daddy is now."

David must have realized what Benjamin meant because he immediately began to wail. He shoved a fist into his mouth and bit down on it, either to suppress his sobs or stifle his terror.

"Why don't you come out here?" Benjamin said, feigning calmness. He offered his hand. "You know, I've got a son about your age. The two of you can get together, have a nice time—"

David turned around and yanked on the car door handle. The door swung open. He uttered a shaken cry as he went sprawling out onto the muddy earth.

Benjamin chased him, leaping across the seat like a flame in the wind. He thrust his right arm forward and latched on to David's bony ankle, the only part of him still in the car. He fastened his other hand on to David's calf and squeezed with fury-driven strength, drawing a panicked scream out of the boy.

Benjamin outweighed David by at least a hundred pounds, but still managed to use his grip on the boy to pull himself across the seat. David twisted around and looked up at Benjamin, eyes wide and rolling beneath a mask of mud and dead grass. Benjamin grabbed on to the waistband of David's jeans, thinking, *No godly assistance needed here. I am in full control of the situation.*

He jerked backwards, hauling the boy back into the car. David flailed like a landed fish, black mud streaking across the seat as he bounced against the car's frame. "Come to me, boy! Your parents are waitin' for you!"

David's right hand, until this moment hidden from Benjamin's view, swept around in a wide curve. In it was a screwdriver, ten inches of cold, muddy steel. It sliced into Benjamin's forearm, and Benjamin howled

in white-hot pain. He let go of the boy, who skittered
backwards out the door with a cry.

For a flickering moment, as the pain bulleted
through Benjamin's body and the blood trickled
warmly down his hand, he felt disconnected from reality. An unclear image of Osiris flashed before his eyes,
giving him the immediate will to press on, to not let
anything interfere with the ritual. *This is how it's supposed to happen, how God wants it, how Osiris wants it. . . .*

"You come back here, boy!" Benjamin launched
himself across the seat and . . . *Slash!*, the screwdriver,
quick and sharp in David's hand, lanced across Benjamin's bare chest, bisecting his scar. Fresh blood
sprayed across the seat of the car, then flowed down his
chest in bright red rivulets.

Benjamin screamed, the savage pain all-consuming.
A gray cloud seeped into his line of vision, and he
made every effort to look past it at the fallen boy, who
was scampering backwards through the mud, eyes wide
with terror. In his slipping mind, Benjamin thought he
could see aggression beyond the fear in the boy's
face—that he intended, right here and now, to kill the
man who had killed his mother.

"You murderer," David muttered.

"The Lord took your parents, boy!" Benjamin
crawled out the door after him, blood dripping down
his chest. He realized now that this was the same
screwdriver that had loosened the screws on the
church lock's clasp. "*He* speaks through me! *He* told
your mother to put that gun of hers against your father's head! *He* told me to—"

With catlike agility, David leapt forward. The
screwdriver came down again, punching a savage hole
into Benjamin's shoulder. Blood shot out in a quick, vi-

cious spray, then streamed down his arm. Pain lanced into his brain, yet still, he pressed forward, teeth clenching against a scream. He fell out of the car, onto his hands and knees. He crawled through the mud and wet leaves like an injured soldier in the trenches.

A shadow fell over him. He looked up and at once caught sight of David, the muddy shaft arcing down again. With no thought he seized David's thin wrist, squeezed it and twisted it back. David cried out in agony. Benjamin scrambled to his feet, got a hammerlock on him, and bent David's arm around his back. The boy released a breathless scream. His feet slipped in the mulchy earth as he tried to run away. Benjamin jerked David's arm upwards, once, twice, three times. David shrieked and the screwdriver fell from his slender grasp, down into the wet earth between Benjamin's feet. Benjamin laughed and wrapped his left arm around David's neck and squeezed. David scratched and clawed at Benjamin's arm. Benjamin squeezed, harder, drawing his forearm into David's adam's apple. David's knees buckled as he fought for air.

Putting all his body weight behind it, Benjamin jerked up on David's wrist again, yanking the hand all the way up to the nape of his neck. There was a loud, sudden *crack*, like the pop of a champagne cork on New Year's Eve. He felt David's arm bone give way from his shoulder. David stiffened like a plank of wood, then released a shriek of searing pain.

Feeling sick and faint and short of breath, Benjamin let go of the boy. David stood tottering for a moment, then stumbled crookedly away from Benjamin, his left arm dangling obscenely.

Benjamin bent down and picked up the screwdriver, then started after him. He could feel the throbbing of his wounds as he ran, the mud and blood both wet and sticky on his skin.

"C'mere boy!" he yelled, a fresh rage coming on. "Gonna teach you a lesson!" His mind floated as the words exploded from his throat, and he fought off a sudden surge of dizziness threatening to take him down.

In a matter of seconds, he reached the boy, who was swaying more than running. He clutched David's injured shoulder, and David screamed deliriously, then spun around and groped for Benjamin's face with his good hand. The pain barely registered as the boy gouged Benjamin's cheek with his fingernails.

Benjamin wasted no time. Without a sound, he thrust the screwdriver into David's left eye.

David's mouth creaked open. He wheezed once, then started shaking, as though charged with volts. His stabbed eye oozed droopily from its socket. Blood poured down his cheek in a shocking stream. Benjamin marveled at his handiwork and was almost caught off-guard when David lurched forward again.

Benjamin sidestepped him. He grabbed David by the hair, then, holding the screwdriver to his neck, dragged him back toward the woods. He stopped by an old oak tree and lifted the boy, keeping the flat of the screwdriver against his chin. He gazed into the boy's gory face, sniggered once at what he saw, thinking *Like mother, like son*, then dully slammed his skull against the rock-solid tree trunk. The sound was shocking: a hard, unyielding thud. Benjamin let go. David fell facedown to the ground like a wind-torn branch, leaving behind a jagged smear of blood on the tree's bark.

Benjamin backed away, watching with amazement as David writhed on the ground, sneakers digging irregular trenches in the mud, arms pumping crazily, as though still determined to fight. He flipped over and used his one good eye to peer up at Benjamin. His mouth opened. A thin line of blood trickled out across his cheek. Then his remaining eye rolled up in its socket.

Heart pumping furiously, Benjamin backed away. At that moment he realized that no one and nothing could stop him from completing the ritual. He ran to the car with the screwdriver held out in front of him. He saw the stiff body of Helen Mackey's husband in the front seat. The bullet hole in the man's head stared back at him like an accusing black eye.

Ever so slightly, it twitched.

Benjamin drew back. With his free hand, he rubbed the fatigue from his eyes. *That didn't happen*, he thought.

But when he opened his eyes, blinked, then stared back at that terrible black hole in the man's head, he saw that it was indeed moving, like tiny puckering lips. Benjamin assumed that from somewhere beyond this plane, something wholly spiritual was trying to touch him, to make certain that he was aware of its presence—to alert him to make preparations for its physical arrival.

Osiris . . .

Black oily blood spurted from the bullet hole as if a vein had been slashed. It splashed across the dashboard of the car, then poured down the man's face, onto his soiled shirt, soaking in and spreading out in a puddle.

Revolted and confused, Benjamin released a choking gasp. He shoved himself away from the car, feet splashing in a muddy puddle. He nearly slipped, but managed to keep his balance, eyes still fixed on the bullet hole, which now oozed a spiral of wet brain matter like soft-serve ice cream.

"Oh God!" Benjamin cried. The twisting brain curled across the man's face like a horn, wriggling as though it had a life of its own. As Benjamin gathered his breath to scream, the bullet hole snapped shut and cut off the growth. The mass plunked down in the man's lap, where it writhed like a worm.

Benjamin turned away. He squeezed his eyes shut and stared into the swirling blackness, begging for the strength to continue. He smelled something rotten— decaying leaves and sitting water. Another sharp pain pierced his head like a nail. It dulled his senses, and when he opened his eyes, he saw sepia-toned clouds floating across the late-afternoon sky.

"Benjamin Conroy," called a voice inside his head, cold and bonelike.

And when Benjamin looked at the dead man again, he saw there was no oozing brain. And no blood. Just a clotted bullet hole in the center of his pasty forehead.

"The ritual . . ."

Heeding the voice in his head, Benjamin staggered away. Horrific pain, sudden and sharp against his skull, seemed to echo the throbbing from his stab wounds. He spun left and right, holding the screwdriver out, swinging it through the air as he shambled around the back of the car. Drifting in and out of reality, he circumvented the church. Out front in the dirt parking lot, sat his truck. Benjamin raced toward it, realizing only after jerking open the driver's side door that he didn't have the keys, that he'd dropped them on the floor upon first seeing Helen Mackey sitting behind his desk.

He slammed a fist against the door. "Damn it to Christ! Damn! Damn! Damn!" Bathed in sweat and blood, he reeled back toward the church, pressing a hand against his chest wound. Blood seeped sluggishly between his fingers. As he approached the front doors, a sudden, strange weight bore down on him. His muscles felt numb, lethargic.

He climbed the steps and staggered inside. His footsteps echoed throughout the church as he stumbled down the aisle. He fell, then crawled awkwardly toward the open office door.

The keys were on the floor where he'd dropped them, amidst the photos that had fallen from his diary. The eyes of the women in the Polaroids stared up at him, accusing. A series of sharp pains stabbed at his brain, and he had to grip his skull tightly to ease them.

A voice whispered, "*The ritual . . .*"

Only this time it hadn't come from his head. It had come from somewhere in the room.

Helen Mackey.

There she was, lying spread-eagle on the floor with her dress hiked up around her pale thighs; her face unrecognizable, jaw hanging, dead lips split wide, smiling crimson-stained teeth.

Grabbing the keys, Benjamin crawled back against the doorjamb, staring incredulously at her, squeezing both the keys and the screwdriver firmly. Her eyes suddenly came to life, wet and yellow and glaring reproachfully at Benjamin. Her voice seemed to come from very far away: "*The ritual . . .*" Her teeth and gums showed in a repulsive, leering grin.

"Osiris . . ." Benjamin said. "Is it you?"

His question went unanswered. In a blink, Helen Mackey had returned to her old dead, milky self, unmoving and unspeaking, eyes clouded over, jaw slack in a lifeless gape.

Benjamin pulled himself up and ran from the office.

Agony ripped up from his wounds as he fled past the altar and down the center aisle. *I have to get out of here,* he thought. *I must complete the ritual now.*

As he made his way outside, dizziness beset him. His feet tangled, and he spilled down the wooden steps. He dropped the keys and the screwdriver and threw his hands out to block his fall. He lay sprawled in the dirt for a moment, rasping, shivering coldly.

He stood, retrieved the keys and the screwdriver. He leaned up against the truck and looked back at the church. Its chipped surface was swelling, breathing as if it had a life of its own. Terrified, he turned away. He looked at the blood on his hands, his chest, his legs. Grayness overwhelmed him, and he had to grab the open door to keep from collapsing.

Suddenly, something brushed up against his ankle. He jerked away from it.

On the ground next to his feet, was a dead bird, its feathers black and ragged, blanketing a withered skeleton. Maggots crawled in its eyes.

A voice from the unmoving bird whispered: *"Go to the house. . . ."*

Wheezing, he scrambled into the truck, shut the door, and locked it in a panic, noticing only as he backed away that the dead bird was now perched on the roof of the church, staring down at him.

CHAPTER TWENTY-SIX

September 8, 2005
12:09 P.M.

Johnny tried to move but was paralyzed, his body and thoughts frozen in shock. The floor swayed and rolled beneath his feet. A thick, muted ringing filled his ears.

He couldn't believe what he was seeing: a disfigured man—a baseball-size portion of his forehead missing, his left eye little more than a dark, empty void—repeatedly stabbing the man who'd brought him here.

Blood spurted onto the floor. It spattered the disfigured man. It saturated the front of Judson's white dress shirt. Judson himself was twitching and jerking in a death seizure, hands and feet tapping out discordant rhythms on the dirty wood floor.

The crazed man yanked the garden spade out, hesitated, then leaned back and carefully inspected his work. He cried hoarsely, "You are *not* his blood!"

He drove the spade back into Judson's chest. A gargled moan escaped the lawyer's bleeding lips. The man jerked the spade upward, twisted it, and pulled it out. Judson bucked and thrashed, then fell motionless, arms and legs spread out, a sickly wheeze escaping his lungs.

In silence, the murderer peered over at Johnny.

Gasping, Johnny sidestepped along the length of the wall and threw himself out of the room. His feet slid through the puddle by the steps. He lost his balance and thumped heavily to the moldy floor. A burst of pain lanced up his spine, and he realized with horror that the one-eyed man who'd just murdered Andrew Judson was the same man whose picture he saw on the news that morning—the escapee from the mental institution.

He scrambled to his knees and looked back over his shoulder. The madman was standing in the doorway, staring at Johnny with his terrible, glowering eye. Johnny could see the spade in his hand, dripping blood. The black robe he wore hung open like a drape, exposing green institutional scrubs underneath, tattered and soiled with mud. His breathing was heavy and labored, as though clogged with phlegm.

Johnny leapt to his feet and ran back through the living room, the kitchen, then out the back door. Not once did he look back. The killer had looked possessed, his one eye wide and wild, lips cracked and coated, hair raked with mud. Johnny stumbled across the porch. He lost his footing again as he went down the steps. He reached out for the iron handrail, but couldn't manage a grip. With a yell he went sprawling into the knee-high grass. The tight swarm of horseflies he saw upon his arrival flew apart.

A swaying shadow covered him, and when he looked

up he saw the killer standing on the top step of the porch, the dripping garden spade in his hand. Here in the sunlight, he looked even more crazed.

"Conroy . . ." he moaned.

Johnny gained his feet and raced around the side of the house. He cut to the right, sprinting across the weedy driveway to the driver's side of Judson's car. The killer screamed, and Johnny could hear him close behind on the gravel of the driveway. Johnny yanked furiously on the door handle. It popped open, and he lunged inside, locking the doors a split second before the attacker's bloody fingers reached the handle.

The madman pulled and pulled, grunting with each failed attempt. Unable to get in, he leapt on top of the hood and pressed his face against the windshield.

Gasping, Johnny pressed back against the seat. He could hardly breathe in the oppressive heat of the car. His heart beat like a drum in his chest. He groped at the ignition, just as he remembered that Judson had taken the keys with him.

Face still against the windshield, the madman shrieked, then clawed at the glass, leaving behind squeaky fingerpaint-swirls of blood. "Conroy!" he snarled, spewing spittle. He slammed his fists against the windshield, the bloody spade still clenched in his right hand. Johnny flinched, then clambered over into the backseat, watching with nightmare terror as the madman leaped off the car and ran toward the house.

With surprising strength, he grabbed the rusty handle of the water pump and ripped it free of its brace.

Johnny scrambled back against the door, watching through the opposite window as the madman limped back to the car, the iron handle gripped in both his hands.

There was a moment of terrible silence as the attacker stopped, looked in at Johnny, and grinned. He
laughed . . . then swung the iron handle around in a
wide arc, smashing the rear passenger window.

Johnny frantically reached behind his head and felt
for the door lock, all the while kicking at the maniac
clawing his way in through the shattered window. "You
know, I've got a son about your age," the maniac
barked, shards of glass slicing his skin. "The two of
you can get together, have a nice time!" He grabbed at
Johnny, who turned, pulled the door handle, and
lunged out into the tall weeds. Honeybees and damselflies rose up and away around him. He pushed
through the weeds, looked back, and saw his attacker
crawling across the seat after him.

"Conroy! Your blood is mine!" he called.

Johnny stood and raced back around the front of
the car, tripping through the weeds, hardly feeling the
hidden brambles poking at his arms and hands. He
fled into the high grasses of the backyard, his legs
nearly buckling as he eyed his two choices: the woods
or the barn.

Before he had a chance to choose, the madman shot
out from around the side of the car and stumbled awkwardly through the weeds after him. His arms were
outstretched, covered with bloody gashes from the
broken glass he'd crawled across. He yelled, "Come to
me, boy! Your parents are awaitin' for you!"

My parents . . .

Johnny shrieked, then spun and raced toward the
barn, praying for all this to be some crazy nightmare,
one he'd soon wake from, sweating and shivering in his
bed . . . alive.

. . . thump . . . thump . . . thump . . .

He shoved the thought aside and raced toward the dilapidated barn. He could see a rusty clasp on the barn doors. There was no padlock. If he could get inside, maybe get his hands on a shovel or a pitchfork or some other makeshift weapon, he might have a shot of coming out of this alive. It was better than getting lost in the backwoods of Wellfield.

Johnny reached the barn and yanked on the doors. The hinges screeched like braking train wheels, and the madman echoed the noise with a shriek of his own. Johnny quickly slipped inside, grabbed the rusted handles, and tried to pull the doors shut . . . but not before the madman shot an arm in and latched on to Johnny's left wrist.

Johnny yanked on the doors, trapping the maniac's arm. He howled in agony, but his grip was strong, fingernails biting into Johnny's skin. Johnny pulled the handles furiously and watched as the splintered wood on the edge of the door sliced into the madman's skin. Johnny was only barely aware of the blood bursting from the wounds he was inflicting on his arm.

"Let me go!" Johnny cried. He braced his foot against the lower frame and pulled on the handles with all his strength. The madman's grip began to give, allowing Johnny to break free.

Johnny stumbled backward and thumped down on the ground. The maniac had fallen, too; the door was cracked open and Johnny could see him outside, already climbing to his feet. Coughing, eyes stinging and tearing from the dusty air, Johnny quickly collected his bearings and raced toward the rear of the barn. The light faded as he approached the underside of a loft. A old wooden extension ladder was perched against it, leading perhaps fifteen feet high. He looked all around, but saw no useful weapon. Then, with no other choice, he began climbing the ladder.

The madman burst into the barn and barked something incoherent.

"No!" Johnny cried. "Leave me alone!" He scrambled up the ladder, his heavy breathing taking on a flat, dull tone in the empty barn. He was about three-quarters of the way up when he felt the ladder tremble. He looked over his shoulder and saw his attacker had begun making his way up after him. He had a limp, and it was keeping him from scaling the ladder with any sort of speed. "Oh God!" Johnny screamed, then climbed up into the loft and glanced about in a panic. He saw a small window beneath the peak of the ceiling. Dim light seeped through, coating the loft and the drifts of dusty hay covering the planked floor. On the floor below the window was a moldy mattress, a graveyard of cigarette butts, and a cluster of empty beer bottles.

Johnny reeled over to the beer bottles and grabbed one by the neck.

The ladder shifted slightly from left to right . . . and then the madman's face appeared.

"C'mere boy!" he yelled. "Gonna teach you a lesson!"

He reached over the top of the ladder and started climbing up onto the loft.

Gripping the beer bottle tightly, Johnny raced forward and smashed it over the man's head. He howled, hands groping for Johnny's legs. The ladder tipped back from the loft, though not enough to send it flying backwards. A stream of blood burst from the man's forehead and ran into his good eye. He squeezed his eye shut.

Now he was blinded.

Holding the jagged base of the beer bottle, Johnny drove it forward into the madman's face. It tore open his forehead and ripped into his shut eye.

The man squealed and his hands flew to his face. Blood gushed out between his fingers. Johnny thrust the beer bottle at him again, pushing with all his weight. The ladder tipped away from the loft. The madman pinwheeled his arms for balance, but to no avail. The ladder fell back, taking the man with it.

Johnny watched in fascination as both man and ladder slammed into the front wall of the barn. The man's head hit the wooden wall with a sickening crack, the top rung of the ladder pinning him there for a few awful seconds before he plummeted to the hard ground. His torso fell forward and his head slammed against the dirt floor. He remained in this position like a spent animal, surrounded in a cloud of dust, legs splayed out under him. Blood cascaded from the back of his head like a fountain. Sickened, Johnny turned away and saw blood on the wall where the madman's head had come in contact.

Johnny waited, half-expecting the man still to be alive, to get up and come after him again. The world spun around him. He felt himself teetering and nearly toppled over the edge before backing up into the dusty recesses of the loft. He tucked himself into the corner, too scared to move. He stayed there for an indeterminable amount of time, standing motionlessly, staring at the moldering mattress and the assortment of empty beer bottles.

Flies flitted about his head. He swatted at them, then scratched his neck, feeling as if the maniac were touching him with ghostly, blood-sticky fingers. *Your blood is mine, Conroy!* the man had yelled, his hideous visage flashing in Johnny's mind like a bolt of lightning.

Soon Johnny came to realize that he needed to find a way out of here, off the loft, then off this property forever. He wanted no part of it—or the money that came with it. As far as he was concerned, the mayor and his businessmen friends could have it for free.

He shifted and the wood beneath him gave slightly.

Curious, he kneeled down. He stared at the floor for a few seconds. Then, using his hands, slowly began clearing away the thick layer of yellow hay dust.

A ghostly voice whispered: *"Bryan . . ."*

He coughed as the dust flew into his face. "Hello," he called, immediately feeling foolish. The voice had come from his own head. It was nothing more than his traumatized mind playing cruel games with him. He shuddered. He wondered if this was what it felt like to lose your mind. *Hey, maybe the psycho's bed at the insane asylum is still available.*

But then he saw something in the wood, something that brought him hope. He cleared away as much of the dust as possible, then ran his fingers along a thick, dust-caked groove in the floor. He reached a right angle, wheeled around and continued to move his fingers along the groove, wishing madly for an awl or a screwdriver to dig out all the dust. The groove gave way to another right angle, and in less than a minute he came to realize that the ladder hadn't been the only access to the loft.

Thank God!

Here was a trap door.

There was no handle, but he was able to squeeze the tips of his fingers into the groove.

The voice came again. This time it was louder, joined by another forceful whisper: *"Our dying souls . . ."*

"No . . ." Johnny said aloud, trying to shake his head free of the spine-chilling voices. *It's all in my head.* Sweat rolled down his face. He yanked on the door. At first it didn't budge, but he pulled and pulled until his hands cramped painfully.

The caked-in dust began falling into the dark recesses of what lay beyond.

He edged his fingers into the groove and continued to pull against the hard wood. The door creaked, came up an inch—enough so that he could wedge his fingertips onto the underside.

With a yell, he pulled the heavy door up.

Just then, the light reaching in through the barn's window dimmed, as if a dark cloud masked the afternoon sun. A gust of hot, stinking air pushed up from below, forcing the door wide open; it thumped loudly against the wall and remained open. Johnny cowered as a chorus of whispering voices ascended from the darkness below, like animals bounding from a cage. *"Our souls are free!"* they shouted, echoing one another, penetrating Johnny's body like tiny charges of electricity. They swam in his blood and tasted his soul, and then yanked him down into the darkness beyond the trapdoor. He bit against the pain as the steps splintered beneath his weight. He crashed onto the rock-solid floor with a loud thud.

And there he remained, paralyzed, exploring the

shifting darkness. He tried to move his arms, his legs, his neck, but couldn't. All he had control of were his wide open eyes, somehow seeing in the surrounding blackness ghostly wooden crosses doused in blood, the bodies of four people crucified upon them, their eyes pleading.

CHAPTER TWENTY-SEVEN

August 24, 1988
7:27 P.M.

Eddie Carlson stood in the kitchen of the Conroy house, the scream he'd heard still ringing in his mind from the few seconds it took for him to race inside. He looked around but saw no one. There *was* a foul smell, however, and when he circled the butcher-block table and peeked into the sink, he saw a tapestry of dried vomit coating the white porcelain.

From somewhere in the house came another scream, louder than the first. He gripped the counter, tense and white-knuckled, peering into the living room, but there was no one there.

"Hello?" he called. "Elizabeth?" How long he would have stood there, waiting for Elizabeth to come waltzing in all clean and rosy and assuring him that everything was fine, he did not know; it was the muffled

thud upstairs—as if someone had fallen to the floor—
that eventually set him into motion.

He walked cautiously into the living room, past a
small table topped with an empty vase, then down a
short wallpapered hallway toward a set of stairs leading
to the second floor.

He gripped the banister and looked up into the
gloom.

He took one step up. The wood creaked beneath
his feet.

From upstairs came moans of anguish, of pain.

Then, a cry of terror:

"*Get . . . it . . . off!*"

"*Go to the house, go to the house,*" the voice in Benjamin's
head said, and he faithfully complied, speeding down
Pine Oak road toward his home. He spun the pickup
into the driveway, a shower of gravel pitting the dull
red finish.

He stopped the truck and got out, waving away the
dust in his eyes. The evening air was chilly against the
blood drying on his skin. His wounds throbbed along
with the pain in his head. Despite the heavy pressure in
his ears, he could still hear the fields of wheat and corn
swaying richly in the distance.

He limped into the shadows cast by his home. He
could smell the death of one of his own. This startled
him, but he accepted it graciously, assuming it a gift
from God. He gazed toward the basement well and
saw his son Daniel, the young boy's life spilled out onto
the earth in a dark, patchy river.

Alongside him was the damned dog, right where he
left it.

Benjamin stopped . . . then smiled, not at all surprised, and rather tickled, by what he saw. *Thank you, Osiris, for your assistance.*

From the boy's body, Benjamin heard the voice of the spirit call out: *"Commence with the ritual."*

He nodded, proceded up the steps and stared into the house through the open kitchen door. He could sense their presence, *smell* them as he did Daniel just moments earlier: his family, still alive and intently waiting, in the heated throes of preparation. *I shall carry out your destinies.*

He closed his eyes and embraced the agony piercing his brain and skull, the stab wounds on his arm, shoulder, and torso. Behind his closed eyes, ghostly flashes of white light blazed—lights that flickered and revealed a dark, gray shape: the silhouette of the Lord Osiris. And as the shape moved into focus, Benjamin could make out the spirit's black robe of watered silk, his black Egyptian nemyss, and even the long dark hair pouring over his shoulders.

Benjamin reached a bloody hand toward the spirit.

The spirit reached a glowing hand toward Benjamin.

The windows to the astral plane are opening! he thought dreamily. *Osiris is here to assist me with the ritual.*

Their fingertips touched.

Benjamin smiled, feeling the power of the spirit within his entire body, his entire soul. His breathing quickened. His skin rode with a gentle charge of electricity. The agony of his wounds converted into a massive surge of power, of euphoria.

"Commence with the ritual," the spirit whispered, and then like a fire doused with water, it disappeared, leaving behind only a shadow and rotting feathers.

Benjamin opened his burning eyes. He rubbed the tears away, then jerked his head around. The hair on the back of his neck stood on end—or at least the hair that wasn't matted down with blood. Somewhere in the distance, he could hear a bird caw.

He peered down at his dead son.

"Commence with the ritual . . ."

Nodding, he went down the porch steps, keeping his eyes on the boy. He felt oddly calm and unafraid, sensitive to the evening breeze breathing cool air on his heated body. He could hear the wind sighing through the trees in the woods behind the barn.

Benjamin noticed a halo of dead horseflies—hundreds of them—surrounding the boy and his dog. *A gift from God*, he reasoned. He looked into Daniel's ashen face. The boy's eyes were closed, his mouth a beaten frown frozen in time. Benjamin crouched down, touched Daniel's exposed scar. It was mutilated like his own, making Benjamin wonder how the boy had met his fate. *By what means did the Lord Osiris deliver your support, my son?*

He prayed: *Thank you, Lord Osiris for—*

There was a flicker of movement to his right.

Flinching, Benjamin looked toward . . .

. . . oh, damn it to hell . . .

. . . the dog, its eyes open . . .

With the suddenness of a lightning strike, the dog's head snapped around, gummy eyes contemplating Benjamin with feral aggression. It lunged and latched its foamy jaws on to Benjamin's left wrist. He screamed and started pummeling the dog's head with his free hand. The dog snarled, its muzzle wrinkled back to expose huge shredding teeth. Benjamin's fingers closed on the matted fur around its neck and dragged the dog away from the bloody circle, a wash of fresh blood flowing from its wounds.

Dust rose up as the dog kicked its paws into the dirt. Seeing the dog making a desperate attempt to right itself, Benjamin saw no choice but to throw all his body weight on top of it.

He plunged down with a yell. There was an immediate cracking—the sound of Pilate's backbone snapping in two under two hundred and twenty pounds of desperate minister. The gash in the dog's side split open. Blood and guts burst out like piñata treats.

Benjamin fell away. Lying on his back, he pried his wrist free from the dog's jaws. Pink blood and frothy saliva strung away like syrup. He heaved and gagged, spit on the ground, then rolled over onto his stomach and climbed to his feet. He stood teetering for a moment, examining his wrist. There was hardly any feeling in it. It was cold and numb. For a moment, all the pain of his prior injuries shot back into him, alerting him to the fact that he couldn't waste any more time here—the time to complete the ritual was now.

Shaking off the burst of pain—*Thank you, Osiris*—he stooped down, scooped his arms beneath the body of his dead son, and picked him up.

For a moment he stood there, gazing at the dead boy's face, feeling an unexpected, clear-headed flood of accomplishment: The moment he'd been waiting for all these years had finally arrived. The final stages of the ritual were about to be set into motion. *Osiris is with me. I touched him, and now he is watching me, guiding me, relieving me of my pain and soothing my injuries so that I may complete the ritual.*

He carried Daniel across the backyard, tripping and staggering but finally making it to the barn. He hoisted the boy's body over his shoulder, then pulled open the clasp on the doors and went inside.

He placed the boy down alongside the mess of ashes from the morning's ritual, then hurried to the extension ladder leaning against the loft. He climbed halfway up, reached to his left—fresh blood trickled from his injured shoulder—and pulled down a bale of hay from underneath the fifteen-foot platform. Then he climbed back down and shifted aside two more bales to allow access to the rear of the barn. He picked up Daniel's body and carried it into the concealed area under the loft.

He placed the boy's body down. Taking a deep breath, he admired his handiwork, visible beneath the dusky light seeping in through the small window: five wooden crucifixes, all of them different sizes, ranging from six feet long, to one only three feet.

He retrieved four nails from the pile of twenty-five on the ground. Each one was six inches of honed iron, its point as sharp as a razor.

Benjamin grabbed the boy's arm and dragged him across the hard dirty floor to the second-smallest crucifix.

He placed the nails at the foot of the cross and recited a prayer of thanks to the lord Osiris.

Then bequeathed upon Daniel Conroy the gift of ancestral afterlife.

Eddie raced up the steps to the second-floor landing. Behind the closed door of the room closest to him, a baby cried. He moved to the door and listened. Just a baby. Not the adult he'd heard pleading for help: *Get . . . it . . . off!*

He took a deep breath, then backed away from the door. He continued down the corridor and turned the corner.

Here he saw Elizabeth.

She was standing in the shadowy hallway, pale and terrified, her right hand cupped over her mouth, tears pouring down her face. She was staring unblinkingly into a room.

"Elizabeth?" Eddie called, his voice an injured whisper. "What's going on here?"

She shook her head in a quick panic. "No . . . no . . . no . . ." she sobbed, her gaze still fixed on whatever was in the room.

Eddie ran to her. He smelled something horrible. He grabbed her hand, still crusted with grime and blood. "What is it? What's going on?"

Finally she turned toward him, clearly in shock, her eyes wide and frozen. Her body was stiff as a board, the dirty robe pulled tightly around her waist. "We're . . . in . . . hell . . ." she muttered.

Eddie turned and looked into the room.

My God, we are in hell.

It was a bathroom. There was a naked woman inside, sitting on the floor in a pool of vomit. To Eddie, she seemed shrunken, her face and body shriveled like an old skinless apple. Her skin was a sickly yellow with jagged splotches of tan. She trembled like a frightened rabbit.

The woman saw Eddie. "Get it off me!" she screeched. "*Get it off!*" Her eyes bulged as she clawed at what appeared to be a large scar on her chest, the skin bloody and raw beneath her long, yellow fingernails.

Elizabeth had a scar just like that, in the same spot, he thought.

Eddie shook his head in bewilderment and disgust. He looked at Elizabeth, who continued to stare in a catatonic stupor.

"Jesus . . . we've got to get out of here," he said.

An earsplitting cough came from the woman in the bathroom. Eddie looked back toward her.

"Oh . . . my . . . God . . ." he cried, drawing back.

The woman vomited something. Eddie's mind instantly rejected what his eyes saw: a kidney or a spleen falling from her mouth to the wet floor.

Abruptly, from somewhere downstairs, a howling voice shot through the house like a burst of fire: "Faith? Elizabeth? I've come to save your souls!"

Benjamin stood in the kitchen. He was staring into the living room, an ear cocked to the ceiling. He sniffed the air. He could smell them. All of them. His daughter, his wife, his baby, and . . . something else, *someone* else here in the house. An interloper determined to take him down, crush his lifelong attempt to bring his family ancestral afterlife. *Nothing can stop me!* He massaged his forehead as the pain made its way back. His wounds began to burn and throb again, and when he looked down at his shirtless body, all he could see was blood, coating him from his chest to his feet.

He moved to the kitchen counter. With a quick jerk, he removed the largest stainless steel knife from the butcher block alongside the sink. It made a *sleek!* sound that sent shivers down his spine.

He held the knife up and studied his beaten reflection in the twelve-inch blade. *I am all-empowering. I am working alongside the Gods. Nothing can stop me now!*

Slowly, step by methodical step, he made his way into the living room.

"Faith?" he called, holding the knife out before him. "Elizabeth?"

He walked down the hallway and stood at the bottom of the steps.

He gazed up toward the landing. He could hear baby Bryan whimpering from behind the closed door of his room.

He hesitated, licked his dry, scabby lips.

Then, firming his grip up on the knife, he started up the stairs.

"You've got to get out of here!" Elizabeth whispered urgently, her catatonia seemingly shattered. "Now!"

Eddie looked back from the sick woman on the floor in the bathroom to Elizabeth's tortured eyes. "Who is it?"

"He's coming up!"

"Who?"

"My father . . . this . . . this is all his doing. . . ."

Eddie heard the approach of footsteps on the stairs, slow and heavy. "Elizabeth, listen, you have to come with me."

She shook her head, fear painted heavily on her face. "I . . . I can't. . . ."

Eddie peered back down the hall, then grabbed Elizabeth by the shoulders. "I can't go back that way. . . . He's coming!"

She pulled away and opened the door across from the bathroom. "In here, now!" She motioned frantically with her arm. Eddie looked over his shoulder. "Quickly," she said, "hide under my bed."

He ducked into the room. She immediately shut the door behind him, leaving him in near darkness.

In a panic, Eddie rushed to the bed, conscious of a stale burnt smell in the air. At the foot of the bed he saw what looked like an occult symbol on the floor with a small mound of charred remains. *Jesus, what the hell is going on here?*

He kneeled beside the bed. He could hear the minister's plodding footsteps moving slowly down the hall. He dropped to his stomach and wriggled under the bed, head toward the footboard.

The footsteps stopped. From the hallway he could hear a muffled cry. A shuffle of panicked feet. Then a loud thump.

Threatening silence followed.

Slowly, the door to the bedroom creaked opened.

Elizabeth's dirty bare feet came into view. Directly behind them, a pair of muddy brown work boots. He could see out the side of the bed as Elizabeth's feet rose off the ground. They hung oddly motionless. For a moment he thought about leaping out from beneath the bed and braving a rescue attempt . . . until he saw the blood, thin winding lines of it dripping down over her ankles to the floor.

Eddie cringed back. He tried to breathe but couldn't. The dripping blood began to pour, and then her body collapsed to the floor, twisted in a broken heap.

Eddie could only stare at the horror Elizabeth had suddenly become: her eyes darting back and forth; her lips twitching, as though she were trying to whisper something; and a thick purple gash running across her neck from ear to ear, pumping blood out onto the floor toward him.

The minister's boots moved off to the left, deeper into the room. Eddie's gaze followed them. The boots stopped before the charred mess inside the painted circle at the foot of the bed. The minister kneeled before it. A blood-coated hand came into view, sifted through the ashes, and removed what appeared to be a black feather.

At that moment, Eddie felt something warm and

wet against his cheek. He jerked his eyes back toward Elizabeth.

She was no longer alive, that much was clear now. Her eyes were glassy, lips unmoving. The blood draining from her had traveled under the bed and was now puddling against his face. He tightened his lips, but he could still taste it, sharp and metallic against his tongue.

The boots moved across the room, back alongside Elizabeth's body; in their wake, Eddie could see bloody tracks on the floor.

A knee came into view.

Eddie shuddered, feeling sick and light-headed. *Dear God, help me! He's going to murder me like his children.*

His children . . .

Oh . . . my . . . God.

The baby!

He couldn't hear the baby crying anymore.

More tears welled in his eyes and blurred his vision. He blinked frantically in an effort to clear them away, and saw the minister's ashy, bloody hand grab Elizabeth by the hair and drag her out of the room. Eddie heard a thud in the hallway. A second later, the door to the bedroom slammed shut, nearly wrenching Eddie's heart from his throat.

He waited, keeping himself tightly squeezed beneath the bed. He would wait until he had a chance to get the baby and run.

But in the meantime, he could do nothing but remain beneath the bed and listen to the gruesome sounds of the minister murdering the sick woman in the bathroom.

Benjamin swung the knife around and plunged it into Faith's chest. The twelve-inch blade went through her scar, and the point came out her back. He twisted it back and forth, and with a quick flick of his wrist, jerked it out.

He watched with fascination as his wife dropped face-first onto the slimy wet floor. He slammed the knife into her upper back, just to the right of her spine. Droplets of blood flew across the room. Then he let go. The handle jutted crookedly out of her back like a tombstone.

He leaned down and grabbed Faith by the hair. Making certain not to slip on the wet tiles, he dragged her out of the bathroom, a thick trail of crimson behind her. He halted momentarily to take hold of Elizabeth's body, also by the hair.

Struggling to harvest his strength, Benjamin leaned his weight forward and dragged both bodies down the hall. His perspective seemed skewed. The walls were too tall, the hallway too. Even the floor seemed to slope up and down.

Eventually he reached the top of the landing. Here he stopped and listened . . . to the baby's exhausted whimpers seeping out from behind the closed door of his room. Benjamin sniffed the air for guidance, but his newfound sense was clogged from the sooty stench in Elizabeth's room. He couldn't smell the baby.

Or the intruder, he thought.

Then he thought of the ritual that morning, how it had played out so perfectly until . . .

"Commence with the ritual, Benjamin. . . ."

Heeding the warning in his head, Benjamin pulled the bodies across the hall. One at a time, he shoved them down the stairs. Elizabeth tumbled head over heels like a sack of potatoes and hit the bottom in a twisted, bone-shattering sprawl. Faith's arm got caught up in the banister about halfway down. Her elbow broke, but her withered, bloody body traveled no farther, and remained stretched out on the steps. Benjamin lumbered down after them. He unhinged Faith's arm and pushed her down on top of Elizabeth, then continued down the steps. He stepped carefully over the twisted bodies, resecured his grasp on their tangled hair, and dragged them across the living room floor.

In the kitchen, he saw it was going to be a tight squeeze. His leg struck one of the kitchen chairs as he went by, which tipped against the heavy table and pressed against the wound on his arm. Pain burned through his body like a poke from a brand, and he howled.

He sidestepped the chair and shoved the butcher-block table aside with his hip, never releasing the hair in his fists. He managed to work the bodies past the table, then slammed into the back door and went outside.

At once he saw the black bird. It was standing on the wooden porch railing beneath the dreamy moonlight. It cocked its head and contemplated Benjamin with beady, oil-drop eyes.

"Osiris . . ." Benjamin whispered.

The bird flew off toward the barn and Benjamin watched as it settled on the peak of the roof.

Keeping his eyes on the bird, he pressed forward, hauling the bodies down the porch steps, and across the backyard. By the time he reached the barn, both bodies were coated with soil and grass, and had stopped trailing blood. He dragged the bodies inside and placed them before their designated crucifixes.

He took a moment to gather his breath, standing there in the back of the barn, gazing at Daniel, now nailed upon his very own cross. The boy's face was gray and riddled with splotches of blood, his eyes yellow. His tongue was black and swollen, peeking out from between his bloated lips.

What a fine job I've done, Benjamin thought. *Osiris will be proud.*

He said a prayer to God, performed the sign of the cross, then sent the souls of Elizabeth and Faith Conroy to join Daniel in his wait for ancestral afterlife.

As silently as possible, Eddie struggled to relieve the cramps in his body. He flexed his muscles, but it did little good.

Through the solid, incessant beating of his heart, he'd heard a variety of painful sounds in the house: thumps, crashes, and inhuman grunts. He'd felt utterly helpless, lying there under the bed, where he would remain until the minister left the scene of his crimes. He also realized he would almost certainly hear the murder of the baby in the other room.

There'd been a banging noise downstairs, a grunt of pain followed by a loud slam, which Eddie recognized as the screen door in the kitchen slamming shut.

He'd waited, breathing a bit more easily now that the minister was outside. His eyes darted back and forth. He moved his arms and legs. The seconds trickled by. The silence he'd hoped for was now at hand.

Finally, he slid out from beneath the bed and rose into a stoop. He stared at the door, nearly invisible in the shuttered gloom and listened for the minister's plodding footsteps to return in the hallway. But Eddie heard nothing. All was silent.

He looked down and saw that he was standing in drops of blood on the floor—Elizabeth's blood. He touched his face and could feel her blood on his cheek, his lips. Feeling sick, he stood up straight. A surge of light-headedness beset him, and he had to stretch his arms out for balance.

He waited. He heard nothing.

He stepped softly to the door and pressed an ear against it.

Still, he heard nothing.

He slowly turned the doorknob. The latch made a gentle popping sound. He cracked the door and peered out into the hallway, visible in the glow of the bathroom light. He could see thick streaks of blood on the floor leading down the hall toward the landing. Toward the baby's room.

He stepped out of the room and silently shut the door behind him.

He went to his right, into the tacky-wet blood—there was no avoiding it. Keeping his back pressed flat against the wall, he skirted along, taking very small steps, the floor creaking slightly beneath him. He approached a closed door, perhaps Elizabeth's dead brother's room. As he moved by, he imagined the boy's ghost reaching through the wood, cold dead fingers grabbing the nape of his neck.

Though terrified, he could move no faster—his legs were bloodlessly numb, his breathing shallow, his mind unable to think clearly. All he could do was sidestep slowly and listen to the silence enveloping the house.

He crept to the corner of the hall, paused, then peeked around the edge, his eyes following the blood streaks as they angled to the left. The hallway was empty, apart from the blood that led downstairs.

Across the hall from the stairway was the room he thought the baby's cries had come from. All was deadly silent now. There was no whimpering, no crying from behind the closed door.

Eddie thought he'd missed his chance to save the baby's life.

Without hesitation, he turned the doorknob, and opened the door just enough to slip through.

The room was smaller than Elizabeth's. In the soft amber glow of the plug-in nightlight, Eddie could see a crib, the only piece of furniture, by the room's lone window. On the floor before the crib was a white drawing similar to the one in Elizabeth's room. It too had a small pile of ashes at its center, plus melted candles and a small brass censer.

Eddie tiptoed around the ashy mess.

He glimpsed into the crib.

And shuddered.

The baby was here . . . sleeping, thankfully. What had made Eddie shudder was the tightly wrapped gauze around its chest, and he wondered if something had happened recently, something that had left the baby with a scar—a brand—upon its chest. He'd seen the mark on Elizabeth and had thought it was a birthmark, but he saw a similar marking on her mother's chest. And then there were the drawings on the floor. Eddie's stomach turned as the truth sunk in: This innocent little baby had been the focus of some sick ritual.

He reached into the crib and plucked the baby out. It lay motionless in his arms. If it hadn't been for the ripe stench of urine and the slow rise and fall of its bare belly, he might've believed he were holding a lifelike doll.

Clutching the baby under his arm like a football—a force of habit—Eddie stepped across the room and moved out into the hallway.

Now he had his legs back—and it was a do-or-die moment, escape or be killed. He listened for the slam of the screen door, as that would be his cue to hide.

Stepping through the blood on the floor, he went downstairs, one hand gripping the iron banister tightly. When he reached the bottom landing, he paused. The front door was ten feet ahead, across the foyer.

The baby fidgeted, head twisting, eyes opening slightly then closing. Eddie looked at the baby, then quickly crossed the room to the front door.

He unhooked the chain, then gripped the knob.

The door didn't budge. He yanked on it more forcefully, but it was deadbolted. And he didn't have the key.

He would have to go out the back door. The same door the killer went through, judging by the blood streaks leading from the stairs to the kitchen.

He tightened his grip on the baby and staggered down the hall toward the living room, staring all the time at the back door.

Which opened.

"Osiris, I pray for your empowerment, your continued guidance in my quest for ancestral afterlife. Soon, I shall join my family—oh, my family, how easily their bodies were crucified, thanks to your guidance—in the astral plane. And like Jesus Christ, who employed your magic to rise from the dead and deliver the earth from evil, we shall summon your greatness and pass on to the astral plane, where we will remain together as a family for all of eternity, under your spiritual guidance, forgiven of all our sins.

And then we, the Conroy family, will be known for eternity as those who have risen in the spirit God's shadow. We will become gods ourselves. . . ."

*   *   *

The minister emerged from the darkness, into the bright light of the house. The screen door slammed shut behind him.

The baby flinched and began to wail.

Eddie drew back, swooning with horror at what he saw . . . this grotesque image of a man staggering into the kitchen. He was tall and thin, with ragged hair that fell into wide and bloodshot eyes. The skin of his face, aglow beneath the kitchen light, was gore-streaked, lips spread into a ghastly grin baring dark, craggy teeth. His bare chest was covered in filth, riddled with cuts and wounds. His pants were dark with blood, and Eddie could see the familiar boots, swathed in mud and grass.

"Give me my child, boy," the man growled.

Eddie peered from side to side. There were two closed doorways in the hall, one on his left, the other to his right. *I'll take what's behind door number one*, he thought crazily, taking a step back and lining himself up with the doorknob.

"Give him to me!" the minister barked, coming forward, and it was then that Eddie saw the hammer in his right fist, dripping with blood.

Hugging the bawling baby under his left arm, Eddie frantically tried the door on his right. It occurred to him that it might very well be a coat closet, but he was overjoyed to find wooden stairs disappearing down into chilly, dank darkness.

"Come here!" the minister yelled. He reeled into the hallway, the pound of his boots sending vibrations into the floor beneath Eddie's feet. Eddie gripped the inside doorknob with his free hand and shoved his weight against the door. The minister crashed into the solid wood with a painful grunt and Eddie could hear him slide down onto the floor like an iron weight. For a moment Eddie heard nothing, but then the minister began struggling to his feet, the hammer in his hand hitting against the wall. The baby squirmed and bawled in Eddie's arms. Eddie, grimacing from the pain in his shoulder, fled into the cellar.

His most immediate thought was to protect the baby—and the only way he could do that was to hide it somewhere and then distract the minister. At the bottom landing Eddie tripped over something hard and heavy that shifted gratingly upon the cement floor. He shouted, not in pain, but from fear of nearly dropping the baby. He landed on one knee. The cement floor dug a jagged hole through his jeans and bit into his skin—he could feel a warm trickle of blood on his leg.

There was a sharp thud—the sound of the hammer slamming onto the floor. Eddie looked up and saw the bloody fingers of the minister grasping the edge of the partially open door.

Eddie scrambled to his feet and limped toward a stack of boxes, knocking into a standing lamp base that tottered back and forth. He ran past the boxes, deeper into the cellar.

Here the room grew a bit brighter, caught beneath the moonlight trickling in through the small windows. The space was packed tightly with a wide array of shadowed clutter, boxes and lamps and dusty furniture. Rafters and pipes crisscrossed on the ceiling, swathed by gauzy webs.

He scampered to the farthest corner and hunkered down, listening as the pounding footsteps of the minister made their way down.

"*I want my son!*" the madman shrieked.

Eddie became vaguely aware of a cool draft behind

him. He spun and looked. There, coated in dust and cobwebs and a few greasy cloths, was a crawlspace.

"Give me my baby boy!" The minister was in the cellar now. Eddie could see his head over the maze of boxes, bobbing as he lurched toward a large oil tank in the opposite corner. The man swept aside a stack of books, leaned down, and peered beneath the tank.

Keeping to his knees, Eddie crept over to a burlap bag on the floor a few feet away.

The baby was breathing raspily, eyes wet and swollen.

"I'm sorry . . . I'm sorry . . ." Eddie whispered, tapping a gentle finger over the baby's lips. Quickly, he shrouded the baby in the bag, stood up, and tucked it deep into the dark crawlspace.

"Bring me my boy, you son of the devil!"

Head down, Eddie immediately raced back toward the stairs. The minister launched across the cellar toward him, hammer raised high. Quickly, Eddie stepped aside and pushed the standing lamp down. The minister tripped over the iron shaft and fell into a stack of boxes. Both minister and boxes crashed to the cement floor.

Instead of fleeing, Eddie fell to his knees and groped for the hammer. His fingers closed around the iron claw and he could feel the blood on it, sticky and warm. He rose up on one knee and pulled. The minister tightened his grip on the handle and yanked back.

They struggled. The minister managed to climb to his knees. Now both of them were kneeling, eye-to-eye, grimacing madly. The minister yanked and Eddie saw his opportunity. He let go of the hammer, and the minister plummeted back against the crushed boxes.

Eddie scrambled to his feet. He glanced about, looking for a weapon. The standing lamp was his best chance. In one fluid motion, he grabbed it and swung it around. The exposed socket jabbed into the minister's wounded chest.

With a scream of agony, the minister clutched the end of the lamp with his free hand, and before Eddie could jerk it back, levered himself to his knees. Black blood, glistening in the pallid light, fell down his chest in a stream.

Eddie let go of the lamp. He tried to kick the minister in the chest, but lost his balance and missed. The minister dropped the lamp, and with a grunt, swung the hammer into Eddie's shin.

Eddie screamed. He collapsed to the cement floor and immediately started pushing with his good leg in an attempt to crawl away. The minister lurched forward, panting and growling. Eddie rolled sideways. His hand brushed against the heavy thing he'd tripped over. A full can of paint.

The minister screeched and leapt forward. The hammer's claw swept down over his head. Eddie grabbed the can of paint with both hands and held it up just as the hammer came down.

The driving force of the hammer, and the weight of the can, proved too much for Eddie. The heavy can slid from Eddie's grip. It came down on his nose, shattering it. A silver burst of pain shot deep into his head, and he gagged and choked as blood poured into his throat.

He knew quite well that the hammer was on its way down again, so Eddie skittered back against the steps, and, despite his shattered shin and broken face, made a valiant effort to clamber up. The hammer hit the cement floor between his legs. Eddie jerked his body up a step. The minister crawled after him. This time Eddie was able to plant a foot squarely into the minister's forehead. The crazed man fell back and spilled to the floor.

And that was when Eddie, even with the sheen of blood in his eyes, saw the knife, its blade twelve inches of wet, bloody steel staring back at him. *The minister must've kept it on him*, he thought. It rested on the cement floor between them. Eddie moved first. The minister also saw the knife and leapt up.

But he didn't go for the knife.

He raised the hammer instead.

Eddie latched on to the knife and stabbed upward as the minister swung the hammer down. There was a ghastly popping sound as the knife sunk into the minister's left eye.

Warm blood drenched Eddie's hand and his mind reeled.

In the distance, the baby cried.

The minister shrieked. Eddie tried to back away, but couldn't move. Time fell into a frame-by-frame progression. Eddie held his bloody hand up—beyond it, he could see the minister, one hand groping his bloody eye-socket . . . the other swinging the hammer down.

Eddie squeezed both his eyes shut, the final image imprinted clearly upon his dying mind was the hammer's claw descending, just before it punctured the top of his skull.

A feeble scream trickled from his lips. He fell back down onto the steps, the hammer sticking out of his head like a tomahawk. Caught in a void of darkness, he lay motionless as his life spilled out through the hole in his skull, his heart forcing its last few beats deep into his mind:

Thump . . . thump . . . thump . . .

* * *

Benjamin howled in pure agony. With his good eye he could see the intruder, the baby stealer, lying in a pool of his own blood, the hammer's claw buried in his skull.

He tripped over the body and faltered up the steps, wholly intent on getting back into the barn, thinking of his bawling son, whom he was leaving behind in the basement.

"Bryan will come later," the voice in his head promised. *"I will bring him to you. But now, finish the ritual."*

He wove through the house, burst through the kitchen door, and went into the waiting night.

We will be waiting for you, Bryan. Osiris will bring you to us.

As Benjamin staggered across the backyard, all the pain of his injuries returned. He collapsed just feet from the barn. He peered up at the doors and reached out with his slashed arm.

In the doorway was a figure—a looming shadow in the darkness.

And Benjamin knew it was not the spirit of Osiris. It was something else, a rolling shapeless thing with sagging flesh crawling with buzzing horseflies. It filled the doorway, stretching and moving. Stinking, withered feathers floated down from its roiling bulk and landed on Benjamin's wasted body.

"Osiris . . ." Benjamin pleaded vainly, his voice barely a whisper.

A black, shadowy appendage crept out from the thing. It latched on to Benjamin's neck and with brutal speed, wrenched him into the barn, where the crucified souls of his family awaited the ancestral afterlife.

PART TWO

THE LIVING, DEAD

"What happens after death? Only the body dies. The soul . . . it lives on forever."
—Scott Cunningham, *The Truth About Witchcraft Today*

CHAPTER TWENTY-EIGHT

September 8, 2005
6:37 P.M.

Visiting hours were in full swing. She'd heard a nurse in the hallway telling someone that they ran from six to eight, but she expected no one to come. Not Ed and not even Johnny. She gave God credit for giving her this knowledge.

While the nurses hustled and bustled out in the hallway with their clipboards and their stethoscopes, her acceptance of abandonment was replaced by a focused anxiety. It forced her to silently and furtively dress herself in the clothes she came here with and sit on the edge of the bed to wait for a sign of when to leave.

As the hallway grew more alive with activity, as more visitors came and went, her answer came, perching on the sill of the window in her room. A large black bird, a crow maybe, its feathers shiny-wet, glistening in the late-afternoon sun. The sounds of the city coalesced into a blur, acting as a backdrop to the low whisper of the bird's command.

"Go to the house. . . ."

She remained on the bed, staring out of the window at the bird, which hopped back and forth on the sill, cocking its head in a curious almost intelligent fashion, aiming its little gleaming eyes in at her as if waiting for her to heed its instructions. Although its beak did not move, she could distinctly hear the hollow whisper that seeped into her head.

"Go to the house. . . ."

She stood from the bed, which creaked slightly, and stepped over to the window.

She placed her hands against the cool pane and again looked out at the bird. In the past few seconds the bird had not only died, but had rotted, becoming host to a swarm of wriggling larvae.

A single black feather, healthy and glistening, unlike the rest of the bird now, billowed in the breeze against the window's edge. Mary Petrie cracked the window the entire four inches it would go and retrieved the feather with two reaching fingers.

Holding the feather, she backed away, suddenly confused, and yet at the same time strangely focused. She placed the feather in her pocket, then gripped the steel railing of the bed, taking a few moments to catch her wits.

The house, she thought, looking out at the dead bird, its small bony legs curled against its wasted body. She looked down and was surprised to see she was wearing street clothes, not remembering how or when she got dressed.

The bird's whisper returned: *"I will guide you."*

Mary Petrie, who was to be released from St. Michael's Presbyterian Hospital in the morning, walked out into the hallway, looking no different than the scattered visitors seeking their loved ones. People barely glanced at her as she walked by.

She passed a doctor in the hall and moved into a stairwell that released her one floor below into the busy lobby of the hospital.

Without delay, she hurried out the main entrance into the night, a covert mission in her mind: *Go to the house*.

She walked and walked, for miles it seemed, blind to every distraction as darkness spread its cloak against the city's bright lights. Eventually, she arrived at her apartment building on East 88th Street, where she rode the elevator to the third floor. She got out and went down the hallway to her apartment.

The door was unlocked.

From inside came a noise, a dull, jarring thud . . .

. . . *thump . . . thump . . . thump . . .*

She walked into the apartment. The kitchen table was just as she remembered leaving it, with the mail scattered, a lone torn envelope tossed aside like the peel of a banana. The chair she fell from was still on the floor, her rosary lying beside it.

Johnny . . .

Then the smell hit her: feces and urine and a hint of decay. She crossed the living room, curious yet strangely expectant, listening to the noise.

Thump . . . thump . . . thump . . .

Her bedroom door was ajar. Through the slight opening, she could see the curtain billowing in the night breeze like a ghost making its way into her home . . . a home that had become a place of death— of evil making itself known once again in her life.

Benjamin Conroy . . .

She entered the room and saw her husband.

Here was the man who'd been dead for nearly two days. Whose body, pallid and blue in the room's dim light, swung from the leather belt looped around his neck. Whose head was twisted, whose eyes were bulging from their sockets, whose tongue was protruding from his open mouth. Who was covered in a thick black sheath of tarlike blood.

The body swayed in the breeze gusting in through the open window. It hit against the wall, *thump*, adding to the solid *O* there—the *O* that was the first letter of the word scrawled in large *wet* bloody letters on the wall: *Osiris*.

Mary leaned against the doorjamb, staring at the man she'd been married to for twenty-seven years, the man who'd agreed to move away from the evil in Wellfield that had slaughtered her family.

The evil that had given them a son.

Despite her initial hesitation to accept this gift . . . this gift resulting from the devil's work, she'd not been able to deny her incapability to bear children. She'd spent endless hours trying to convince herself that the boy who'd become her son had in fact been a gift from God—His way of repaying her for her tragic loss.

Now, gazing at Ed's hanging, lifeless body, she realized that she'd never been so wrong.

The blood on the wall is wet, as though the words were just written. . . .

She took a step into the room, beating back her gorge as the image she faced engraved itself into her mind: Ed's feet and legs, mottled black, his upper body and face blanched white with blue veins showing though translucent skin. The bed had been moved aside, his body dangling over a clotted spot, a line of thick, dry blood following his movement as the breeze pushed him up against the wall.

Thump . . .

Osiris . . .

The body of her husband swung back, and the instant Mary looked into his face, his head twisted up. The bulging eyes rolled toward her.

Ed Petrie, in death, spoke to his wife, his voice deep and hoarse and seeming to come from inside his rotting lungs: *"Save my dying soul. . . ."*

And then he fell still and silent, back to dead.

Mary stood frozen, staring at Ed's body and trying to will him back to life again, just for a moment, to confirm that she had indeed heard him speak to her. It had seemed only logical, at least in her current state of mind, that he in fact *had* spoken to her—that the evil of Benjamin Conroy had found its way back into her life, via Johnny. Johnny, who she knew, just *knew*, wouldn't be here—who was likely in Wellfield now, unwittingly allowing Conroy's evil sin to come back into existence. Into her life. And here, into Ed.

Save my dying soul. . . .

"I will, Ed," she answered, uncertain of what it meant or how she would accomplish the task. She knew, however, what she needed to do next, and that was to return to Wellfield . . .

. . . go to the house . . .

. . . go to the house, save Johnny and . . . and save Ed's dying soul.

CHAPTER TWENTY-NINE

September 8, 2005
8:53 P.M.

Johnny awoke in darkness. It enveloped him, *grasped* him, much like a womb would a fetus. He struggled to his knees, eyes tearing, head thudding. A cold chill pervaded his body; his lungs rattled as breathed.

He looked up . . .

. . . and remembered the crosses he'd seen, dead human bodies crucified on them. And then . . . something else there in the darkness, looking at him, something dark and shifting and definitely alive. . . .

He grimaced in pain and the memory drifted. His bruised back screamed as he stretched. The chill faded, and he realized suddenly how hot and stifling it was.

Staring into the darkness, he crept forward, arms outstretched and groping blindly. His hands came in contact with what felt like a wood wall, damp and pulpy.

He stood and began to feel along the length of the wall, gouged and grooved with decay. Some of the planks budged slightly. He kicked at one, gently at first because his legs hurt so damn much, and then a little harder as he managed to muster a bit of strength. In the dark it seemed he was doing little damage, but he kept kicking and pushing anyway, and soon enough the rotted wood splintered outward.

He leaned down with his hands on his knees, breathing heavily, drained of strength. Streaks of sweat dripped down his face and body. A wave of oppressive heat assaulted him, and for a moment he was sure he was going to faint. *God helps those who help themselves*, his mother used to say, and he found it in himself to at long last heed Mary's godly counsel and maneuver through the jagged hole he made, back into the barn. *She also once said that those in pain who turn to God after a life of denial shall not find His guidance.*

The front doors of the barn were still open. Silver moonlight seeped in and splayed across the hard soil in a single wide beam. He could see the ladder lying across the ground like a fallen soldier. Alongside it was a dark splotch of blood where the crazed attacker had fallen.

The dark splotch was the letter *O* in the word *Osiris*, scrawled in lurching bloody letters on the ground. Instinctively, he felt for the plastic bag holding Ed's suicide note, still in his pocket. *Osiris* . . .

"Jesus Christ . . ." he whispered.

The body was gone.

Every plausible scenario tore through Johnny's

mind. He was certain that the maniac was dead. Could someone have come along and taken the body away.

But what if he's not dead?

There was a sudden sound . . . a rustle of something sifting through the tall grass outside. He jerked his gaze to the doors, waited, then limped toward them. When he reached them, he pressed a tentative hand against the jamb, listening intently; cool air, like a gift from God, bathed his sweat-soaked body.

He took a deep breath. Then he stepped outside into the waist-high grass.

First he looked toward the driveway, where Judson's car sat like a fossil beneath the pale blue moonlight. He peered at the house, its back door still open.

The rustling continued. It was closer now . . . or maybe it was just the wind talking.

Slowly, Johnny looked to his right . . .

. . . not the wind . . .

. . . and not ten feet away, emerging from the shadows of the waist-high grass, was the madman. Johnny had only a moment to realize that, despite having no eyes, the maniac could, by some unnatural means, still *see* Johnny.

Johnny screamed, looking not just at the maniac's vacant sockets, but at the rest of his face: his cheeks, stripped of their skin, wet and glistening beneath the moonlight.

He widened his grin. One mangled hand reached out and he whispered: "Brother . . ."

Johnny lurched away. He tripped through the high grass, beating back the pain lancing through his guts. A gray cloud of terror filled his sights. His breath came and went in speeding gasps. He could hear the madman's feet behind him, and he pleaded in a silent panic,

Oh God, help me! He glimpsed Judson's car, fifteen feet away, its shattered window dimly aglow from the soft domelight, still lit from the open door he'd fled though hours earlier.

He skidded on the driveway. A small cloud of dust rose up around him. Someone was sitting in the backseat of the car.

He staggered along the length of the car, leaned down, peered inside.

The figure in the back seat twisted toward him.

Johnny jumped back. But then the figure lunged across the seat and thrust its face through the broken window.

It was Andrew Judson . . . but there was no conceivable way this monstrosity could actually be the friendly lawyer Johnny had met earlier in the day. In fact, there was no way it could be alive. Its chest was an open cavity. Johnny could see the white bones of its ribcage imprisoning its motionless heart. Its lungs, blue and mucousy, sagged lifelessly atop exposed intestines. Its face, mostly intact, was white and horribly bloated. Its lips were blood coated, teeth jabbing out in a scathing grimace.

It plunged its arms through the jagged window. Fragments of glass ripped into the pulpy skin of its forearms. Its hands, grasping and groping, were covered with deep lacerations.

Panting and wheezing, Johnny lurched backwards against the house. He clutched his chest, his scar burning as though a razor were tracing its shape. The Judson-thing stared at him with cloudy yellow-brown eyes. "Brother . . ." it groaned, reaching both hands out like a baby wanting to be picked up.

Johnny shambled along the length of the house, his

heart chugging in his chest. The Judson-thing was halfway out the car's window now. Shards of glass ripped into its exposed guts—Johnny could see its blood, running down the car door in dark, glistening stripes. Johnny backpedaled across the cracked walkway, watching in terror as the thing nose-dived out of the window onto the ground, a rope of small intestine caught on a fragment of glass in the window frame like a pull from a sweater. It gazed up at Johnny with its sunken eyes, arms and legs twisting and grasping for equilibrium as it tried to right itself. It opened its mouth. "Brother . . ."

Johnny reached the front of the house. He continued backing away on buckling legs, thinking, *This can't be happening, it just can't.* But Judson, and now the maniac—once dead human beings now terribly alive—were very much *real*, moving crookedly in the weedy driveway with their clutching hands and gaping mouths and injuries still fresh and gleaming in the bright moonlight.

Johnny screamed. The maniac-thing tottered after him. The Judson-thing fought with the intestinal rope still leashing him to the car.

Johnny spun and dashed away into the night, head down, arms pumping back and forth as he pushed himself past the pain trying to bring him down, past the rotting fingers he imagined he felt grasping the back of his neck. The darkness of the country road welcomed him, and he embraced it as a sanctuary from the evils that shouted out in his wake: *"Brother . . ."*

CHAPTER THIRTY

September 8, 2005
9:46 P.M.

"Four-seventy-nine, East Eighty-eighth Street. Apartment 3B. Yes, ten P.M. A van with wheelchair access. Yes, with an automatic lift. I'm also going to need the driver to help me with my luggage, so please tell him to double park with his hazards on. There's an elevator in the building, so it'll only take a few minutes to come back down. Thank you."

Mary Petrie hung up the phone. She studied her wrinkled hand—*How peculiar it looks in the bright light,* she thought—then checked the clock on the kitchen wall. 9:47.

Go to the house.

From the very moment she woke in the hospital Mary had become overwhelmed by an inexplicable, compulsion to get out of bed, get dressed, and leave the hospital. It had consumed her like a wildfire.

Now, this compulsion had her functioning with a degree of strength and concentration she'd never known in the past—suddenly she felt no anxiety, no depression, no weakness dragging her down. She had become a new woman, one who didn't need medication, one brimming with the rigid will to comply with her husband's posthumous demand.

Save my dying soul.

After leaving the hospital, she'd gone straight home, where she'd packed a small bag and dug out of the closet the collapsible, dust-coated wheelchair she'd used years before when she broke her hip. The only thing that mattered was her furious, undying need to save Johnny—the bird on the sill had convinced her of this. *Go to the house.* She would go to the house, deliver Johnny from the hand of evil, and save Ed's dying soul. And then she would bring them both home, safe and sound, where they would live the remainder of their lives as the happy family she always imagined them to be.

She snapped open the wheelchair, locked up the safety arms, and rolled it over to Ed's hanging body. She inched the chair forward and locked the wheels so it was just below the rear of his blood-soaked jeans. The leather seat brushed against his legs, and he swayed forward a few inches. The beam he hung from creaked like a rusty hinge.

She retrieved the tailor's scissors she kept in the top drawer of her bureau—big heavy-duty stainless steel ones, the best of their kind, good for the woman who does all her sewing at home—then reached up over Ed's head and cut into the leather belt halfway between the ceiling and his matted hair.

The scissors went through about a third of the way before Ed's dead weight did the rest. The belt tore in half and he thumped down into the wheelchair. Mary dropped the scissors and grabbed the handles, shifting her weight against the chair so it wouldn't tip forward. Her heart drummed madly in her chest as she steadied the chair ... and for a moment her old insecure, mentally ill self broke through, striking her with a lightning bolt of fear and uncertainty. She was instantly terrified, but her new awareness immediately returned, dousing her insecurities and fears before they could stop her.

She remained motionless for a moment as her mind-set settled. Taking a few deep breaths, she looked blearily around the room.

In the kitchen, the clock struck ten. The sound of the tolling bell set her back into action. She hooked her arms firmly beneath Ed's armpits and shifted him up with a previously unknown strength.

She rolled him out of the room and into the kitchen. She searched the linen closet and pulled out a set of queen-sized sheets. Like a spider securing a captured fly, she swathed Ed's body, tucking the edges of the sheets firmly between him and the wheelchair. She made certain that he was fully covered, from neck to feet, then grabbed a cap from the top shelf of the closet and fitted it on his head, which she had to keep readjusting because it kept tilting over. She dug out a pair of sunglasses from the junk drawer in the kitchen and covered Ed's hollow-milky eyes.

It was a sad sight, but one that wouldn't raise any

eyebrows—Manhattan pedestrians saw much odder things on a daily basis. As long as there was no blood visible Mary would be able to transfer him into the van and get away.

Of course there was the driver to worry about, but Mary's new mental state had already come up with a plan to deal with that.

On the counter next to the microwave, sat the butcher-block set of stainless steel knives. With a quick jerk, she removed the largest one in the upper left-hand corner of the block. It made a *sleek!* sound, and somewhere in her mind she saw a man's bloody hand performing the very same deed, preparing to do the very same thing she planned to do.

The intercom buzzed. She answered it: "Yes?"

"Your ride," a man's voice said over the tiny speaker.

"Come in," she answered blankly, pressing the release button to let him in.

She waited just to the right of the threshold, the knife poised in her sweating hand, listening for his footsteps, which emerged from the elevator two minutes later.

Six steps. Then a knock.

"Come in," she answered, holding the knife up, its polished point aimed squarely at the opening door.

The driver entered the apartment, and with a thin cry, Mary plunged the knife into his waist.

The driver yelled, staggering into the kitchen, hands groping for the exposed handle. Mary slammed the door shut behind him and watched with odd fascination as the driver slammed into the refrigerator. His knees buckled, and with a yell, he collapsed to the floor.

Mary leaned forward and snatched the knife out of

his waist. He made an attempt to stand, staring dumb-foundedly at the old lady who'd decided for some reason to murder him.

Without thought or hesitation, Mary lunged forward and drove the knife into his left eye . . .

. . . and again, somewhere in her consciousness, she saw the man's bloody hand again, performing this very same act.

Their dying souls . . .

The driver shouted again and collapsed face-up on the kitchen floor. His eye gushed blood and vitreous fluid, body twitching as if charged with electricity. Mary leaned down and yanked the knife out . . . and drove it into him again, this time into his heart. She twisted it, watching for a moment the blood sputtering from his wounds, his body stiffening, his lungs wheezing their final gasp of air.

And then, all was quiet and still. She ferreted out the man's keys from his jacket pocket, careful not to get too much blood on her hands, then backed away, deliberately, almost peacefully. She turned, leaned down, and with a smile kissed Ed on his cold, stinking cheek. "That was for you, dear . . . and for Johnny."

Then, as if nothing unusual had happened, she placed her bag on Ed's lap and wheeled him out into the hallway, stopping only once to feel the soft comfort of the feather in her pocket.

CHAPTER THIRTY-ONE

September 8, 2005
10:04 P.M.

Guided only by the moonlight, Johnny sought refuge in the night. His legs moved and his arms pumped as he ran. Giddiness filled his head, caused by exhaustion, fatigue, and pain.

He wondered whether this was still earth as he'd always known it. He wondered whether this was some other reality now, where the dead walked the earth.

The dark road he traveled was endless, bounded on both sides by fields of wheat and rustling weeds. Beyond, an unending symphony of crickets filled the air.

After endless minutes, he heard a car behind him. A wash of bright light opened out on the road, pinning him like a prison escapee.

Johnny continued running at a slow, staggering pace. The road ahead was illuminated by the approaching car lights. Finally, he lurched to the roadside and waited for the car to pass. In his pocket, the plastic bags holding the feather and Ed's note seemed to shift slightly.

The car drew up beside him, soil and pebbles crunching beneath its tires. On the verge of hyperventilating, Johnny leaned with his hands on his knees.

The car stopped, engine idling. Johnny could hear the passenger window go down, and when he looked he saw a red sedan.

A voice emerged: "Hey . . . you all right?"

It depends . . . are you dead or alive? Johnny peered into the car, listening to the crickets and the gentle rumble of the car's engine. In the moonlight and broken shadows before him, a man—one very much alive with no guts or blood on his clothes—leaned across the seat. He was old, pushing sixty, with a gray mustache and a Red Sox cap on his head. His face was a white patch beneath the brim.

"You okay, kid?" he asked, scrutinizing Johnny's soiled clothes.

Johnny shook his head. "No." His voice was just a whisper.

"Are you hurt?" the man asked, brow furrowed. "Do you need to go to the hospital?"

"I . . . I don't know."

"What's your name, son?" Johnny saw the man lean over and open the glove compartment. He figured he might be reaching for a weapon of some sort—in case the strange boy in the road got unruly.

"You got a name?" the man asked again, looking back at Johnny.

Johnny nodded and opened his mouth to speak . . . but what leaped off his tongue wasn't what he'd meant to say.

"Conroy."

The man froze. His eyes, studying Johnny intently now, narrowed.

"Conroy . . ." the man replied. He sighed nervously.

Johnny nodded gravely, uncertain what made him give that name.

And then the man said, "Bryan Conroy," as if he recognized Johnny. He leaned across the seat and opened the door. The dome light came on, revealing the man's elderly features. "Get in."

Johnny hesitated, uncertain if he should get in the car or run. It didn't take him long to realize that there'd be no dead people inside the car, and only heaven knew what waited for him deep in the darkness of Wellfield's farms. He slid into the car and pulled the door shut . . . then turned and faced the man.

Indeed, the man *had* retrieved a weapon from the glove compartment: a large hunting knife. It lay across his lap, sheathed in leather. But he didn't seem all that concerned with using it. Instead, he regarded Johnny for a moment and plucked a cell phone from his waist.

"Give me a minute, okay?"

Johnny nodded. His scar itched and throbbed, as if warning him of something.

The man dialed the phone and placed it to his ear. With his free hand he shifted the car into drive and started down the road. After a few seconds he said, "Henry? Carl. Evening. Don't mean to be botherin' ya at this late hour, but . . . well, I have a young man here in my car. Found him wandering around about on Brunswick Road, 'bout a half mile from the old Conroy place. Yep, that's right. Looks like he's been through the war, too. And Henry . . . he's telling me his name is Conroy. Yep. *Bryan* Conroy. Uh, I'd say about eighteen, nineteen tops. So I figured I'd call you first before bringing him over. Okay then, we'll be there in five minutes."

He clipped the phone back onto his belt, shifting his girth as he did so. "I'm gonna bring you over to see someone."

"Who?" Johnny asked. He felt a little light-headed.

"Someone who's going to help you."

"Help me?"

"Someone who's been expecting you."

His heart started pounding furiously. Goose bumps formed on his arms. His light-headedness grew much worse. Numbness gripped him, an equal combination of shock and exhaustion. His head dropped forward and a fibery grayness seeped into his sights. He drifted toward it. . . .

And he saw himself back in the barn, at the bottom of the broken steps, staring into the darkness and seeing five makeshift crucifixes jutting crookedly from the hard ground. Nailed upon them were the bodies of a man, a woman, a girl, a boy, and . . . something else on the smallest one, not a human . . . and they were all alive, staring at him with bulging eyes and bloody faces, calling for him to join their quest. . . . He tried to pull away but all of a sudden a gray shadowy limb oozed out of the darkness and latched on to his arm. . . .

He screamed.

He jolted up and looked around.

The car was stopped and his door was open. Another man about the same age as the one who picked him up was gripping him gently by the arm.

"It's okay, it's okay, I'm here to help."

Johnny gasped, his mind rolling crazily. *Dead men, coming after me!* He licked his cracked lips with his dry tongue. The fibery grayness that had taken him down slowly cleared. His shirt was torn, bunched up around his neck.

"My name is Henry Depford, and I'm here to help you."

Johnny nodded, unable to wrestle the images from his mind. He took a few deep breaths, then struggled to his feet and followed the man. He thought he was going to throw up, but it quickly passed. Both men helped him along a short walkway toward a house with a bright yellow porch light. Bugs flitted about the light in droves.

"You just come with me," the man said, leading Johnny up the porch steps. "You'll be safe here."

The man, Henry, showed Johnny into a living room with two blue plaid sofas and a planked wood floor that glowed richly. The cool clean air inside was refreshing, making him feel a little more connected to the world . . . a world where only kind, living people existed.

He noticed a woman standing in the entrance to the kitchen. She had auburn hair and bright blue eyes that gazed at Johnny from behind a pair of wire-frame glasses. She wore a bathrobe with an embroidered rose on it. In her hands was a wooden rolling pin, and since Johnny couldn't smell anything cooking, he assumed it was for self-defense. Indeed, she didn't look all too pleased to have a filthy stranger invading the privacy of her home.

"Don't just stand there, Teresa," Henry said. "Get him some water."

The woman grimaced and disappeared into the kitchen. The two men eased Johnny down into a chair next to a small round table. Johnny saw both of them pacing and fidgeting, seemingly impatient for the woman to return with a glass of water. Soon enough, she did, and she handed it to Henry, who then gave it to Johnny.

"Drink up, my boy. Mrs. D. will fix you something to eat—you must be hungry."

Johnny drank the glass of water, and Teresa—Mrs. D.—was there to refill it, albeit tentatively. He looked around the room. Straight ahead, a needlepoint tapestry of a barn hung on the wall above an old stereo. On the right stood a breakfront overflowing with ceramic farm animals.

"Please . . . what's going on here?" he asked.

"We were fixing to ask you the same thing," Henry said, regarding Johnny with what appeared to be deep fascination. "Are you hurt?"

Johnny shook his head. "A few bumps and bruises . . ." He took another sip of water, wondering if he should tell them about the men coming back from the dead. Instead, he said, "Something terrible is happening."

Henry nodded grimly. "I know."

Johnny gazed up at Henry, realizing with dismay that whatever in God's name was going on, it was far from over. In fact, it was probably just beginning.

Henry said, "We'll get you washed up, get some food into you, and then we'll talk about everything that's been going on, okay, Bryan?"

Johnny sipped the water, then responded, "Johnny . . . my name's Johnny Petrie."

Henry hesitated. For a moment he looked at the man who drove Johnny over, then back at Johnny.

"But . . ." Johnny added, "I *am* Bryan Conroy."

Henry nodded, lips pursed. "You look just like your father."

"So I've been told."

Henry got down on one knee and placed a gentle hand on Johnny's thigh. At once, Johnny felt a cautionary tightness in his chest. "Johnny," Henry said, "I'm gonna need to hear everything that's happened to you. It'll help me decide what to do next, although I do have an inkling as to what lies in the road ahead." He paused. "I'm going to need your help, son. Can you help me?"

Johnny didn't know what to do. Common sense told him that he should insist on a ride to the nearest bus station and get the hell out of Wellfield, now and forever . . . but his heart told him otherwise.

Henry really did seem genuine in his desire to help, though he hadn't yet said why.

Johnny saw no alternative. He said, "I'll help you, but please, tell me . . . what the hell is going on here?"

Seeming both nervous and secretly pleased, Henry smiled. "Okay."

CHAPTER THIRTY-TWO

September 8, 2005
10:29 P.M.

Fatefully easy.

That's how the journey from the third-floor hallway to the sidewalk was for Mary Petrie. She hadn't run into anyone inside, and just as she'd assumed, the pedestrians outside did nothing more than wrinkle their noses at the strange odor in the air. Yes, they'd all eyed the swaddled, wheelchair-bound man wearing sunglasses and a pea cap, but they all moved on, perhaps blaming the stink on garbage or dog crap or dead rats in some nearby sewer. Even to Mary, whose new consciousness interpreted Ed's rotting state as "natural," had imagined it would take a few good applications of bleach to rid the building's elevator of its nearly visible stench.

She used the remote on the driver's keyring to open

the sliding side-panel door of the minivan. Set into the frame of the door was a red, quarter-sized button. She pressed it, leaving a wet smear of blood on it. With a mechanical whir, an automatic lift slid out and dropped to the sidewalk. She rolled the wheelchair onto it, back-stepped into the van, and pressed the button again. The platform rose.

She pulled the chair in the van and anchored the wheels to the braces in the floor; there were no rear seats at all, affording enough room for four wheel-chairs if needed. Once the second wheel was locked in place, she settled in behind the wheel of the van, where she stared at her dead husband in the rearview mirror.

Don't you worry, Ed. I'm taking you to see Johnny. He's at the house. That's right, the same house where we're going to save your dying soul. There'll be no stops, no reunions. We'll just do what we have to do, and then we'll get Johnny and leave. And rest assured, he'll be getting the whuppin' of his life when we get back home.

She started the van, but before leaving, removed the feather from her pocket and tucked its quill into a slit in the passenger seat beside her. *Guide my way*, she thought, then pulled away from the building where she and Ed and Johnny had lived for the last seventeen years, blending into all the sights and sounds of the city, just as she had upon leaving the hospital.

Twenty minutes later, she was driving in light traffic on the George Washington Bridge, looking for signs to Interstate 95, which would take her north, all the way to Wellfield, Maine.

And not once did she consider that, up until this moment, she'd never driven a car before.

CHAPTER THIRTY-THREE

September 8, 2005
10:56 P.M.

The shower in the Depford home was hot and strong. For nearly twenty minutes, Johnny scrubbed himself from head to toe, desperate to get rid of every speck of Wellfield. Teresa—Mrs. D., as she was so cordially known—was kind enough to place his clothes in the trash; but first he'd retrieved the plastic bag containing the feather and Ed's final note,

OSIRIS

plus the initial letter from Andrew Judson, which having gone through a war of sorts, looked much older than it was. While toweling off and quickly dressing himself in Henry Depford's clothes (the pants given to him were a bit too big, but Johnny still had his belt and was able to fasten them around his waist), he shuddered at the cruel fact that Judson had essentially waited around for eighteen years to get murdered, and, as it turned out, come back from the dead.

Dead men, coming after me . . .

Brother . . .

Massaging his head with the towel, Johnny shook the harrowing thought from his mind. He tucked the plastic bag and Judson's letter in his pocket and left the bathroom.

He smelled the aroma of fresh coffee brewing, and upon reaching the dining room, found Henry Depford sitting at the small round table sipping from a small mug. Johnny sat at the table across from Henry, and Mrs. D. appeared from the kitchen with a sandwich and mug filled with black coffee.

Henry said glumly, "Better get some food and caffeine in ya. Gonna need your energy."

Feeling exhausted and fatigued, these weren't the words Johnny was hoping for, but he didn't argue the point. He was suddenly starved, and given the events of the day, didn't think he'd be able to sleep at all anyway. He attacked the sandwich in silence, peering at Henry once and seeing a man who seemed to have aged quite a bit in the last half hour. As had Johnny himself, he was sure.

When Johnny finished the sandwich, he inquired about the man who'd picked him up.

"Carl Davies."

"Why'd he bring me here?"

"Because he knows me better than anyone else in the world, Mrs. D. included." Henry took a sip of coffee. "Used to be my deputy. But like myself, he's retired now."

"Your deputy?"

Henry nodded. "I used to be the sheriff here in

Wellfield. Retired almost seventeen years ago, though."

"You're not old enough to be retired that long."

Henry rubbed a thumb along the handle of the mug. "I was thirty-eight at the time, had been the sheriff for five years." He cleared his throat, then added, "Something happened right here in Wellfield that'd not only made me step down from my sheriff's post, but also forced me to devote my life to a new field of study."

Johnny took a sip of coffee, his gaze fixed questioningly on Henry Depford.

Henry stood from the table. "Come with me, Johnny. I've got something to show you."

Johnny rose and followed Henry through a short hall to a set of carpeted steps that creaked as the two climbed to the second floor. Once in the top foyer, Henry made a left. Johnny kept close behind, noticing a closed paneled door about four feet away. Across the foyer was an open door, and Johnny could see another bathroom, the synthetic smell of cherries wafting from it.

Henry stopped at the closed door. He gripped the knob, then turned toward Johnny. His face was solemn, icy, and pale. "Here's where I've spent much of the last seventeen years. Here's my life's work."

He opened the door and ushered Johnny into a study roughly twelve by fifteen feet. Perched in the far right corner was a studiously neat pinewood desk that held a computer, a small wrought-iron lamp, and a steel mesh document tray piled with notebooks. Against the walls were a series of rolling corkboards—Johnny counted seven in all—each and every one jam-packed with a wide variety of neatly arranged documents: newspaper clippings, photographs, and scribbled notes. A floor-to-ceiling bookshelf alongside the window was clogged with hard- and soft-cover books. A cursory glance revealed a few titles relating to religion and the occult. Johnny couldn't help marveling at it all.

Henry shut the door behind them.

"What is all this?" Johnny asked—and was about to add, *And what does it all have to do with me?*—when he noticed an eerie black-and-white photograph on one of the display boards. He walked over and placed a finger on it.

My God . . .

It was a photo of him, and one from not too long ago either. It appeared to have been taken from a distance; Johnny had been looking to his left, and the photographer, on a street somewhere in Manhattan, had snapped the photo at the perfect moment, capturing his face.

Johnny looked at Henry Depford questioningly.

"There are many more where that came from, Johnny. I've got some so old that you were just a toddler holding Mary Petrie's hand."

Johnny was stunned . . . and yet at the same time not entirely surprised, given everything else that had happened.

"And I thought Andrew Judson was the only one keeping tabs on me."

Henry grinned knowingly. He walked over to the bookshelf and pulled down a spiral-bound photo album. He handed it to Johnny.

"Andrew Judson couldn't hold a candle to what I know about you. His motives are purely financial. Mine run much deeper than that." He gestured to the photo album. "Go 'head. Take a look."

Johnny opened the album and saw a picture of himself at about ten or eleven years old. He'd been standing in a crowd outside St. Michael's Church alongside Mary. He was wearing blue slacks and a white short-sleeve school shirt. Taped below the picture was a note indicating the time, date, and place the photo had been taken: *July 20, 1997. Ten A.M.* Johnny thumbed through the book, each page, perhaps twenty in all, displaying a single photograph of him at various ages, along with the details of its taking.

Johnny felt scared . . . and yet, in some strange way, secure. It was as though he'd just come face-to-face with a guardian angel who'd been watching out for him his entire life.

He handed the photo album back to Depford, then sat in the metal folding chair in front of the bookshelf. The corkboard before him held a number of laminated newspaper articles, many of them yellow with age.

One in particular caught his eye: WELLFIELD MINISTER MURDERS FAMILY, LOCAL WOMAN, BOY

His scar throbbing like a heartbeat, Johnny stood and touched the blurry black-and-white photo of Benjamin Conroy.

"I was the first to arrive at the scene," Depford said, unpinning the article and handing it to Johnny. "It'd been late in the day, and I was driving home after working late because a group of local thugs had roughed up some kid . . . who later on turned out to be Daniel Conroy. Your brother."

Johnny stared mutely at Benjamin's photo.

"I'd passed the Conroy farmhouse," Depford continued, "and noticed Bill Carlson's red Mustang in the driveway. Now, it wasn't at all odd for Bill to loan the car to his son Eddie—who at the time was heading into his senior year—but I did think it odd to see the car there; you see, the Conroys kept mostly to themselves, and, of course, to the more generous members of Benjamin's church. And let me tell you, Bill Carlson was no advocate of Conroy's preaching."

Staring at Benjamin's photo—*my family was murdered, my father murdered them, my father*—Johnny absorbed every last word of Depford's story.

"I'd had it in my mind to ring up Bill Carlson, but didn't want to cause him any alarm. If he'd been keeping an eye out for Eddie to come home, then the entire town would've been ringing my office, and I didn't want to set anyone into any sort of panic. So I pulled into the driveway and thought for a second that young Eddie Carlson had been making nice with the Conroy girl. Though that didn't seem all too likely.

"So I pulled in behind the Mustang, got out . . . and right away I knew it was going to be a long night."

"What'd you find?" Johnny asked, handing the article back to Henry.

Henry hesitated, then took a deep breath and said, "Your family, Johnny. And Eddie Carlson. They'd all been brutally murdered."

Eddie felt a sudden, sharp pain in his head. Again the feather in his pocket seemed to grow warm, and his scar itched furiously. He sat back down and ran a hand though his hair, then touched the sudden comfort of the feather through his jeans, which eased the burning in his scar. God, he was scared. Scared of Henry Depford. Scared of the truth that, once he heard it, would grip him like a fever and never let go.

But he had to know.

"I was there when it happened, wasn't I?"

Henry nodded.

"How, Henry? How'd he do it? And why not me?"

Henry hesitated, then licked his lips and said, "First, Johnny, what did you see up at the Conroy house today?"

CHAPTER THIRTY-FOUR

September 9, 2005
12:03 A.M.

Mary Petrie was driving north on I-95 at eighty-five miles per hour. Traffic continued to be light. She avoided being noticed by highway patrol, a stroke of good fortune credited to her "lucky feather." Every minute or so she would glance over at it, with its quill tucked firmly into the tear in the seat beside her, its glossy surface wavering gently beneath the cool breeze of the air conditioner.

While on the GW Bridge, she discovered that the van's radio didn't work—which didn't bother her at all. *God wants me to think about the task at hand. Save Johnny. Save Ed's dying soul. The bird was sent to me, and I have heeded its word.*

Yes, Mary was quite certain that God was close by, guiding her.

The van shot its way through the night, chasing its headlights through Connecticut and Rhode Island. A bit of traffic built up on the interstate around Boston but thinned out once she headed north away from the city, where she was able to move even faster, pressing past ninety at times.

Gonna save my family, she thought as the van crossed the Maine border, running between blurred blue spruce and pine. *Gonna save my family, gonna save my . . .*

And it was here, for the first time since leaving Manhattan, that Mary's new consciousness began to wane, leaving her confused and unsure. She reached to her right and grabbed the feather—to Mary, this was her only hope of hanging on to the perception that had guided her this far . . . the *false* perception now struggling against the harsh surge of reality rearing its ugly head.

CHAPTER THIRTY-FIVE

September 9, 2005
1:05 A.M.

It had taken Johnny nearly an hour and a half to relay his entire experience to Henry Depford. Henry had sat riveted as Johnny spoke, taking vigorous notes and asking frequent questions, sometimes getting up and pacing nervously about the room. As anticipated, Henry had been particularly interested in Johnny's confrontations with the madman and Judson. Twice Henry had asked if Johnny was absolutely certain, but Johnny vehemently reassured Henry he was. Henry had nodded both times, fully trusting him.

"You're lucky to have found me, Johnny."

"You found me, Henry."

Henry leaned forward, whispering as though trying to hide their conversation from Mrs. D., said, "Here in Wellfield, like anyplace else, most things run like nature intends them to. But . . . and I've spent the last seventeen years studying Benjamin Conroy, and I can say with the very same conviction as you, that everything surrounding Benjamin Conroy's legacy does *not* run according to nature. There's another force at play here, one we can't see or feel or hear, but it's powerful and *it is there*. Johnny . . . it's influencing us right now. Yes, we may have found each other—and it may very well have been by accident—but it knows we're in this together."

Nodding, Johnny said, "I've told you everything. Now it's your turn. What did you find when you got to the house?"

"Blood," Henry answered without hesitation. "A trail of it, leading from the house all the way to the barn out back."

"The barn . . ." A cold shudder marched along Johnny's spine. He closed his eyes, remembering. . . .

A gust of hot stinking air bounding up from below . . . a chorus of whispering voices ascending from the darkness. Their souls . . . free of the ghostly wooden crosses drenched in blood, free of the four bodies crucified on them, chasing me as I drift into the gloom . . .

"What is it, Johnny?"

Johnny shook his head. "Nothing . . . please, please go on."

Henry eyed Johnny suspiciously, but continued. "I thought I heard some voices coming from the barn, and given the blood, well, I ran over to it like a bat out of hell. When I got there, I took a second to say a prayer, then drew my gun and went inside.

"The first thing I saw was an odd occult painting on the ground. There were some charred remains in the middle of it, plus a shattered full-length mirror on a pivot stand. I saw the bloody trail that continued to-ward the rear of the barn. And that was when I heard a groan. It was a woman. There'd been a wall of hay bales stacked up under the loft that had hidden the back part of the barn. One row had been pulled down. I walked toward the opening."

Henry hesitated.

"Henry?" Johnny said. "What did you find?"

But Johnny already knew. *Four human bodies crucified on wooden crosses . . .*

"Hell . . . It was the entire family, all of them. Ben-jamin Conroy. Faith Conroy. And their kids, Daniel and Elizabeth. They'd been . . . crucified. There were four wooden crosses, each one sized to fit a family member's body. There was a fifth cross, maybe two feet tall—just the perfect size to fit a baby. But there was no baby on that cross . . . it was . . . it was . . ."

"That tiny cross," Johnny said. "It was meant for me, wasn't it?"

Henry nodded. "But Benjamin couldn't get to you, so he crucified the family dog instead."

Sickened, Johnny sighed heavily.

Henry stared at Johnny, eyes welling with tears, and continued . . .

"I couldn't move, my legs were paralyzed with fear. It took me a few seconds to realize that they were all still alive! Benjamin. Faith. Their kids. And the dog too. I couldn't possibly see how—they'd sustained in-juries that no human could ever live through. Stab wounds, gougings, harsh beatings—the damn boy'd been disemboweled! Yet, there they were, writhing on these wooden crosses, moaning, each and every god-damned one of them tugging at the nails driven into their hands and feet. They had no idea I was watching

them. Oh dear Lord, there . . . there was so . . .
much . . . blood . . ."

Tears welled in Johnny's eyes. "Where was I,
Henry?" But Henry seemed not to hear him. The man
was lost in memories. . . .

"After a while, I realized I was still holding my gun.
I pointed it, at no one Conroy in particular. I knew that
by shooting them, I wouldn't be putting them out of
their miseries. No. These people had already died. And
they'd risen from the dead."

Johnny nodded. "Like Judson and the psycho."

"I could only assume it had something to do with the
occult painting on the ground. Jesus, they were all
groaning, these monsters, bleeding . . . bleeding and
hanging like slabs of meat in a slaughterhouse. Jesus,
there was no way for me to describe the scene, with the
blood and the human innards on the ground below
each of them. I began to wonder who could have done
this to them, but that lasted only a second, because
Benjamin Conroy said something. . . ."

"What, Henry? What did he say?"

"I could see Conroy staring at me with his only good
eye, and he was grimacing, and I went over to him, and
I saw he was different from the others. He . . . he
hadn't died yet. His wounds were brutal, but unlike the
others, his chest was heaving and I could hear a sick
wheeze in his lungs. Somehow he'd lived through it all.
With a horrible tearing sound, he pulled an arm free
from the crucifix, leaving the nail still set deep in the
wood. Blood spouted from his hand onto the ground.
But it didn't seem to hurt him. I walked up to him and
asked, 'What happened here, Benjamin?' and he said in
a croak, 'I was wrong.' And then he started to sob, and
I could only stare. And then Benjamin howled, 'Don't

let them come back! I was tricked. It was not Osiris! It was not Osiris!' "

"Osiris . . ." Johnny, keeping his eyes on Henry, dug into his pocket and pulled out the plastic bag containing Ed's suicide note. He plucked the note from the bag, but before he had a chance to show it to Henry, the man continued on.

" 'Who?' I asked. The others were aware of me now, and they were moaning. Benjamin Conroy looked over at his family: Faith, Elizabeth, and Daniel, all of them moaning like mad, and he was stricken with grief. His free arm reached toward them but he couldn't get their attention. 'Benjamin, who's this Osiris?' I asked, but he was dying. He slumped, one arm still nailed on the cross, his other dangling. I leaned in and heard him croak: 'I was wrong . . . don't let them come back.' I took aim with my gun, twelve inches from Faith Conroy's head. 'Is this what you want, Conroy?' I shouted, and with every last bit of strength left in his dying body, he nodded. So without hesitating I pulled the trigger. The woman's head exploded. There was a sound like no sound I'd ever heard before, like the howl of a jackal with its leg in a steel trap, and then a gush of foul air sprung up and hit me like a fist and nearly knocked me over. I staggered back, Benjamin nodded again weakly, telling me to do the same thing to his children . . . his children. The kids understood the end was close, and they were jerking and bucking like crazy on the crucifixes, screaming, trying to get down. Quick, with no thought, I planted bullets in each of their heads. Then there was a storm of howling wind that stunk of sulfur and rotting vegetables. It grabbed me and threw me to the ground. I crawled to my knees and waited until the storm faded. I struggled to my feet and went to help Benjamin, but he refused and said: 'The baby . . . in the basement.'"

"The baby," Johnny said. "Me."

"So I tore away from Benjamin Conroy and raced out of the barn, across the backyard, and into the house where the bloody trail was at its thickest. I found the basement door and pulled the tiny ball chain in the foyer leading downstairs. It lit up the tight staircase and I saw the sprawled body of Eddie Carlson lying at the bottom of the steps in a pool of blood. I ran down, but I could see immediately that Eddie was dead. Really dead. I knew he wasn't Conroy blood, and he hadn't been crucified. Maybe I was lying to myself, but my sole purpose, as it has been since stepping foot in the barn, was to save anyone in danger. In the basement there should have been a baby, but I couldn't hear anything and I thought for a moment that Benjamin tricked me into some trap. I stopped in my tracks. But then I heard something: a baby whimpering! In a mad rush, I followed the sound toward a crawlspace in the cement wall. Inside was a bundle of burlap and rags. I pulled it out, and found baby Bryan Conroy. . . ."

"Me," Johnny said.

"I unwrapped the baby. His face was swollen from crying, but he appeared OK. I ran back through the basement, stepping over poor Eddie Carlson's body. Holding the baby close, I got up the stairs and followed the bloody trail back outside, and that's when I realized that Benjamin Conroy, devoted father and husband, revered minister of the 'Organization of God,' had done all this. He killed his family and Eddie Carlson. And then when I reached the bottom step of the porch I wondered: Who crucified Benjamin?"

Henry paused, and Johnny asked, "Who was it? Who *did* crucify Benjamin?"

Henry's eyes glistened with tears.

"No sooner did I ask myself that, than it was answered. Benjamin appeared in the doorway of the barn. He was on his knees, hands and feet shredded and bloody from the crucifix; I could see a nail still in his right hand. Clutching the baby tightly, I took a few steps but Benjamin Conroy yelled 'stop!,' and I saw no choice but to stop. I opened my mouth, but he yelled, 'It wasn't my doing! It was the darkness—the bird who carries its soul. I was tricked! It wasn't Osiris. It was the darkness!' At first I didn't understand him. But then I saw it, the darkness, and I knew it was the darkness that had crucified Benjamin during the ceremony. As I watched, it grabbed him . . . a shadow of a thing with black arms and withered feathers floating down from it. It came from inside the barn and it swallowed Benjamin. It saved his face for last . . . his face with its one eye bulging in terror and a bleeding mouth that shouted, 'Don't let it have Bryan, take him away!' I tried to step back, but there was something holding me, pulling me closer to the barn, and I saw a bird perched on the roof of the barn. It was whispering to me. 'Henry. Save our dying souls. Bring us our blood, bring us our blood.' I watched Benjamin Conroy disappear into the blackness, the blackness that filled the doorway to the barn and called to me. . . ."

Johnny swallowed past the dry lump forming in his throat. "You saved my life, Henry. It was you."

Henry, finally pulling himself away from his memories, gazed at Johnny and shook his head. "It was Eddie Carlson, who saved your life."

Johnny needed a moment to soak it all in. The dream

he had just two nights ago came back to him, where he was being carried by a young man, and he could see the young man with his keen features and blond hair and intense gray eyes, how he'd looked so frightened, how he was running and crying and clutching Johnny close to his chest, how they were in a house, somewhere dark and musty, how the young man in his panic had wrapped Johnny up in burlap and slid him into a cool dark space, then turned and disappeared into the shadows, where he screamed and screamed and screamed. . . .

"I remember him, Henry. I remember Eddie Carlson. I don't know how, but it's as clear as day to me now."

"There's a lot more you won't be able to understand. I've spent the last seventeen years trying to understand, Johnny. And I still don't understand it all." He sighed. "But I believe things are about to change."

Without hesitation, Johnny said, "I'm ready . . . but first, please tell me, what happened after Benjamin disappeared into the darkness?"

Henry took a deep breath. "I remember standing there for a very long time. Who knows how long? I was in shock, I guess, and whatever it was that got Benjamin was trying to lure me in as well. A part of me wanted to give in too, surrender the baby and explore the hidden mysteries in the barn. But there was another part of me that fought the urge and probably saved my life. At the time I didn't understand what it was, but I think now it was the baby in my arms protecting me. Protecting itself."

Johnny nodded, somehow understanding.

"A couple hours later, I was found by my deputy, Carl Davies, who got a frantic call from Mrs. D. and followed my usual path home and found my car in the Conroy driveway. I came to in a panic and told him about the bodies in the barn, and Eddie Carlson, and that I'd found the baby in the house and tried to get away. I remember carrying the baby to my car while Carl investigated the barn. He came back a minute later choking, almost in a panic.

"The investigation lasted a couple of weeks. After an autopsy proved that I hadn't killed the Conroys, that they were dead before I shot them, the bodies were cremated at the request of Mary Petrie, the family's only known relative, who immediately took custody of you. Soon after that, the rear of the barn under the loft where the crime took place was boarded over, mainly to discourage curiosity seekers. Of course, I couldn't honestly explain why I'd shot all the 'dead bodies,' so I kept silent in my defense. Everyone assumed I'd cracked from the stress and it was recommended that I relinquish my post as sheriff, which I agreed to. Carl took my place and was extremely cooperative in letting me investigate Benjamin Conroy's past by going through all his papers and journals."

"And what did you find?" Johnny asked.

"I found the work of a man who was on to something incredible."

CHAPTER THIRTY-SIX

September 9, 2005
2:24 A.M.

Mary Petrie drove on a Maine back road, the full moon she followed tossing its ethereal glow across the hissing wheat fields surrounding her. Her new consciousness had won the battle against her old powerless ways, and she was once again in full control.

She peered at Ed in the rearview mirror. The pea cap on his head had shifted down and was now covering his sunglasses. The wheelchair, still anchored to the floor, squeaked with every turn, cautioning Mary to take the sharp bends slowly.

She made a right turn onto Flower King Road, which in a few miles would escape the sea of wheat fields and cross over onto Farland Avenue, the lifeblood of Wellfield's business district. In her right hand she still gripped the feather, its silky surface coated with sweat. *Johnny needs me*, she thought, glancing at the feather. *Ed needs me too. And I'll do whatever it takes to help them, to save them.*

Save their dying souls.

She drove along at a reduced speed, taking in all the sights that had made up her life prior to seventeen years ago: the wheat, the cracked road, the faded street signs jutting crookedly at every back-road intersection.

Again she looked in the rearview mirror.

Ed was no longer there.

With a sudden, violent bang, the wheelchair slammed against the rear of the van. Mary screamed with horror, her new consciousness instantly gone, not even a whisper of it left to battle the weakness that had previously dominated her life.

And didn't know how to drive.

In a panic, Mary slammed her foot down on the accelerator. The van lunged forward. She screamed again and jerked her foot to the left and slammed down on the brake. The van's tires squealed. The wheelchair rolled forward and thumped into the back of her seat. She fought with the wheel but couldn't gain control. The van fishtailed, then careened off the road and crashed into the six-foot-tall wheat stalks, where it came to a rubber-burning standstill ten feet deep.

Here she remained, panting, shivering with shock. She counted out the seconds in silence, then noticed something gripped in her sweating hand: a feather. She had no idea how it got there and shook it away with disgust, as though it were a large spider.

A thump in the back of the van startled her. She heard a loud wheezing gasp and glanced into the rearview mirror.

A set of hands—bloated, black, and bloody—reached up over the back of the seat.

She clawed at the door handle. It popped, but the door wouldn't budge against the confining wall of wheat. She looked over her shoulder and saw the horribly mottled hands, their groping fingers gripping the headrest of her seat.

She screamed again. She sprawled across the seat toward the passenger door, peering up at the hands that were advancing over the seat, now visible to the forearms.

Mary looked up at the passenger-side window. Here the swaying wheat was partially crushed, affording her some room to open the door. She yanked the door's handle, but it was locked. Her hand shot up to the lock and pulled it.

The demented wheeze behind her grew, and for a moment it sounded like an attempt to speak. She saw the gripping, flexing hands, and the words *save my dying soul* filled her head. Then something shifted, and a head surfaced over the back of the seat.

Mary, mother of God!

It was Ed. His face was a bloated mess, as bloodlessly white as his hands were black. His cheeks were caked with blood and mold. His eyes, a clouded gray-blue, were filled with dreadful consciousness. His lips split open with a tearing sound. Black blood oozed from the corners of his mouth in twin rivulets. A pair of plastic sunglasses dangled from his right ear like a wind-torn branch.

Mary yanked on the door's handle. Leveraging her feet on the steering wheel, she drove her weight against the door. It swung out into the wheat, granting her perhaps twelve inches of fleeing space. She wriggled forward, grabbed the edge of the door, and pulled her body forward. The bitter smell of wheat and soil swam over her.

Ed wheezed again, and when Mary glanced around she saw a thick gouge in his neck widening like a mouth. With alarming speed, he clambered over the seat, laid hold of her legs, and yanked her backwards. Mary fought vainly against him, grabbing blindly at the glove compartment, which flipped open and spilled its contents on the floor. He yanked her again. She rolled over the seat, then down against the hard floor. There was a loud crack somewhere inside her. White hot pain lanced across her torso.

Through blurred vision, Mary gazed up at her monster of a husband, his coated, milky-white eyes rolling obscenely toward her. The horrible gash in his throat flapped open and wheezed again. Coagulated blood flew out from it and spattered Mary's face. He regarded Mary with no recognition, only purposeful anger.

Mary sputtered, "Ed . . . w-hat . . . is . . . this . . . ?"

Ed wheezed. Again it sounded as if he were trying to speak. Finally he succeeded. *"Dying souls . . ."*

He then sprung at Mary, incredibly fast and incredibly powerful.

CHAPTER THIRTY-SEVEN

September 9, 2005
2:48 A.M.

Johnny held a Bible in his hands. It had seen better days, tattered and torn and frayed at every corner. On nearly every page, a vast array of lines crisscrossed back and forth between circled letters and words.

"If you'll notice," Henry said, "in the spaces between the crossing lines are bold black letters, which, if written down alongside one another, spell out a phrase. It's in the same pattern on every page. It's a code."

"A code . . ." A sense of wonder washed over Johnny, and despite feeling tired and achy and scared, he wanted to hear more of Benjamin Conroy's—his father's—mysterious past.

Appearing fidgety and nervous, Henry leaned forward and began telling Johnny about the rituals Benjamin had performed on himself and his family. "It was Benjamin's belief, based on the code he found in the Bible, that Jesus could rise from the dead because Jesus himself had explored the magical rituals spelled out in the Egyptian *Book of the Dead*." Henry reached over and retrieved a notebook on his desk. He opened it and showed it to Johnny; it was filled with scrawled text. "Conroy found this phrase in code in seventeen different places in the New Testament:

"I, Jesus Christ, son of God, beseech thee, O Spirit Osiris from the underworld, by the supreme majesty of God, so that I may benefit from your empowering gift."

Henry turned the page. "And then here, this phrase is present in fifteen places:

"Grant thyself with everlasting afterlife by sacrificing thy skin with life's symbol."

At once, upon hearing the second phrase, Johnny's scar began to itch and burn. He unbuttoned his shirt and displayed it to Henry. "An ankh," Johnny said. "Life's symbol."

Henry stared at the gnarled skin, and Johnny could see him shudder. "I saw it when I came out to get you from Carl's car. You were out cold and twitching, having a bad dream perhaps. . . ."

Five makeshift crucifixes jutting crookedly from the hard ground. Nailed upon them were the bodies of a man, a woman, a young girl, a boy. . . .

"Your shirt was rolled up around your neck, and I saw the scar, and I knew it was you."

Johnny buttoned his shirt back up, thinking of his mother and how she'd always told him that the scar on his chest was a birthmark, a will of God. *And I believed her*, he thought incredulously. He felt sick to his stomach.

"Henry . . . are these code phrases for real?"

Henry nodded methodically. He leaned back in his chair and hurriedly returned the notebook to his desk. "Benjamin Conroy was wholly convinced that Jesus had known all along he would be crucified, and had performed a spell from *The Book of the Dead* prior to his death, with the intention of returning as a savior." Henry grabbed another tattered notebook, opened it, and flipped to a page somewhere in the middle. In a deep tone he read Benjamin's words: " 'I have proof of this . . . I have cracked a code in the Bible that reveals Jesus's use of Osiris's name in the New Testament. It is proof that Jesus himself had studied portions of the Egyptian *Book of the Dead* prior to his fall! Jesus rose from the dead because he evoked the spirit of Osiris! It is my opinion that these rituals can be utilized to allow me to repent for my sins in life, and allow me to bring my family with me into the afterlife, where we may remain together for an eternity, in peace.' "

Johnny swallowed nervously; all this talk of Jesus and dead men and Benjamin Conroy was overwhelming. He started to feel a little light-headed again. "So . . . was he right?"

"Yes. The codes are there. According to Conroy's interpretation, Jesus did indeed evoke a spirit to assist him in his quest to return from the dead as a savoir. But . . . it may not have been Osiris."

"Who was it, then?"

Henry shrugged. He looked away from Johnny toward some nondescript place on his desk. "That's exactly what we need to find out."

Abruptly, Henry stood. He picked up Ed's suicide note and stared at the repeated word intently as if *it* might contain some secret code. "According to *The*

Book of the Dead, Osiris was a benevolent god, and upon being summoned from the underworld, or astral plane, he would grant the deserving conjurer his wish. If there'd been any disruption in the ritual, then the spirit would depart, leaving the conjurer with nothing more than the will to try again. Benjamin had written in his journal that during his final ritual, his son Daniel had created a disturbance that made everything go wrong.

"He blamed Daniel's noncompliance for all the evils that befell the family that fateful afternoon. But his final written ramblings show a change. He'd had numerous affairs with local women, and had sought a way to repent for his sins. He felt God would never forgive him for what he'd done and that he and his family would burn for his transgressions. So he turned to another god in a quest for forgiveness. On the surface, it'd seemed to work for him. But he'd been misguided, and ultimately, he'd come to fear that it was something *foul* that had ruined his lifelong efforts—that in his conjurings, he had unwittingly become a demonologist of some sort."

Henry peered out the window for a second. "Right after that, Benjamin Conroy murdered his family, a local woman by the name of Helen Mackey, and Eddie Carlson."

After a moment of silence, Johnny said, "You were expecting me to come here, weren't you?"

Henry nodded. "As you know, I've kept close tabs on you over the years—I had your pictures taken so I'd know what you looked like when you eventually arrived."

"And I'm assuming you did this, not only because you *knew* I would return to Wellfield, but because I'm part of the puzzle, and you need my help."

Henry nodded again.

Johnny sighed, feeling no choice but to resign himself to Henry's still undisclosed plan. "So then, what's going to happen to me?"

"Honestly, I don't know. But what I do know is that I'm the only person in Wellfield who knows what's happening, and that it's my job—my destiny—to put an end to it all before someone else gets killed."

And comes back from the dead, Johnny thought.

Brother . . .

Johnny looked into Henry's eyes. "Well . . . *I* know now. And I believe."

Henry smiled thinly, and Johnny could see a measure of gratitude in his tired eyes. Still, that did nothing to assuage Johnny's fear.

"What was it, Henry?" Johnny asked.

"Pardon?"

"The spirit Benjamin conjured up. If it wasn't Osiris, then . . . what was it? And I know you know, so please don't avoid the question."

Henry looked out the window again, took a deep breath, then confessed, "A malevolent spirit. It's my opinion that it had appeared to Benjamin that fateful day as the spirit Osiris. But . . . it was in disguise." Looking suddenly nervous, Henry stood and paced back and forth, looking around the room as if the evil spirit he spoke of might suddenly appear. "Once the spirit was evoked, it began to work its evil on those present—on the Conroy family."

I was there, Johnny thought. *What evil did it work on me?*

"It used Benjamin to kill his family. As soon as they were dead, it corralled all their souls and sealed them in its domain; the place it came from."

"The barn," Johnny muttered, thinking again of the

trap door in the loft and how a gust of hot, stinking air geysered up from below when he had opened it; how the whispering voices ascended from the darkness below.

Our dying souls are free. . . .

"Correct. But because you were never crucified, it wasn't able to follow through with its intentions to deliver all their souls to hell. It's been holding them all these years, waiting for you to return to Wellfield so it can gather up your soul and complete what Benjamin started. I've spent years studying the ritual—the one hidden in the Bible and many related ones, and even though I can't be certain of the spirit Jesus himself conjured, I do know that somewhere along the line, Benjamin failed and the spirit he conjured was anything but benevolent. Johnny, the souls of the Conroys *have returned.* They believe that once your soul is gathered, they'll be released to continue toward ancestral afterlife in the astral plane. But it's not true! They're being misguided by the evil that possesses them. Once they retain your soul, you and the rest of the Conroys will be ushered into hell!"

"And that's how you knew I would eventually return here," Johnny said. All of a sudden, the feather in his pocket grew warm.

Henry nodded fearfully. "We have to stop them, Johnny. Stop *it.*"

"So just how *do* we stop them?" Johnny asked.

"We need to ask the only person who knows."

"Who's that?"

"Eddie Carlson."

Chapter Thirty-eight

September 9, 2005
3:11 A.M.

Beneath the cool blue light of the moon, two bodies emerged from the back doors of a still-running van that sat in a wheat field ten feet from the edge of Flower King Road. They staggered down the road, the glow of the van's taillights pointing the way. There wasn't a soul or a vehicle within miles, as they moved steadily, purposefully, toward the outskirts of Wellfield.

Toward their home. The Conroy house.

CHAPTER THIRTY-NINE

September 9, 2005
3:17 A.M.

"Eddie Carlson? The dead kid? I don't understand."

"Soon you will."

"But he's *dead*—been dead for seventeen years."

Henry grinned. "If I told you the lawyer promising you a small fortune would be murdered by an escapee from an insane asylum, only to come back to life in an attempt to kill you, would you believe me?"

Johnny stared expressionlessly at Henry, then shook his head.

"Which leads me to another important factor: the the man who murdered Judson is in fact David Mackey. His mother, Helen Mackey, was having an affair with Benjamin Conroy. The bodies of Helen and her husband were found murdered at Benjamin's church on the same day the Conroy family was killed.

Their boy, David, who was fourteen at the time, was there as well. Somehow he survived the attack but came out of it severely injured, partially blind, and brain damaged. He fell into a coma for three years, and up until his escape a few days ago, had lived out his days at the Pine Oak Institute for the Mentally Insane, about ten miles from here."

"I suppose it's no coincidence that he escaped when I returned to Wellfield."

"And it's no coincidence that both he and Judson were killed." He paused for a moment, seemingly trying to collect his thoughts. "It's my belief that the souls of the Conroys need the bodies of those close to their blood in order to walk the earth. And walking the earth is the only way they can come to gather your soul—to *murder you.*"

Johnny's jaw dropped. "So what you're saying is . . . the bodies of the psycho and Judson contain the souls of two dead Conroys. . . ."

Henry nodded.

Brother . . .

Johnny shook his head. He was tired, confused. His eyesight blurred.

Henry moved to the closet and opened the door. "Since the animated bodies of Judson and Mackey called you brother, we can assume that the souls within them are Daniel and Elizabeth Conroy. The souls of Benjamin and Faith are out there as well, and at this moment are seeking recently deceased people who have held some association with you."

"But I don't know anyone else here."

"Then the evil driving their souls will lure them in."

"How—?"

"I don't know for sure. But it happened with Andrew

Judson, a man who'd spent years waiting for you to turn eighteen, and then David Mackey, whose parents were murdered by Benjamin Conroy. And . . . I'm afraid it just may happen with me." Henry rubbed his cheek solemnly. "Once all four Conroy souls walk the earth again, they can retrieve you and complete the ritual Benjamin wasn't able to finish all those years ago."

Henry reached into the closet and dragged out a huge black trunk, nearly six feet tall. Johnny helped him and together they carried it into the middle of the room. At once Henry undid the twin clasps, opened the lid, and gestured toward the contents.

Inside the trunk were a number of crudely cut wooden planks, all different sizes. They were stained with dark brown Rorschach test–like blotches.

"What is this?" Johnny asked in a near-whisper, his scar itching ferociously again.

"The wood from the crosses your family was crucified on." Henry dug inside and pulled out a small leather pouch; it too was old and worn. He untied the sash at the top. "And these," he said, emptying the contents of the bag in his hand, "are the nails they were crucified with."

Johnny studied the six-inch spikes, each one as thick as a pencil, rusted and stained with blood. "Seems like Carl Davies let you keep more than Benjamin's journals."

"He's always been sympathetic to my efforts. He was there that night. He saw the bodies on the crosses."

Johnny hesitated, unable to look away from the bloodstains on the nails. *Conroy blood. My blood* . . . "So why are you showing me all this, Henry?"

"Because it will help us contact Eddie Carlson."

"How?"

"At some point they're going to come for us, Johnny. I think it's best we move on and get this over with." He shut the trunk, latched it, and grabbed one end. "Help me carry this downstairs, and I'll try to explain."

Heart thudding, Johnny gripped the worn leather handle on the opposite end, and helped Henry haul the trunk down the steps into the foyer, where they placed it on the floor next to the front door.

Henry stepped aside and peered out the front window, cupping his hands against the glass. Johnny asked, "Is Eddie Carlson's soul out there too, looking for a dead body to inhabit?"

Henry turned from the window and walked into the dining room. "No, he was never crucified," he responded absently. "His soul is at peace."

"So then how are we supposed to contact him?" Johnny did his best to catch up with Henry, who was now walking quickly down the hall.

"A séance," Henry said. "Eddie Carlson saved your life once before, and I'm afraid we'll need him to save it again." He went into the kitchen, where he stopped dead in his tracks, his face a sudden, sweaty white.

Johnny, trailing Henry, nearly slammed into him. He leaned to his left and peered around him.

The back door was wide open. He could see a wash of blood on the exposed jamb . . . and then the wind gusted in from outside and brought with it a horrible stench of decay that was instantly familiar. Johnny looked up and saw mosquitoes the size of tiny birds dancing across the kitchen ceiling.

"Oh my God!" Henry shouted.

Johnny fell in behind Henry as he lunged outside. Henry halted at the top of the porch steps, staring wordlessly into the darkness. Johnny saw Henry's eyes bulge and his mouth gape in terror.

And then Henry Depford screamed. Johnny followed Henry's line of sight and realized that the inconceivable horrors of the day had started again.

There were two bodies sprawled in the moonlit grass just feet from the porch steps. One of them was David Mackey. His body was motionless, arms and legs outstretched from a torso bent back into a hideous *C* shape. A thick wash of blood flooded his open mouth and glistened wetly beneath the silver light of the moon. Alongside him was Mrs. D. She too was lying in the grass, her head skewed at an impossible right angle—cheek-to-shoulder—a huge gaping wound in her exposed neck gushing redly from where Mackey had gnawed at her flesh.

Henry and Johnny both stepped forward, and Henry saw Mrs. D.'s body twitch. "She's still alive, Johnny!" Henry cried.

For a moment Johnny was prepared to agree with Henry, until her head creaked sideways and he saw her eyes, bright and bulging and glistening malevolently beneath the moonlight, her mouth opening and closing.

She croaked, *"Brother . . ."*

Seized with horror, Johnny gripped Henry's biceps and said, "We need to get out of here." He yanked on Henry's arm and the two of them ran back into the house.

Once inside, Henry walked unsteadily into the front foyer and grabbed one end of the chest. "Johnny . . . c'mon . . ." he uttered weakly, eyes wet with tears.

Johnny grabbed the opposite handle and helped Henry lug the chest out the front door.

Here, in contrast to the scene out back, the night

was eerily silent, save for the trees that whispered in the distance. Henry and Johnny took the porch steps one at a time, then scrambled as quickly as possible to the driveway and rested the trunk against the bumper of the black pickup. Henry lowered the tailgate, and Johnny helped hoist the trunk onto the flatbed.

Together they slammed the tailgate shut, then quickly skirted around the truck and into the cab. Henry secured the locks as soon as the doors were shut.

"David's body . . ." Henry exclaimed, panting, shaking his head. "It-It was probably too battered . . . the soul inside . . . my God, it *switched*."

Suddenly, the front door to the house burst open, and dead Mrs. D. was there. Her head rolled from her broken neck, making her look like a child's rag doll. She tottered down the steps, heaving, staring, snatching at the air. *"Brother!"* she snarled, her voice deep and guttural.

"God rest her soul," Henry sobbed. "My dear God . . ." For a moment Henry stayed frozen, staring at his wife, who had become a living monster. She tottered unsteadily across the lawn, bathed in the ghostly amber glow of the porchlight, head lying on her shoulder.

"Henry," Johnny said, "start the car."

Henry groped at the ignition. There were no keys.

"Jesus, Henry!" Johnny shouted, his mind racing with panic. "Please tell me you have the damn keys!" He glanced out the window.

Mrs. D. stretched her arms toward Johnny, her wound spitting blood as she moaned: *"Brother!"*

Henry yanked down the sun visor. The keys jingled out onto his lap. He fumbled for them desperately and finally ferreted out the right one.

"Thank God!" Johnny said. "Now! C'mon! She's coming!" His blood went cold. In his peripheral vision he could see Mrs. D. just a few feet away from his window.

Henry slid the key into the ignition and started the truck.

What used to be Mrs. D., who not two hours earlier had fixed Johnny a sandwich and a hot cup of coffee, slammed her bloody hands against the window. Johnny leaped, staring wide-eyed out the window at the woman whose head rolled repulsively on her broken neck; whose blood-matted hair was home now to mosquitoes and buzzing horseflies.

"Henry! Please!" Johnny shouted as Mrs. D. pressed her sideways face against the window and peered in at Johnny, her mouth yawning up and down, leaving smears of blood and foamy saliva on the glass.

Henry, staring with horror at the thing that used to be his wife, yanked the shift into reverse and launched the truck backwards up the driveway. Mrs. D. fell away from the truck and collapsed to the ground like a wounded soldier. In the cloud of dust they left behind, Johnny could see her grappling with the gravel in her struggle to rise back up.

The truck's tires squealed against the road as they sped backwards out of the driveway. Henry, not once looking back at his living-dead wife, pulled away from his home in terror-filled silence, tears streaming down his face.

CHAPTER FORTY

September 9, 2005
3:46 A.M.

The man and woman who'd staggered away from the van in the wheat field thirty minutes earlier stepped down the driveway of the Conroy house, their deadened eyes staring at the barn out back. A third figure appeared from the porch of the home, a man. He was naked, but earlier he had worn a shirt and a tie and a pair of dress pants, which now lay in a tattered pile in the driveway. His abdomen was a gaping cavity, devoid of its innards. Together, the three figures entered the barn.

In the darkness of the loft above, a single black bird watched them, fluttering its wings and cocking its head as they began to gather wood from the splintered stairway in the back of the barn. . . .

CHAPTER FORTY-ONE

September 9, 2005
3:48 A.M.

A minute of brutal silence passed before Johnny said, "This is all my fault. I'm so sorry, Henry."

Henry shook his head firmly. "It's Benjamin Conroy's fault. Don't blame yourself for any of this. You're an innocent pawn in this. Nothing more." He turned the truck left onto Brunswick Road, the same road where Carl Davies had found Johnny aimlessly wandering. The trunk in the back slid across the metal bed and slammed against the side panel with a jarring thud.

Johnny cracked his window a few inches, trying to steady himself with a lungful of fresh air. "What are we gonna do now? Where are we going?"

"We have v-very little time," Henry replied, his voice cracking. He sounded suddenly disoriented, lost in thought. When Johnny looked over at him, he saw a pale, blank expression on his face. *Seeing your wife getting killed and coming back from the dead will do that to a man*, Johnny thought.

Henry continued, "I never imagined it would happen this way, this *quickly*. I mean, how could they have known to find you at my home? Unless . . ."

"Unless what?"

He coughed loudly, eyes tearing, then said, "It states in *The Book of the Dead* that evil's messenger will leave behind an object, a homing device if you will, to help keep its target in sight. Something must have drawn them to us, Johnny. It's the only logical explanation."

At that moment, the feather grew warm in Johnny's pocket. Another wave of fear settled in his stomach like an icy weight. "Oh my God . . ." He dug out the plastic bag, gazing speechlessly at the long black quill within.

"What's that?"

"A feather. I found it on the fire escape of my apartment the night Ed killed himself. I . . . I think it may be what attracted them to us. To *me*."

"Get rid of it, Johnny," Henry said uncomfortably, not looking over at it. "Now!"

Johnny hesitated. His hands trembled at the mere thought of ridding himself of it. Whatever this feather was, whatever it represented, it was still working its magic on him, maintaining its hold on him. Johnny knew it, but couldn't do anything about it. "I . . . I . . ."

"*Now!*" Henry shouted.

Johnny beat back his lying instincts, and in a quick fluid motion, let the bag fly out the cracked window. As soon as the bag and its feather vanished into the night, a tidal wave of weakness, both mental and physical, washed over him. The grayness that had pulled him away from reality earlier in the evening threatened to bury him again. His head bobbed forward, and his breathing suddenly grew ragged.

"Stay with me, Johnny," Henry pleaded, slowing the truck so he could focus on Johnny's wavering state of mind. "That feather carried with it an illusion of strength . . . it was given to you by the evil spirit, furnishing you with a false energy to continue on. But now, it's lost its grip on you—now you have the ability to break free of its commands. You have the strength and the will to carry on without it. You've come this far, don't give up now."

Henry's words filtered into Johnny's consciousness like a hypnotist's commands—he felt himself being pulled away from the invading blackness, back toward the living world. He started to come back around again. The grayness in his sights cleared. He opened his eyes, took a deep breath, then looked over at Henry.

"You okay?" Henry asked.

Johnny shook his head. "I don't think so. I feel weak. Confused. *Scared.*"

"And understandably so—the evil influence that gave you the strength to carry out its plan is gone now. It's your own resolve now that'll let you defeat it. You have control of your own destiny. Be strong, Johnny."

A massive wave of anxiety rained down on Johnny, and he began to panic. "Oh my God, I . . . I . . . don't think I can do this. . . ."

"We're almost there, Johnny," Henry said. "You have to take control and be prepared."

Johnny didn't answer. He closed his eyes and wished it all away.

"Johnny?"

"Henry . . . I can't . . ."

"You have to! If you want to live, you have to find the strength to confront the evil that wants to destroy you!"

"Why can't I just leave?" Johnny shouted, despite knowing the answer.

Henry reaffirmed what Johnny already suspected. "It won't let you go. The only way out of Wellfield is to face the evil here and defeat it."

"But without the feather . . . how can it follow me now?"

Henry paused, seemingly thinking, then shocked Johnny by saying, "I won't force you to do anything you feel you can't do. If you insist on leaving, then I'll just drive right past the Conroy house and take you anywhere you want to go. But understand this: For seventeen years I've studied the hidden rituals in the Bible, the Conroy events, and so much more above and beyond what I've told you. When evil wants you, *requires* you, there's no avoiding it. And, Bryan Conroy, the evil here most definitely wants you."

Johnny bit his lip. His heart pounded furiously with the urgent need to escape once and for all. "Keep going, Henry. I can't do this."

Henry grimaced, then gripped the steering wheel tightly and stepped harder on the gas pedal. The truck sped up. The Conroy house appeared on their left like a looming monster.

Henry shouted, "Oh my God!" and slammed on the brakes.

Johnny, heart leaping, braced against the dashboard with both hands, knuckles white. Through the windshield he saw a dog, a large yellow lab, leaping out in front of the truck. Henry fought with the wheel in a desperate effort to avoid hitting the dog. The truck skidded, back wheels fishtailing to the right, but slammed into the dog with a sickening thud. There was a loud explosive sound of a tire blowing. The dog's bulk got caught up beneath the chassis, slowing the truck down before it crashed into an oak tree directly in front of the Conroy house.

The engine ticked, then died. Dreadful silence followed.

When he could breathe again, Johnny looked sideways at Henry. "You okay?"

Henry nodded and coughed. Strips of wispy gray hair dangled in his eyes like cobwebs. "I told you—it's not going to let us leave."

The notion of fleeing Wellfield once and for all was as dead as the dog they'd just hit. Johnny ran a hand across his forehead; it came away wet with blood. *Conroy blood.* He shuddered, and looked out the window toward the house.

"It's waiting for us," Henry said, devoid of emotion.

Johnny saw no alternative but to go along with Henry's plan of defeating Wellfield's evil spirit. *It's either that, or I die. Might as well get it over with.*

"So what do we do now?" His eyes were fixed on the house. It looked bigger, more threatening now in the dead of night than it did when he'd first arrived yesterday afternoon.

"We need to contact Eddie Carlson. I believe he's the only one who knows how to defeat this evil."

Johnny wiped his bleeding forehead with the bottom of his shirt. Suddenly he said, "Is this realistic? I mean, there're goddamned ghouls out there that want to kill us. I really don't think we have time to light candles and burn incense and call out for some dead teenager."

Henry, also gazing at the house, replied, "This isn't

the movies." He leaned over, opened the glove compartment, and retrieved a large utility flashlight and a handgun. He checked the gun to make certain it was loaded, then spun it closed. "This former sheriff wasn't going to give up *all* his privileges." He opened the door and slid out of the truck. "C'mon, help me with the trunk."

CHAPTER FORTY-TWO

September 9, 2005
3:59 A.M.

The two men and the woman dragged the wood from the broken staircase into the center of the barn. They moved slowly, their eyes not focused on the task at hand, but upwards toward the black bird that watched them from the edge of the loft. They used the steps to leverage one of the side beams into a vertical position, with nearly twelve inches of its base buried firmly into the hard soil. Utilizing the rope from the broken extension ladder, they secured a second side beam from the steps against the first beam at a right-angle position about three-quarters of the way up. As soon as their work was completed, a second woman entered the barn. Her neck was broken and her head rested sideways upon her shoulder. She was wearing a nightdress with a dark bloodstain that extended from her shoulder to the lower hem. She looked at the bird, then along with the others gazed vacantly at the six-foot crucifix erected at the center of the barn. . . .

CHAPTER FORTY-THREE

September 9, 2005
4:06 A.M.

"You hear that?" Henry said, stopping to look toward the barn.

"What is it?"

"It's . . . *them*."

Johnny eyed the barn nervously. It sat beneath the moonlit gloom amidst the tall grass like a huge spider preparing to leap across its web. The lone window frame beneath its peak stared down at them like a reproachful eye. *I can smell it*, Johnny thought. *It reeks of death*. His hand cramped terribly beneath the trunk's worn leather handle, a result of having to lug it from the front of the property all the way to the back porch.

Henry squinted. "I can't see them, but I know they're back there. I can *feel* them." He stood stiff and motionless, staring, listening.

A few tense moments passed, and Johnny saw something in Henry's face that worried him. Perhaps it was the man's eyes, glassy and glued unwaveringly to the darkness—a darkness that revealed nothing to Johnny. Finally, Johnny whispered, "Henry?"

Henry remained still, oblivious to Johnny's voice.

"Henry . . ." Johnny tried again, now using his free hand to nudge Henry's arm.

The former sheriff shook his head, then, after blinking his eyes, stared blankly at Johnny.

"We need to get the trunk into the house, and then you have to tell me what to do."

Henry nodded indifferently, clearly disoriented and confused. He took a deep, labored breath. "Okay, let's go."

They went into the house, Henry sluggishly wielding the flashlight's beam. A dusty and bitter odor struck Johnny immediately, and he wrinkled his nose with disgust. *It didn't smell like this earlier today. It smells like dead things*, he thought.

After Johnny locked the door behind them, he followed Henry through the kitchen, down the hall into the living room. When they reached the bottom of the steps, Johnny peered up into the pitch darkness of the second floor and wondered with dismay what kind of evils lurked up there.

Henry continued into the dining room, and Johnny followed, shuddering as he crossed the threshold.

"Haven't been here since the day it all happened," Henry whispered, eyeing the moldy mattress leaning up against the wall. "I remember it like it was yesterday."

Johnny had heard Henry's words, but he was distracted by Andrew Judson's blood on the floor. Suddenly panicked, he stopped and released his end of the trunk. It thumped loudly on the floor, rattling the windows and shaking the dusty light fixture. There he remained, unmoving, staring at the dimly lit puddle. It was still damp and tacky and glistening, peppered with mosquitoes and moths that had met their fates in the mess.

"Dying souls . . ."

Johnny gasped. His hand went to his mouth and his eyes widened with horror. Had he just heard a voice come from the blood? No, it couldn't be. He was instantly aware of the hair on the back of his neck standing on end. He looked away from the black pool, thinking for a split second that he had seen a slight ripple of movement in its reflection.

"Dying souls," the voice whispered in his head again.

Henry, unaware of Johnny's fear, hunkered down on one knee and opened the trunk, grimacing painfully. "They'll be here soon. We have to get started. Help me with the wood." He began removing the planks, placing them in a neat row on the floor beside him. As he worked, he said, "There are three crucial factors that must be present when conducting a séance: the purpose, the quality of the sitters, and the location. We have a perfect combination of all three."

Trying to discount the voice in his head, Johnny grabbed a plank. His hand came in contact with a faded bloodstain on the rough surface, and in his head, the ancient voice returned, louder and clearer than before: *"Bryan . . . save our dying souls. . . ."*

His body froze, and he dropped the wood as if it were burning hot. The plank dropped and banged on the floor, producing a dead echo in the vacant house. His eyes shifted to the pool of blood and this time he *did* see a shadowy ripple in it, as though a ghostly finger were painting a line in its surface.

"What's wrong?" Henry asked worriedly, brows drawing together.

"They're here," Johnny replied softly. His throat felt as if it had been coated with tar.

"Then we have to begin now." Henry opened the the pouch of nails tied around his left wrist, then squatted down on the floor alongside the row of wood. He looked somehow *different*, pale and sickly. "The wood and the nails and the house will all serve as symbolic connections to our purpose." He set the flashlight between them, so that its beam provided enough light for them to see each other. He then removed the gun from his belt and placed it between his legs.

Johnny remained standing. He kept looking back at the moving puddle of blood; then at the sitting room doors, which were still open from when David Mackey leaped out and stabbed Andrew Judson with the garden spade.

"Johnny, please," Henry said urgently. "Sit down here and take my hands." Henry held his hands out, palms up, the pouch of nails hanging from his wrist like a carcass from a tree limb. Johnny shook his head and drew back, afraid to come any closer.

From the kitchen came a rattling sound at the back door.

Henry pinned Johnny with a severe stare, lips now drawn with anxiety and fear. "Now, Johnny! Come here now!"

Outside, the breeze picked up and shook the cloudy panes of the window. Johnny glanced toward the window and glimpsed a shadow stirring just beyond the grimy surface. He tried to step back, but his legs were numb with fear.

Henry leaped up and grabbed hold of Johnny's wrists. The fierce, abrupt move startled Johnny. They looked at each other for a second and then Henry collapsed, pulling Johnny with him . . . right on top of the wooden crucifix planks.

"Bryan Conroy, save our dying souls. . . ."

Johnny whimpered in pain. He made a weak attempt to pull away, but Henry held him tight.

The door in the kitchen rattled louder. The moving shadow at the window began clawing against the panes. Somewhere outside, Johnny heard a muffled banging, like an incessant fist against a door.

Thump . . . thump . . . thump . . .

Henry closed his eyes and almost silently began to pray. He was still gripping Johnny's wrists with both hands, pulling them now into his chest. All the noises beyond the walls of the house grew louder, closer.

Johnny made another attempt to pull away from Henry, but still to no avail. At that moment, Henry began to mutter in some odd foreign language Johnny didn't recognize. Henry's eyelids shot open, divulging wet, bloodshot eyes. His grip tightened painfully on Johnny's wrists.

Somewhere in the house, glass shattered.

Johnny startled. He yelled, "Henry! They're here!"

But Henry didn't hear him—he was buried in some type of powerful trance. His face was ashy, eyes twisted up into their sockets. Beads of sweat stood out on his forehead. There was a banging sound in the room and Johnny twisted his head toward the window, where the looming shadow was striking against the grimy panes. One of the panes shattered, and a bloody, wasted hand clawed through, the fingers swollen and creaky, flexing blindly in the air.

In a panic now, Johnny struggled even harder to jerk away from Henry's powerful grasp. Henry only tightened his grip and continued mumbling.

Until, suddenly, Johnny heard one intelligible word amid all the gibberish: "Eddie . . ."

Somewhere in the house, another window shattered. The clawing hand at the dining room window hacked away at the rotted frame, dislodging the paned glass. It dangled over the sill, scraping against the water-stained wall below like a wind-torn branch. Strangled moans crept in from outside. A second deadly, festering hand bludgeoned its way inside. Henry pulled hard on Johnny's wrists. Johnny didn't look at Henry or at the doorway where the sounds of dragging footsteps approached, but to the pool of blood on the floor . . . Andrew Judson's blood that now bubbled and rippled as though something was surfacing from its depths.

"What the hell . . ." Johnny's words were cut off by Henry's sudden, violent choking fit. Johnny tried to stand, and managed to climb to his knees, but Henry wouldn't allow him any further. Johnny looked back to the blood on the floor and watched with fascination as the liquid began to branch out from the jagged puddle like trickles of water crawling down the surface of a windshield.

They seemed to be forming letters.

"Henry!" Johnny shouted, turning back to the window. The bloated hands were gripping the sill. There was a moist, squashing sound. Blood and yellow matter trickled down the wall and dangling glass. Then, Andrew Judson's dead face appeared from the darkness beyond the frame. It was white and swollen and streaked with blood. The hair was a muddy and matted mess. His eyes, although coated milky white, sparkled with wicked intelligence and consciousness.

Johnny finally screamed. It broke the trance Henry was in, at least enough for Johnny to break away from his grasp. He climbed to his feet and backpedaled toward the door. Henry, in his half stupor, was fumbling for the gun in his lap.

Johnny looked back at the blood, and the twisting, veiny streaks were indeed forming letters along the edge of the puddle. He couldn't make them out in the darkness. "Henry! The blood! Look!"

Henry looked quickly. But he only shrugged his shoulders and shook his head.

In his peripheral vision, Johnny saw a flicker of movement to his left.

He whirled and saw them, standing in the doorway. His parents. His *dead* parents. Ed and Mary Petrie.

Johnny staggered back, tripped over his own feet and thudded down on his rear. The familiar invading grayness that had swallowed him earlier seeped back into his sight, threatening him with unconsciousness. Yet, in spite of everything, he was still able to clamber back against the moldy mattress, all the while gawking incredulously at the two monsters that had once been his parents. He wondered how they managed to get to Wellfield—and what had happened to them.

Ed killed himself. But Mary?

Mary. As she stepped into the flashlight's beam, Johnny could tell that she hadn't died that long ago. Unlike Ed and Judson, she still retained most of her facial features, despite having turned a pale blue. Her hair was Einstein wild, infused with bits of hay and dead grass. Her mud-spattered dress was torn open and her pale, flattened breasts swung as she shuffled into the room. Both she and Ed carried an unbearable stench, like a heap of dead fish beneath a hot summer sun.

Mary's mouth dropped open. Thick black fluid oozed jellylike from it as she croaked, *"Son."*

So here was the soul of either Faith Conroy, or Benjamin Conroy himself, free after seventeen years of otherworldly confinement to retrieve Johnny's soul.

To his right, Andrew Judson was battling his way into the room, fighting with the broken window. He was completely naked, his torso an empty pit gaping blackly like a huge opened mouth. His legs were caked with dried blood and debris. Henry aimed the gun at Judson, but his eyes were focused on Ed and Mary Petrie, the expression on his face one of mixed bewilderment and fear. Henry knew who these two dead people were, having spent many years keeping tabs on Johnny, and was just as baffled as Johnny as to how they ended up in Wellfield, as dead as Andrew Judson.

Johnny climbed to his feet, but saw no clear way out of the room. Ed and Mary were blocking the door, Judson the window. He tried the sitting room doors twenty feet away, but it was too late: Mrs. D. was there, clawing at the jamb with her sideways head and vertical mouth chomping back and forth, whispering, *"Brother."*

Andrew Judson turned his head toward Johnny. He moaned, *"Brother."*

In unison, both Ed and Mary Petrie, their voices deep and whistling, groaned, *"Son . . ."*

Johnny took a shaky step forward, keeping himself at a fair distance from all the living-dead Conroys. He caught a glimpse of the blood puddle. He could see the meandering lines now, branching out from the jagged edge to form two words:

Fifth Nail

"Henry!" Johnny shouted, pointing. "The blood! Look!"

Henry fired the gun at Andrew Judson. The bullet entered his midsection and exited through his back, punching a hole in the wall behind him. Plaster and dust flew everywhere.

But it didn't stop him.

"Jesus Christ!" Henry shouted in a panic, firing again, this time tearing out a hole in Judson's neck. Judson collapsed, flailing like an upturned cockroach. Something black as oil oozed from his neck, onto the floor.

Johnny shouted, "Fifth nail. It says fifth nail!"

Henry's eyes locked with Johnny's. "Where, Johnny? *Where does it say that?*"

Johnny felt a burning frustration rise in him. He turned to Ed and Mary. Almost instantly he sensed the true feelings of the souls within the rotting husks of the couple who had raised him. He sensed that they were hurting, had suffered terribly all these years, trapped by an evil force that had lied to them.

Johnny shouted again, "It says 'fifth nail'! It must be a message. From Eddie! In the blood!"

"Eddie didn't come!" Henry yelled, now staring despondently at his living-dead wife, still clawing at the doorway to the sitting room. Unexpectedly, Henry spun around, face drawn with hatred and anger. He pointed the gun at Ed Petrie, and fired. It punched a fist-sized hole into Ed's chest. A shower of bloody gristle sprayed the wall behind him like sauce on a stovetop. Ed staggered and fell. His head, having been nearly severed, rolled to the side, exposing a ghastly white strip of spine.

"Eddie *did* come, you said his name, and there's his message!" He pointed to the puddle.

Henry cried, "I can't see it!"

"It's there, God damn it! It says 'fifth nail!'" he screamed, huffing and puffing, then asked, "What . . . what in hell does it mean?" There was a movement to his right. He spun. Mary was perhaps six feet away from him . . . and approaching. She held her arms out toward Johnny.

Henry pointed the gun at her and fired. The bullet hit her in the skull, just above her left ear. The top of her head exploded, displaying her dead brain like a walnut in a broken shell. She staggered back and tripped over Ed, who was struggling to his feet. She crumpled down alongside him, her dress hiked up to her waist.

"It's a myth!" Henry cried out, more to himself than to Johnny. He was waving the gun around in an erratic semi-circle, ready to fire at any approaching ghoul. "Th-there were f-five nails crafted for Christ's execution, n-not four . . . the fifth nail . . . it was meant to pierce his heart . . . but the gypsies, hid the fifth nail from the Romans . . . they were p-punished by God for prolonging Christ's suffering!" His eyes lit up. "My g-good God . . . it m-makes sense, yes it does! The fifth nail . . . it ends all suffering!" He kept waving the gun in a wide arc, joggling it up and down as if it were too heavy to hold. "The Conroy souls are dying," he said, pointing at each with the gun. "If they succeed in gathering your soul, then they'll end up as dead souls in hell. We must save their dying souls and pierce their hearts! It's the only way!"

Mrs. D., who until now had been wavering in the entrance to the sitting room, shouted abruptly, *"Son!"* She leapt across the room toward Henry like a lion pouncing on a gazelle.

Henry, fumbling to remove the pouch of nails from his wrist, never saw her coming. Johnny shouted *"Henry!"* But too late. Her hands swung up like grappling hooks and closed around his neck.

Johnny tried to leap forward, but a hand reached out and closed around his ankle. He lost his balance and collapsed to the floor. He looked over his shoulder and saw Mary, his husk of a mother with her stained rag of a dress and shattered-open head. She was crawling on top of him, grinning, teeth glinting in the shadows. *"Sonnnnn,"* she croaked, exposed brain gleaming wetly. *"Saaaaaave my dyyyyying soul, Bryaaaaan. . . ."*

Johnny screamed. He had the odd sensation that he was finally dying—as if his soul were being sucked into the twisting storm of hellfire trying to drag him down. A second hand grabbed him, this one on his thigh. A third locked on to his wrist, brutally strong despite missing two fingers. He twisted his head forward and saw Andrew Judson's face, just inches from his own. The dead lawyer had crawled across the floor, leaving behind a slimy, sluglike trail of blood on the floor.

"Cooooome with ussssss, Bryaaaan. . . ." he moaned.

Johnny screamed, again, but it was almost drowned out by the dogged hissing and moaning of the three dead people climbing over him. It didn't seem to matter, though, scream or no scream—Henry would not be able to save him now. Johnny could see him on his knees and sinking fast, Mrs. D. on top of him, strangling him, slamming his head against the floor. The gun dangled loosely in his dying grasp. The pouch of nails . . .

The fifth nail

. . . was still tethered to his twitching wrist.

The dead, pallid hands clawed furiously at Johnny's clothing, his skin. He twisted and bucked, but it did no good. His mind snapped, and the grayness in his sight—that familiar grayness—returned full force, like water filling his head.

Mustering every last bit of strength, he looked once more toward Henry. The dying man lay motionless. The pouch of nails was now open, its contents spilled out onto the floor.

Mrs. D., in all her dead, twisted-headed glory, had abandoned Henry and was now crawling toward Johnny—toward *all* her family members—four of the six-inch nails gripped in her colorless fist.

Blinded by fear, Johnny made one last attempt to crawl away, but the hands of the dead had him in their remorseless grasp, their voices calling out to him as the gray semi-consciousness in his sight turned to black oblivion.

CHAPTER FORTY-FOUR

September 9, 2005
4:47 A.M.

"Noooo!" Johnny bolted awake, gasping, wheezing. His scar burned furiously, agonizingly, and he could smell the meaty stench of burning flesh in the air. Darkness enveloped him like a pool of water. He perched up on his elbows and stared out in the gloom.

Without warning a large black bird landed on his bare chest, its taloned feet piercing his burning scar. He screamed and fell back, wincing in pain as the bird pecked him and a warm trickle of blood jeweled from his chest. The bird, beak smeared with Johnny's blood, contemplated Johnny with beady black eyes that brimmed with cunning and intelligence. It flapped its wings once and took off, leaving behind a sole feather upon his scar. *Like a gift.*

With a groan, Johnny pushed himself up and reached for the feather.

Like a shot from a gun, they were on him, groping hands, putrescent and filthy, pulling and squeezing his arms, his legs, his neck. He fought hard against them, but they were too many and too strong, utterly determined to complete the ritual initiated seventeen years earlier. They hauled him to his feet and secured him in place.

The barn doors creaked open. "*Sssonnnnnn . . .*" crooned a voice. Cool blue moonlight and early-morning mist flooded in, lighting the chilling scene, and Johnny realized with a giddy sort of horror that the voice belonged to his mother, Mary Petrie. She entered the barn, a crooked, looming silhouette against the moon's splaying backlight.

She staggered toward him, managing not to fall. In her right hand was a ball-peen hammer, its weightiness arcing to and fro, parting the mist at her side like a clock's pendulum.

Johnny bucked and thrashed against the dead and rotting hands seizing him: Ed Petrie on one arm, Mrs. D. on the other, Andrew Judson from behind with a cold, stinking, bloated arm wrapped tightly around his neck. In his mind's eye, Johnny envisioned the one-time lawyer's gutted midsection pressing up against his bare back, getting ready to gobble him up like a huge toothless mouth. He looked down at Judson's arm and saw little things crawling busily about the blended sores on his biceps. Some of them skittered up onto Johnny's chin and fled into his hair.

Mary came closer, her footsteps plodding against the hard ground, *thump . . . thump . . . thump. . . .*

"Sonnnnn," she groaned, raising the hammer.

Johnny tried to scream. What came out was a mousy squeak. His lungs were bone dry, petrified. He shook his head furiously, wondering if just giving in and dying would prove a better escape than fighting to live.

His mother faced him, now a foot away and so damn terrifying to look at. He reminded himself that this in fact was not his mother. It was Benjamin Conroy, not in the flesh, but in soul, and that was all that mattered right now.

"Sonnnn," she said with the remains of her mouth. Johnny tried to turn away, but Judson tightened his grip on Johnny's neck, forcing him to stare at the horrible thing that used to be Mary Petrie. The flesh of her left cheek had fallen away, revealing a scrap of white bone covered with brown mucus. Her lower lip sagged. Her upper lip was gone. Her teeth showed, yellow and leering.

She leaned close to him, pressed her cold, ruined mouth against his lips, and kissed him.

Gasping, panting, Johnny tried to pull away, but the living-dead family held him firmly in place. He could hardly breathe, and he nearly puked right in her face.

She left little pieces of flesh behind on his lips. She whispered raspily, *"My baaaaby boyyyy,"* and squashed her cold, bloated hand against his exposed scar. Johnny whimpered at the icy touch of his mother. When she took her hand away, the blood seeping out from the bird's peck on his chest left crimson in the center of her palm, like an image of stigmata. She stared at the blood, then poked a noxious black tongue out and licked it. *"Conroy,"* she cried triumphantly.

"Benjamin," Johnny panted. It hurt his lungs just to

utter the single word. "Please don't . . . it's evil's influence. . . . *there is no Osiris.* . . ."

As if on cue, the three dead people holding him jerked him backwards. Johnny felt his eyes bulge. Judson released his rotting hold, and Johnny made a weak attempt to flee, but Mary advanced on him rapidly, her fetid arms outstretched, rictus grin grinding, moaning.

He slammed into something hard at the center of the barn. Again Judson wrapped his arms around Johnny's waist, pulling him against what felt like a slab of wood against his bare back. He rolled his eyes to the left and saw.

They were going to crucify him.

Oh Jesus, oh God, they're going to kill me now.

With surprising might, Ed and Mrs. D. lifted him off the ground. A flapping shape flew out of the shadows overhead and landed on the loft, right in Johnny's line of sight. The bird. Mary grabbed Johnny's left wrist, and slammed it against the wood. With no delay, Ed placed the point of one of the six-inch nails against his exposed palm.

Pure terror washed through Johnny edged with a type of tragic irrationality that nearly made him laugh out loud: Had Ed ever hammered a nail while he was alive? Johnny felt himself slipping hard. The strength went out of his body. His eyes fluttered, and when he gazed up, he saw the bird still looking down at him from its perch on the loft, fluttering its shiny wings.

For a brief moment, in the time it took Johnny to blink, the bird changed. It was instant, and absolute. The evil running the whole menacing show revealed itself to Johnny, ensuring him that its image would be imprinted on his mind forever.

Oh . . . my . . . God. Johnny struggled to comprehend the hideous thing he saw perched on the loft. It was a giant nightmare that existed far beyond the reaches of space and time—that could exist only in hell. It was eight feet across and four feet high with wings as black as a dark cellar at midnight. Its claws were thin and wiry, parting the air like razors. Its eyes were cruel emeralds bulging from sockets rimmed with silver fluid. It swayed in shadows against the dark backdrop of the loft. Its serrated maw widened. A monstrous tongue rolled out and lapped against its bristly skin.

Then, as quickly as it revealed itself to Johnny, it was gone. Here one second, gone the next, back to being an ordinary-looking black bird. It squawed once. Mission accomplished.

Johnny tried again to buck against the holding hands, but before he could even budge, Mary swung the hammer over her shoulder and drove the nail Ed held right through his palm, securing it to the wood of the crucifix.

It felt as if a charge of dynamite went off in his hand. Bright flashes of light fired and whirled in his brain. He slumped down, pure dead weight now, only semi-conscious as his hot blood flowed.

The living-dead fixed his right hand against the wood of the crucifix.

Johnny managed to come back around. Through distorted vision, he looked back up at the loft. The bird was gone. In its place was another apparition: that of a young man wearing a football jersey. He was holding what appeared to be a gallon-can of paint in his hands. His skull had a large gaping hole in it. A swell of brains was visible through the jagged hole.

Eddie Carlson, Johnny thought, and the apparition

nodded slightly. The dead people holding the souls of the Conroy family didn't seem to sense Eddie's ghostly presence—they carried on with the deadly task at hand.

Johnny remembered what Henry had said back in his office: *Eddie Carlson saved your life once before, and I'm afraid we'll need him to save it again.*

Has Eddie come back to save me?

He gazed up at Eddie's ghost. It immediately vanished, winking out of existence, just like that. Johnny heard a whooshing sound and felt a rush of cold wind.

As Ed and Judson held his other hand against the wood, Mrs. D., pressed a nail against his exposed palm.

Mary raised the hammer.

And then something incredible happened.

Mary froze, her hand still perched in the air, poised to strike. Her partially missing mouth chattered, and then she wailed the agonized shriek of a thousand hell-bound voices. A bloody, seeping patch appeared between her filthy, sagging breasts. Punching out from the center of the spreading wound came the point of a thick nail. The hammer fell from her grasp and clunked on the hard ground.

A pitch-black shadow, dark as crude oil, shot out of her mouth and settled up into the hidden recesses of the loft.

Her body collapsed to the ground, dead and useless.

Behind her stood Henry Depford, one hand soaked with gore, the other gripping the pouch of nails. His eyes were dark empty orbs, devoid of conscious thought and reason. He was working solely on instinct and the will to complete his own lifelong task. *Not unlike the Conroys.* In the pallid light, Johnny could see violet bruises around his neck, deep and brutal, where his former wife had burrowed her cold, dead thumbs.

Moaning incoherently, Ed staggered away from the crucifix, across Johnny's line of sight, his blackened arms raised toward Henry. Henry stepped back. He fumbled through the pouch, drew out a nail, and in a continuous swooping motion, drove it home, right into Ed's unbeating heart. Ed froze, eyes bulging, arms sticking straight out. He opened his mouth hideously wide, and in deadly silence vomited a black, writhing, ectoplasmic cloud that leaped up into the rafters of the loft. Like a grotesque slug, his body writhed for a moment, then collapsed to the ground in a cold motionless heap, alongside his wife of thirty years.

Henry gazed stonily to Johnny's right and removed another nail from the pouch.

Like earlier, Mrs. D. proved herself the quickest of all the dead people. With a rage-filled bellow, she lunged for Henry, hands grasping his neck. Henry shrank back. The pouch dropped from his hand and thunked to the ground. Together, they struggled against each other in a cloud of dust, Henry fighting for his life, Mrs. D., her soul.

Andrew Judson, holding Johnny from behind, released him and slowly staggered around the crucifix. There was a sudden wail of anguish from the bloody battle. Johnny, sucking in a cloud of putrid dust, closed his fingers over the bloody head of the nail and twisted his pierced hand back and forth in an effort to loosen it from the crucifix. Through tearing, agonized eyes, he watched as Mrs. D. rolled off Henry, her chest oozing sloppy blood over his hand as it continued twisting and grinding a nail deep into her heart. Her body twitched, shook, and flailed. Her mouth ripped open and spewed a black-shadow soul up into the dark loft. Her body went immediately motionless.

In eerie silence, Henry, lying on his side, reached for the pouch. Johnny pulled furiously against the nail. It budged slightly, but not so easily—the gushing blood from his hand caused his fingers to slip. From above, the bird squawed loudly and often. Henry crawled forward, his fingers brushing against the leather sash of the pouch. The pouch opened. A single nail slipped out.

Judson leaned down and grabbed the hammer that Mary had dropped. The bloated fingers of this right hand curled around the bloody handle.

Henry rolled onto his back, unnaturally silent despite the looming threat. *He isn't panting,* Johnny noticed.

Johnny bucked and thrashed, digging deep down and unearthing another burst of energy to wrench his blood-soaked hand and the nail driven through it.

The nail loosened from the wood.

Judson, swung the hammer over his head and down. With a deafening crack, it connected squarely with Henry's forehead. Henry dropped to the ground, a pool of blood gushing from his collapsed skull.

Judson turned and faced Johnny. He *grinned.* Terrible lines of pus dripped from his lips.

He raised the hammer.

For a second, just a second, Johnny had stopped thrashing. But then the panic in him rose in full force again, giving him the will to make one last-ditch attempt to yank the nail from the crucifix. His hand poured blood; he could feel it, could *hear* his flesh tearing.

He saw Henry, now twitching . . . moving.

Seemingly unaffected by the blow Judson delivered, Henry popped back up like a grisly jack-in-the-box. His skull was caved in. He reached out and clawed at

Judson's legs, teeth bared. Judson tripped over Henry's grasp.

With a shriek, Johnny tore the nail out of the crucifix. He buckled forward, five and a half inches of nail and splinters protruding from the back of his hand. Blood splashed out everywhere, on his bare chest, his legs, the ground. He twisted his hand around, palm against his chest just as Andrew Judson fell forward. The point of the nail sticking out of Johnny's hand sunk into Judson's exposed heart like a warm knife into butter.

The dead man trembled against Johnny, his face wilting like a flower. It released a gaseous breath of decay and dropped down in a heap. Johnny crumpled down on top of him, his nailed hand ripping free of the blackened heart. There he remained for a few endless seconds, hyperventilating and not knowing how he could still be alive. He nearly passed out before he twisted his head and peered up at Henry Depford. The man was sitting up, grinning at Johnny, the front portion of his head gone.

Johnny knew. *He saved your life once before. . . .*

"Eddie?" he coughed.

The dead thing that had been Henry Depford nodded once, then collapsed to the ground in a lifeless mound of cold, bleeding flesh. Thick white ectoplasm oozed from his mouth and nose and soared up into the loft.

Johnny rolled onto his back, exhausted and unable to move. He stared unwaveringly toward the loft, where the souls of the Conroy family and Eddie Carlson had departed to.

The bird was there, lying on the loft's edge. It was

dead, its clawed feet sticking up in the air like withered flags of surrender.

Johnny closed his eyes and lay there amid the corpses. The gentle warmth of the rising sun provided little comfort as he slipped into the embracing arms of unconsciousness . . .

. . . and dreams of the golden pain. This vision, he knew, would be final—his last confrontation with the horrors that brought him to Wellfield. At last he finds the strength within to shun the growing light and the searing brand that left him scarred for life. The pain fades. He peers ahead and sees another light. This one is softer, less invasive. A white figure emerges from it and stands before Johnny. It is Eddie Carlson. In spite of the white light that envelops him, Johnny sees that he is wearing a football jersey and has a helmet tucked firmly beneath his right arm. He is completely unscarred, as if he'd never met Benjamin Conroy.

"Thank you," Johnny whispers.

Eddie nods and smiles warmly. His eyes twinkle beneath the light enveloping him. "Johnny, please see to it that evil never returns to Wellfield again. . . ."

The apparition fades. Johnny steps forward, heart breaking with thankfulness. He can hear his footfalls on the ground, thump . . . thump . . . thump. He shudders with sudden fear, and is abruptly stopped in his tracks by a pair of dead, bloated hands that grab his shoulders.

A voice whispers in his ear: "Johhhnnnny . . ."

He startled awake, screaming.

A body leaned over him, a dark silhouette before dawn's bleeding light. Its hands grabbed his shoulders, shaking him.

Johnny screamed again, eyes bulging.

Again, the voice: "Johnny, Johnny. It's all right now. I'm going to help you."

Johnny squinted. The person above him came into view, like an angel from a dream. Carl Davies, Henry Depford's former deputy—the man who'd picked him up and brought him to Henry's home. He was hunched, as pale as parchment, his hands warm against Johnny's bare shoulders.

"What in God's name *happened* here?" He was surveying the carnage with wide, unbelieving eyes.

The pain filtered back into Johnny, and he groaned, unable to utter a single word.

"You be quiet," Carl said.

Then, just as Henry Depford did to baby Bryan Conroy—to *him*—seventeen years earlier, Carl Davies scooped Johnny up in his arms and carried him away from the Conroy house, once and forever.

EPILOGUE:
EVIL LEAVES WELLFIELD

October 18, 2005
10:30 A.M.

At ten-thirty A.M., Wellfield experienced its first flurries in a winter that was forecasted to be one of the worst in the last twenty-five years. The winds whipped about Main Street, stealing away the last of the leaves still clinging to the elms lining the sidewalk outside the courthouse.

Inside the brick walls of the courthouse, Johnny sat in a room with the mayor, the current sheriff (a man by the name of Tibbs who looked remarkably like Henry Depford), his deputy, and five serious-faced men that were introduced as lawyers.

"And one more right here," the balding, middle-aged man to his right instructed.

His hand cramped and itched painfully beneath the bandage, but Johnny signed his name anyway. How many dotted lines had there been? A hundred? Two? This was promised to be the last one. He dropped the pen on the cherrywood desk and gazed at Mr. Balding-middle-aged. What was his name again? Baker? Barker? He'd been introduced to all of them, some more than once, but couldn't remember any of their names. Loss of short-term memory seemed to be an ongoing problem.

After a three-week stay at the Glendale Hospital two towns over, Johnny returned to Wellfield. There had been the damage to his hand. Two broken ribs. A concussion. Internal bleeding. Loss of blood. Nothing wholly life-threatening, but nonetheless worthy of a few weeks' healing time. A plain but pretty female psychologist named Dr. Allis ultimately diagnosed him with generalized anxiety and post-traumatic stress disorder.

Carl Davies had been very generous in allowing Johnny a place to stay until he was granted permission to leave town. The mayor was eager to get the land into Wellfield ownership—the Orono businessmen were already lined up, the ink ready in their pens. The Greens Community Homes, scheduled to break ground next month on the northeast end of Conroy's land, would divert the press's attention from Wellfield's stigma of another mass murder—at the same location as the first one seventeen years earlier, no less. The mayor had been able to pull a few legal and financial strings, clearing Johnny of any wrongdoing, as long as Carl Davies was willing to vouch for him, which he readily did.

The murders were ultimately pinned on David Mackey. His medical history and psychological background backed up the long-shot possibility of his repeating a similar attack to the one that Benjamin Conroy had committed upon him and his family seventeen years earlier. *The Daily Observer* reported that after murdering a night guard at the Pine Oak Institute for the Mentally Insane, David escaped the grounds on foot and went on a rather clever rampage, killing Benjamin Conroy's sister- and brother-in-law, the lawyer handling Conroy's assets, plus a local couple who'd furtively amassed a wealth of information on Conroy and his checkered history. The only one to survive the attack was Conroy's only living heir, Johnny Petrie, who'd come to Wellfield to claim the Conroy estate. Of course it was never entirely explained how Mackey learned of the Petrie family's visit. Johnny had been questioned about the murder of the driver in his apartment, but the bus ticket with his name on it showed that he'd left Wellfield prior to the crime. He never found out what happened and didn't really want to know, although he came to assume that his mother had somehow done it.

Last night, on the fortieth night following the end of it all, Johnny had a dream. It had been the first dream after thirty-nine nights of dark, uninterrupted sleep. In this dream, he returned to Wellfield, at sunrise. The town was completely deserted, the buildings crumbling. Sepia-toned clouds filled the sky as he walked down Main Street, his footsteps *thump*, *thump*, *thump*ing along the concrete sidewalk. In the middle of the street stood the entire Conroy family: Benjamin, Faith, Elizabeth, and Daniel. They were whole again, uninjured. They appeared angelic, with hazy white lights behind their heads like halos. Benjamin said: *"Jesus roamed the earth for forty nights before ascending into heaven to be seated at the right hand of God."*

Johnny felt himself waver, then fell down into darkness. But not before hearing Benjamin's final words: *"Son . . . there is one more. . . ."*

He'd awoken in the middle of the night, nearly unable to breathe, thinking over and over again: *on the fortieth night, on the fortieth night . . .*

He'd remained awake the rest of the night.

Now, seven hours later, he stood up from a leather chair in the Wellfield town courthouse and shook hands with eight men who were all smiling greedily. He shook hands with the mayor last.

"In about two hours, Johnny, you'll be a millionaire. How's it feel?"

Johnny shrugged. Smiled. He supposed it felt good to know that he wouldn't have to rush off and find work right away. Two million dollars, after taxes, would amount to about one-point-three million, which would certainly pay the rent for a few years in Manhattan before he'd have to decide what to do with the rest of his life.

I just want the hell out of this God-forsaken town, he thought.

I won't look back. I'll only look forward for the rest of my life here on earth because I know a dark moving shadow will always be right behind me, breathing down my neck, waiting . . .

Johnny left the room. Carl Davies was there. "Well?"

"Done," Johnny said. "The money will be wired into an account in my name today."

Carl held out a hand. Johnny took it, unemotionally. "You've paid the price, Johnny. Enjoy your reward. It's the very least you deserve."

"Thank you, Carl. I truly appreciate everything you did."

They left the courthouse and walked in silence to Carl's car, parked a hundred feet away. Johnny pinched the top of his coat up around his mouth. The wind whipped into his eyes.

And in his mind, the dream voice of Eddie Carlson haunted him: *"Johnny, please, see to it that evil never returns to Wellfield again...."* Then, the voice of Benjamin Conroy: *"Son, there is one more...."*

"Where's the box?" Johnny asked.

Carl started the car. "In the trunk."

Johnny took a deep breath, then said, "There's one last thing I need to do."

Carl drove away down Main. "Where are we going, Johnny?"

"We're going to the bus station. But first, we need to make one stop, okay?"

"And where's that?"

Johnny hesitated, then answered, "The Conroy house."

In less than ten minutes, they were there. Although the property was still considered a crime scene, the investigation was officially over. The posts that at one time had tethered strips of yellow crime scene tape still stood erect from the ground. Strips of the plastic tape whipped in the wind like flags. Carl pulled the car into the driveway.

"Keep going," Johnny said. "All the way up."

The familiar sound of high weeds and gravel crunched under the tires. Carl drove to the head of the driveway and stopped.

"What are we doing here, Johnny?" Carl finally asked.

Johnny considered telling Carl what he already knew, but ultimately decided to keep it to himself. "Just open the trunk, okay?"

Carl nodded, reached down under the steering wheel, and popped the trunk release. Johnny got out of the car and circled around to the back. He lifted the trunk and peered inside.

The box. He reached in and carefully poked through all of Henry Depford's research materials: the Bibles, the papers, the notebooks, the photographs, everything that at one point had belonged to Benjamin Conroy. Johnny had requested the materials, reminding those taking charge of Conroy's estate that these things had originally belonged to his father and were to be included as a part of the inheritance. The small stipulation was immediately agreed to by Wellfield's lawyers, the will was amended, and in two days Johnny and Carl were allowed to search through Depford's study, which fortunately had been held as evidence from his surviving family members. He gathered only those items that at one time belonged to his father.

Including one nail that had been hidden in an envelope. Inside with it was a note from Benjamin Conroy, written seventeen years earlier:

There is one more.

Indeed there is, Johnny thought, grabbing the envelope. He opened it and removed the nail, then walked to the barn, thinking along the way, *Benjamin knew. Somehow, he knew.*

Holding the nail, Johnny entered to the barn.

There is one more. . . .

He walked into the gloom beneath the loft, its rotted wall torn away to reveal its dust-coated walls, as unremarkable-looking as the rest of the structure. There, huddled in the corner, was the last one.

He recalled what Henry Depford had told him when they spoke about Benjamin and the events perpetrated at his home: *Benjamin couldn't get to you, so he crucified the family dog instead. . . .*

Johnny approached it. It had survived here in the same body for forty days: the soul of Conroy's dog, now in the mangled body of the dog Henry ran over with his pickup. It was rotted and full of holes, covered with maggots and horseflies. Its yellow fur reduced to patches of mangy fuzz. It lay on its side, exposed innards dark and still.

It picked its head up and made a weak barking sound.

Tears welled in Johnny's eyes. *One more . . .*

He took a deep breath, then slammed the nail deep into the bare heart of the dead dog.

"Enjoy the afterlife," he muttered, then hurried out of the barn, into the welcoming warmth of Wellfield's morning daylight.

He dreams of light, white light, and it is good. It shows him the future, and in it there is a family: he, the patriarch; his wife; and his son and daughter. They attend church every Sunday, spending all their time together, both good and bad. Sunshine rains down on the Petrie family, and goodness abounds. All of them look ahead to a bright future under God's watchful eye.

But there is a growing shadow in that white light. It represents the temptation to look back. It becomes a secret, one he keeps from his family. It exists as a cardboard box that sits in the attic of his home. The temptation grows stronger and stronger, and quite soon it begins to eat at him and begs him to explore the mysteries within—the mysteries of his past that will never leave him because no matter how long he denies the desire to look back, it will remain with him, always and forever, growing stronger and stronger. . . .